SEVERANCE

SEVERANCE

Ling Ma

FARRAR, STRAUS AND GIROUX

NEW YORK

Farrar, Straus and Giroux
175 Varick Street, New York 10014

Copyright © 2018 by Ling Ma
Printed in the United States of America

ISBN 9780374261597

Designed by Abby Kagan

to my mother and father

SEVERANCE

After the End came the Beginning. And in the Beginning, there were eight of us, then nine—that was me—a number that would only decrease. We found one another after fleeing New York for the safer pastures of the countryside. We'd seen it done in the movies, though no one could say which one exactly. A lot of things didn't play out as they had been depicted on-screen.

We were brand strategists and property lawyers and human resources specialists and personal finance consultants. We didn't know how to do anything so we Googled everything. We Googled *how to survive in wild*, which yielded images of poison ivy, venomous insects, and bear tracks. That was okay but we wanted to know how to go on the offensive. Against everything. We Googled *how to build fire* and watched YouTube videos of fires being lit with flint against steel, with flint against flint, with magnifying glass and sun. We couldn't find the requisite flint, didn't know how to identify it even, and before we tried using Bob's bifocals, someone found a Bic in a jean jacket. The fire brought us through the night and delivered us into a morning that took us to a deserted Walmart. We stockpiled bottled water and exfoliating body wash and iPods and beers and tinted moisturizer in our stolen Jeeps. In the back of the store we found guns and ammo, camo outfits, scopes and grips. We Googled *how to shoot gun*, and when we tried, we were spooked by the recoil, by the salty smell and smoke, by the liturgical drama of the whole thing in the woods. But actually we loved to shoot them, the guns. We liked to shoot them wrong even, with a loose hand, the pitch forward and the pitch back. Under our judicious trigger fingers, beer bottles died, *Vogue* magazines died, Chia Pets died, oak saplings died, squirrels died, elk died. We feasted.

Google would not last long. Neither would the internet. Or any of the infrastructure, but in the beginning of the Beginning let us brag, if only to ourselves in the absence of others. Because who was there to envy us, to be proud of us? Our Googlings darkened, turned inward. We Googled *maslow's pyramid* to see how many of the need levels we could already fulfill. The first two. We Googled *2011 fever survivors*, hoping to find others like us, and when all we found were the same outdated, inconclusive news articles, we Googled *7 stages grief* to track our emotional progress. We were at Anger, the slower among us lagging behind at Denial. We Googled *is there a god*, clicked *I'm Feeling Lucky*, and were directed to a suicide hotline site. In the twelve rings it took for us to hang up, we held our breaths for someone else, some stranger's voice confirming that we weren't the only ones living, despite Bob's adamant assertions. There was no answer.

From this and other observations, it was deduced that we were alone, truly alone.

After weeks of running amok, of running aground, we rallied and organized a game plan. Our self-appointed leader was Bob, a short, stout man who had worked in information technology. He was slightly older than us, though by how much it seemed rude to ask. He was Goth when he felt like it. He knew about being alone. He had played every iteration of Warcraft with a near-religious fervor; it was as if he had prepared for this, this thing, this higher calling. He held his right arm in a sling close to his chest, tucked inside his shirt, after a botched carpal tunnel surgery. Partly enfeebled, he was especially adept at directing others to his will. Things needed to be taken care of, we needed to be told what to do. We received his clear, concise instructions like manna.

I have a place for us to stay, Bob said, puffing on his e-cigarette. The scent of French vanilla wafted through the night air.

We sat around the bonfire, listening. It was this gigantic two-story complex in Chicago that he and some high school buddies had bought.

For what? Janelle asked, blasé. Just in case the apocalypse happened?

For *when* the apocalypse happened, Bob corrected. We always knew it would, though I personally didn't know it would be this early.

We waited as Bob took another drag on his e-cigarette before continuing. The Facility, he informed us, had everything. It had big, high ceilings. The roof had skylights cut into it, so it got plenty of light. There was a movie theater. Maybe the projector would still work. Everyone would have an individual room.

We considered Chicago. The even-keeled, prairie center of the Great Lakes region, its long, hardy winters rife with opportunities for canning root vegetables and stone fruits, the midwestern sensibilities embodied in the large, beneficent scale of its city layout, especially River North and downtown, the larger blocks, the more spacious buildings, and at sunset, the rich, golden light against its stately, modern architecture, structures that had survived fires and floods, so many fires and floods. Such an environment, Bob advised, could only benefit our better natures. We would set up camp in the lake breeze, lay down roots for our new lives, and procreate gently amongst ourselves. We would love the ensuing offspring created by our diverse ethnic offerings. Chicago is the most American of American cities.

It's actually Needling, Bob said. Needling, Illinois. It's right outside Chicago.

I am not living in the suburbs, Janelle announced.

Why, do you have a better place in mind? Todd scoffed.

Making plans heartened us, and as we stayed up late, drinking, we theorized grandly. What is the internet but collective memory? Anything that had been done before we could do better. The Heimlich maneuver. Breech births. The fox-trot. Glycerin bombs. Bespoke candle making. Lurking in our limited gene pools may swim metastatic brain tumors and every type of depression and recessed cystic fibrosis, but also high IQs and proficiencies with Romance languages. We could move on from this. We could be better.

Anything was better than what we felt. We had shame, so much shame at being the few survivors. Other survivors, if they existed, must also feel this way. We were ashamed of leaving people behind, of taking our comforts where we could find them, of stealing from those who could not defend themselves. We had known ourselves to be cowards and hypocrites, pernicious liars really, and to find this suspicion confirmed was not a relief but a horror. If the End was Nature's way of punishing us so that we might once again know our place, then yes, we knew it. If it was at all unclear before, it was not now.

The shame bonded us. In the morning, we Googled *diy tattoos* and boiled a pan of sewing needles. Soused and sorrowed, we inked small lightning bolts on each of our forearms, near the wristbone, to symbolize our bond. Because it was said Crazy Horse divined that he would be successful in war only if he never stopped to gather the spoils of battle, and to remind himself of this, he tattooed lightning bolts behind his horses' ears. Strike fast, strike first.

The key thing, we reminded ourselves, was never to stop, to always keep going, even when the past called us back to a time and place we still leaned toward, still sang of, in quieter moments. Like the canyons of office buildings all the way down Fifth Avenue.

Like all the Japanese and Swiss businessmen leisuring through Bryant Park, sipping hot chocolate. Like the afternoon sun cast through our midtown office windows, when it was almost time to leave for all the pleasures of the evening: an easy meal eaten standing up at the kitchen counter, a TV show, a meetup with friends for cocktails.

The truth is, I was not there at the Beginning. I was not there for any of the Googlings or the Walmart stalking or the feastings or the spontaneous mass tattooings. I was the last one out of New York, the last one of the group to join. By the time they found me, the infrastructure had already collapsed. The internet had caved into a sinkhole, the electrical grid had shut down, and the road trip toward the Facility was already under way.

It had been the nostalgia-yellow of the Yellow Cab that the group had first spotted, parked along the shoulder of a road in Pennsylvania. NYC TAXI, it read on the car door. It was a Ford Crown Victoria, an older fleet model that cab companies had almost phased out. It looked, Bob later told me, as if I'd driven a broken time machine right out of the eighties. It was my in. Entire highways were clogged with abandoned vehicles, but they had never seen a New York cab out in the middle of nowhere, the meter still running, the fare light on.

I was dehydrated and half-conscious in the backseat. I wouldn't speak.

The truth is, I had stayed in the city as long as I possibly could. The whole time, I had been half waiting for myself to turn, to become fevered like everyone else. Nothing happened. I waited and waited. I still wait.

1

The End begins before you are ever aware of it. It passes as ordinary. I had gone over to my boyfriend's place in Greenpoint directly after work. I liked to stay over on hot summer nights because the basement was cool and damp at night. We made dinner, veggie stir-fry with rice. We had showered and watched a movie projected on his wall.

The screening was *Manhattan*, which I'd never seen before, and even though I found the May–December romance between Mariel Hemingway and Woody Allen kind of creepy, I loved all the opening shots of New York set to the Gershwin soundtrack, and I loved the scene in which Woody Allen and Diane Keaton get caught in the rain in Central Park, and they seek shelter in the Museum of Natural History, wet and cocooned in the cavern darkness of the planetary display. Just looking at New York on the screen, the city was made new for me again, and I saw it as I once did in high school: romantic, shabby, not totally gentrified, full of promise. It made me wistful for the illusion of New York more than for its actuality, after having lived there for five years. And as the movie ended and we turned off the lights and lay down side by side on his mattress, I was thinking about how New York is possibly the only place in which most people have already lived, in some sense, in the public imagination, before they ever arrive.

I was saying some of this to him, the shapeless mass lying next to me in the dark, when he interrupted and said, Listen to me. Look at me. I have something to tell you.

His name was Jonathan and he liked to party. Not really. His name was Jonathan and he was high-rolling. He owned a laptop, a coffee maker, a movie projector; everything else went to rent. He ate air and dust. We had been together for almost five years, about as long as I'd been at my job. Jonathan didn't work in the nine-to-five sense. He did odd freelance gigs here and there so that he could spend most of his time writing. Divested of most obligations, he lived cheaply, held jobs when he could find them. Once, for a secret Wall Street club, he was hired to slap middle-aged businessmen for a living. I used to clasp his face between my palms, his expression wrought with worry, with unassuaged anxiety.

Okay, I said. What is it?

He took out his retainer, didn't place it in the mug on the floor but held it there in his hand. It was going to be a short conversation. He said, I'm leaving New York.

What, you didn't like the movie?

No, I'm serious. Be serious for once.

I'm always serious, I deadpanned. So, when are you leaving?

He paused. In another month. Thom is sailing up to this—

I sat up, tried to look at him, but my eyes hadn't adjusted. Wait, what are you saying?

I'm saying I'm leaving New York.

No, what you're saying is, you're breaking up with me.

That's not— He looked at me. Okay. I'm breaking up with you.

Lead with that.

It's not you.

Okay.

No, it's not you, he said, grabbing my hand. It's this place, this city and what it turns a person into. We talked about this.

In the past year, Jonathan had become increasingly disillusioned with living in New York. Something along the lines of: the city, New York fucking City, tedious and boring, its charms as illusory as its facade of authenticity. Its lines were too long. Everything was a status symbol and everything cost too much. There were so many on-trend consumers, standing in lines for blocks to experience a fad dessert, gimmicky art exhibits, a new retail concept store. We were all making such uninspired lifestyle choices. We, including me.

Me, nothing really weighed on me, nothing unique. Me, I held down an office job and fiddled around with some photography when the moon hit the Gowanus right. Or something like that, the usual ways of justifying your life, of passing time. With the money I made, I bought Shiseido facial exfoliants, Blue Bottle coffee, Uniqlo cashmere.

What do you call a cross between a yuppie and a hipster? A yupster. Per Urban Dictionary.

Then he said, You should leave New York too.

Why would I do that?

Because you hate your job.

I don't hate it. It's okay.

Name one time, one time when you really like it.

Every Friday night.

Exactly.

I'm kidding. You don't even know what I do. I mean, not really.

You work at a production firm in publishing. You oversee the manufacture of books in third-world countries. Stop me if I'm wrong.

I had worked at Spectra for almost five years. We worked with publishers who paid us to coordinate book production that we outsourced to printers in Southeast Asia, mostly China. The name Spectra suggested the ostensibly impressive range of book products we were capable of producing: Cookbooks, Children's Books, Stationery, Art Books, Gift and Specialty. I worked in Bibles. The company had huge collective buying power, so we offered even cheaper manufacture rates than individual publishers could achieve on their own, driving foreign labor costs down even further. Obviously Jonathan kind of despised what I did. Maybe I did too.

I changed the subject. Where are you going? When?

Sometime next month. I'm going to help Thom sail on his yacht. The idea is to end up in Puget Sound.

I scoffed. Thom was Wall Street, a client from the club where Jonathan once worked. I said, Right. Like he doesn't crush on you and expect something in return.

You think like that because you live in a market economy.

And you don't?

He didn't say anything.

Sometimes, I said, I think you hold it against me for not being more like you.

Are you kidding? You're so much more like me than you think. In the dark, I could see him winking, bittersweetly. Want to do a sumo roll? he said.

The sumo roll was when he would roll across the bed, and when he reached me, he would compress his body into mine, belly to belly, until I was sunken into the mattress, obliterated, and then he would roll away. This repeated until I convulsed from laughing too hard.

No, I don't want to do a sumo roll, I said.

Ready?

When he rolled on top of me, he weighed into me fiercely, indenting me into the bedding. He could be so heavy when he wanted. I squeezed my hands into fists. I squeezed my eyes together.

I made my body stiff as a board, inhospitable. Slowly, I felt him lessening. I felt him stop. He could feel me shaking. He put his dry, hard palm on my forehead, as if he were taking a sick person's temperature.

Stop crying, he said. Don't cry. Please.

He offered me some water but I stood up and retrieved some Evian from my bag. I sat down on the edge of the mattress, taking small, worthless sips.

Lie down, please, he said. Will you lie next to me?

I lay down, next to him, both of us on our backs. We stared up at the ceiling.

Jonathan broke the silence. In a timorous voice, he said he could see clearly now, could see the future. The future is more exponentially exploding rents. The future is more condo buildings, more luxury housing bought by shell companies of the global wealthy elite. The future is more Whole Foods, aisles of refrigerated cut fruit packaged in plastic containers. The future is more Urban Outfitters, more Sephoras, more Chipotles. The future just wants more consumers. The future is more newly arrived college grads and tourists in some fruitless search for authenticity. The future is more overpriced Pabsts at dive-bar simulacrums. Something something Rousseau something. Manhattan is sinking.

What, literally? Because of global warming? I snarked.

Don't make fun of me. And yes, literally and figuratively.

The thing was, I didn't disagree with what he was saying. It is an impossible place to live. My salary was enough to keep my head above water month to month. Given my rent and lack of financial savvy, I had very little in savings, let alone retirement funds. There was very little keeping me here. I didn't own property. I didn't have family. I'd be priced out of every borough in another decade.

But having heard all this before, I began to tune out, thinking about what I would do next. When he nudged me, I realized he was asking me a question. He was saying, Would I consider leaving New York with him? We could do it together.

What would we do? I asked.

We would live together and take part-time jobs, he said. I would write and finish my book. You could work on your art too. I could make a darkroom for you to develop your photos.

Can you even have a darkroom on a boat?

Well, not during the trip. I was thinking that afterward, we could settle in Oregon. There are some cheaper areas out there in the rural Pacific Northwest.

I guess I'll be a nature photographer, I said drily.

Some R&B track with jumpy bass tremored the ceiling. It was that time of night again, when the neighbor upstairs brooded to sad songs with good beats. I didn't think much of my photographs. When I first moved to New York, I had created a photo blog called *NY Ghost*. It was mostly pictures of the city. The intent was to show new, undiscovered aspects of New York from an outsider's perspective, but in retrospect, the pictures just looked clichéd and trope-y: neon-tinged diners, gas-slicked streets, subway train cars packed with tired commuters, people sitting out on fire escapes during the summer—basically, variations of the same preexisting New York iconography that permeates calendars, romcoms, souvenirs, stock art. They could have been hung in any business hotel room. Even the better, more artfully composed images were just Eggleston knockoffs, Stephen Shore derivatives. For these and other reasons, I hardly updated the blog anymore. I hardly took pictures anymore.

Would you at least consider it? Jonathan asked.

I'm not an artist.

Moving with me, I mean.

You've already decided to move away. You're only asking me as an afterthought, let's be honest.

I didn't think you would go if I asked, he said sadly.

The song ended, then began again. The neighbor had it on repeat. Jesus. It sounded familiar but I couldn't name it.

We spoke until our voices grew hoarse, deepening and breaking and fissuring. It lasted early into morning. Our bodies curled inward, away from each other, dry leaves at the end of summer.

In sleep it came to me. The name of the song, I mean: "Who Is It." Michael Jackson. My mother used to play it in the car when I was a kid. She loved to drive. She drove down long, unfurling Utah freeways on aimless, drifting afternoons, while my father was at work and I was still too young to be left alone. We would go to other towns to buy just one carton of eggs, one pint of half-and-half that she mistook for milk. I was six, and had only been in the U.S. for a few months, newly transplanted from Fuzhou. I was still dazed at the variety and surplus of the supermarkets, miles of boxes and bottles lit with fluorescent lighting. Supermarkets were my favorite American thing. Driving was my mother's favorite American thing, and she drove in a very American way: fast, down empty freeways before rush hour, skimming through cathedral canyons and red rock, her long black hair billowing everywhere, like in the movies. Why move to America if you can't drive? she'd say, never breaking her speed as we veered toward exit ramps, stop signs, traffic lights.

I woke up like I had a cold, my head heavy, my throat sore. Light peeked in through the blinds of the windows above us, and I heard footfalls on the sidewalk. Right away, I knew that I had overslept. The alarm hadn't gone off, and I was going to be late. In his tiny bathroom, rusty pipes cursed loudly for cold tap. I brushed my teeth, splashed cold water on my face. Put on yesterday's work outfit, a pencil skirt and a button-up shirt.

Jonathan was still asleep, swathed in gray threadbare sheets. I left him there.

Outside, the air was surprisingly cold for a July morning. I walked up the basement stoop and crossed the street to the Polish bakery for a coffee. The woman behind the counter was setting out a pan of something. Apple cider donuts. Steam rose off them and fogged up the windows. All the pedestrians in Greenpoint were bundled up in their cold-weather finery, red autumnal plaids and flourishes of thick, lustrous flannel, even though it was summer. For a moment I wondered if I hadn't just slept for months. Maybe I'd Rip-Van-Winkled my way out of a job. I would arrive to find someone else sitting in my office, my belongings in a box. I would return to my studio and find someone else living there. I would start over.

I walked to the J train, thinking up excuses for being late. I could say that I had overslept, though I'd used that one time too many. I could say there had been a family emergency, except my boss knew my parents were deceased and I had no other relatives living in the States. I could say that my apartment had been robbed, but that was too big a story. Plus, it had actually happened before. They'd taken everything; they'd stripped my bedsheets. Afterward, someone had said, You're officially a New Yorker now, as if this were a point of pride.

Looking out at the gray East River as the J crossed the Williamsburg Bridge, I decided that I'd just claim I was sick. I looked like I was sick, my eyes clustered with puffiness and dark bags. At work, they knew me to be capable but fragile. Quiet, clouded up with daydreams. Usually diligent, though sometimes inconsistent, moody. But also something else, something implacable: I was unsavvy in some fundamental, uncomfortable way. The sound of my loud, nervous laugh, like gargling gravel, was a social liability. I skipped too many office parties. They kept me on because my output was prolific and they could task me with more and more production assignments. When I focused, a trait I exhibited at the beginning of my time there, I could be detail-oriented to the point of obsession.

At Canal, I transferred to the N to ride all the way to Times Square. A light rain had begun to fall by the time I emerged aboveground. Spectra's glass office, housed on the thirty-first and thirty-second floors of a midcentury building, were located a few blocks away. The rain scattered the tourists as I ducked and weaved through their dense sidewalk congregations down Broadway, accidentally banging my knees into their Sephora and Disney Store bags. A street saxophonist played "New York, New York," his eyes closed in feeling. The cluster of tourists around him seemed moved, if not by the quality of his playing, which was drowned out by the trains roaring beneath our feet, then by his pained expression, a sorrow that seemed more authentic than performative. When the song ended and he emptied his Starbucks cup of dollars, he looked up, straight at me. I hurried away, embarrassed.

You're late, said Manny, the building doorman. He was sitting behind the reception desk, cleaning his glasses with the same Windex he used to wipe down the revolving glass doors every morning and evening.

I'm sick, I told him.

Here. For your health. From a drawer, he put out a pint of blueberries, and I grabbed a handful.

Thank you. Manny always brought amazing fruit to work. Mangoes, peeled lychee, diced pineapple with salt sprinkled all over it. Whenever I asked him where he bought his produce, he'd only say, Not Whole Foods.

You're not sick, he said, putting his glasses back on.

I'm ill, I maintained. Look at my eyes.

He smiled. You don't know how easy you've got it. He said it without malice, but it stung anyway. I stepped into the elevator, pretending his comment didn't cut me.

When I disembarked on the thirty-second floor and swiped my employee key card at the wide glass doors, the halls were empty. So were the cubicles. The big, sweeping SVP offices that I passed every morning, made of glass as if to suggest corporate transparency, also sat empty. Had I forgotten about some meeting? My heels sank into the newly vacuumed plush carpeting. It was almost eleven. I followed the din of voices down the hall, which opened up to the atrium.

They were in the middle of a meeting. They meaning everyone, all two-hundred-odd Spectra employees standing in the atrium, crowding around the glass staircase that connected the thirty-first and thirty-second floors. The CEO, Michael Reitman, stood on the staircase, speaking into a microphone. Next to him stood Carole, the Human Resources manager, whom I recognized by her severe bob.

Michael was wrapping up a speech. He said: Spectra is a company run by people, and we take your health very seriously. As our business relies on overseas suppliers, especially those in southern China, we are taking precautionary measures with this announcement of Shen Fever. We are working in accordance with the New York State Department of Health and the Centers for Disease Control and Prevention. In the next few weeks, we will keep you abreast of new updates for keeping you safe. We would appreciate your cooperation and compliance.

Scattered applause rained down on us. I joined the flock as inconspicuously as possible. As I scanned the crowd for friendly faces, Blythe caught my eye. She used to work in Bibles, but since her transfer to Art Books, she sometimes pretended I didn't exist. I'd try my luck.

Hey, I whispered, sidling up to her. What's going on?

Public health scare. She passed me a handout, printed on Spectra letterhead, labeled "Shen Fever FAQ." I skimmed it, catching the most alarming parts:

> In its initial stages, Shen Fever is difficult to detect. Early symptoms include memory lapse, headaches, disorientation, shortness of breath, and fatigue. Because these symptoms are often mistaken for the common cold, patients are often unaware they have contracted Shen Fever. They may appear functional and are still able to execute rote, everyday tasks. However, these initial symptoms will worsen.
>
> Later-stage symptoms include signs of malnourishment, lapse of hygiene, bruising on the skin, and impaired motor coordination. Patients' physical movements may appear more effortful and clumsy. Eventually, Shen Fever results in a fatal loss of consciousness. From the moment of contraction, symptoms may develop over the course of one to four weeks, based on the strength of the patient's immune system.

Shen Fever had been in the news through the summer, like a West Nile thing. I swallowed, remembering how I'd woken up with a sore throat. I tried to pass the flyer back to Blythe, who waved it away.

Carole clapped her hands. Okay, now, let's take questions.

Seth, Senior Product Coordinator of Gifts and Specialty, raised his hand. As if reading my mind, he asked, So is this like the West Nile virus or something?

Michael shook his head. West Nile is an easy, but inaccurate, comparison. West Nile is transmitted to humans from mosquitoes. Shen Fever is a fungal infection, so it's transmitted by breathing in fungal spores. And it's not a virus. It rarely spreads from person to person, except perhaps in extreme cases.

Frances, Product Manager of Cookbooks, was the second person with her hand up. Is this an epidemic?

Carole took the microphone from Michael to answer: At this point, Shen Fever is considered an outbreak, not an epidemic. The rate of transmission is not rapid enough. It is fairly contained so far.

Lane, Senior Product Coordinator in Art, said, It says here on the FAQ sheet that Shen Fever originated in Shenzhen, China. So how are fungal spores from China getting here?

Michael nodded. Good question. Researchers aren't sure of how Shen Fever made its way to the U.S., but the popular theory is that it somehow traveled here through the shipment of goods from China to the States. That's why businesses like ours were notified by the health department.

Lane followed up with another question. We handle lots of prototypes and other samples shipped from our suppliers in China, she said. So how do we make sure we're not coming in contact with the fungus?

Carole cleared her throat. The New York State Department of Health has not mandated work restrictions. But, as you know, your health is our first priority, and the company is taking precautions. Can I ask the interns to come around? We are distributing personal-care kits to every employee. I'd like everyone to look through the contents. Inside, you'll find some protective tools, such as gloves and masks to use when handling prototypes.

The interns pushed mail carts piled high with cardboard containers the size of shoe boxes, which they distributed to everyone. The boxes were printed with the company name and its prism logo. We crowded around the mail carts.

Michael wrapped up the meeting. You can send further questions to Carole or me. Look out in your email for any updates to this situation.

We quickly dispersed after receiving our boxes. I opened up my personal care kit on the spot. There were two sets of N95 face masks and latex gloves, each imprinted with the Spectra logo.

There were some New Age–looking herbal tinctures. I opened up the brochure. It detailed an expanded insurance plan. Last, at the bottom of the box, lay a cache of nutrition bars from a health company for which we'd produced a cookbook that contained recipes for transforming nutrition bars into desserts.

I unwrapped a nutrition bar. I hadn't eaten any breakfast.

Out the glass floor-to-ceiling windows, the city didn't look any different, not really. The Coca-Cola sign gleamed, winking. I thought about going downstairs to get a cappuccino before checking emails, but I didn't want to scuttle past Manny and his judgmental gaze. A few employees were talking amongst themselves, the din of their conversation magnified by the respirator masks that they'd put on as a joke.

Hey again.

I turned around. It was Blythe.

I knocked on your door earlier, she said. The Hong Kong office called me, about the Gemstone Bible job. They said they tried to call you.

I stiffened. Maybe the Hong Kong office wanted to tell me that something had gone wrong with the manufacture. They probably called Blythe because she used to work in Bibles.

I'm running a bit late today, but I'll check my messages, I said finally.

She looked at me skeptically. Okay. Well, you know, in our department, we assign two product coordinators per book project— a main person, and another backup. We've found this method pretty helpful whenever one of us is out.

By us, I guess she meant the other girls who worked in Art. The Art Girls, for they were all invariably girls—colt-legged, flaxen-haired, in their late twenties, possessors of discounted Miu Miu and Prada, holders of degrees in Art History or Visual Studies, frequenters of gallery openings, swishers of pinot, nibblers of canapés—carried themselves like a rarefied breed, peacocking through the hallways in Fracas-scented flocks. They worked exclusively on the most detail-intensive, design-savvy projects—coffee-table books and color-sensitive exhibition catalogs. Their clients were galleries, museum presses, and, most important, the big glossy art publishers. Phaidon, Rizzoli, and Taschen. Lane, Blythe, and Delilah. Everyone wanted to be an Art Girl. I wanted to be an Art Girl.

I'll take care of it, I echoed emptily. Did Hong Kong say what was wrong with the Gemstone Bible?

She looked away, embarrassed at my need for specificity. They didn't say. They did mention they want to get a response from New Gate today if possible. With that, she turned and walked away.

I walked back to the Bible department. I unlocked the door of my office, closed the door, dropped all my belongings, and breathed a sigh of relief.

My office was small, the size of a supply closet, with a tiny window. I could close the door and shut out all views of Times Square, though its sounds still penetrated. Back when *TRL* aired, during my first year working at Spectra, in 2006, the afternoon shrieks of bridge-and-tunnel teens outside MTV Studios would resound through the walls. Sometimes I could still hear their phantom hysteria in the afternoons.

The one window was a small circular thing, as if I were aboard a submarine. If I squinted and craned my neck a certain way, I could see Bryant Park. Before the fashion shows moved to Lincoln Center, I would gaze out at the clutter of white tents popping up in the park like umbrellas. The spring collections showed in September. The fall collections showed in February. In this way, five years passed.

My position was Senior Product Coordinator of the Bibles division. No one can work in Bibles that long without coming to a certain respect for the object itself. It is a temperamental, difficult animal, its fragile pages prone to ripping, its book block prone to warping, especially in the humidity of South Asian monsoon season. Of any book, the Bible embodies the purest form of product packaging, the same content repackaged a million times over, in new combinations ad infinitum. Every season, I was trotted out to publisher clients to expound on the latest trends in synthetic leathers, the newest developments in foil embossing and gilding. I have overseen production on so many Bibles that I can't look at one without disassembling it down to its varied, assorted offal: paper stock, ribbon marker, endsheets, mull lining, and cover. It is the best-selling book of the year, every year.

I sat down at my desk. Once I started, I was good at losing myself. I popped some Tylenol, and the morning passed in a blur. I answered emails. I measured spine widths to the exact millimeter. I ordered updated prototypes of Bibles for clients. I drew up specs for new Bible projects, sent them to the Hong Kong office for an estimate. I calculated the volume and weight of books to estimate packing and shipping costs. I received a call from an Illinois publisher, and assured their team over speakerphone that the paper for their prayer-book series was indeed FSC certified, without the use of tropical hardwoods. I don't remember if I took lunch or not.

All day, I kept putting off doing something I dreaded. The Gemstone Bible, marketed toward preteen girls, was to be packaged with a keepsake semiprecious gemstone on a sterling alloy chain. The Bibles were already printed, but the jewelry hadn't arrived, so they couldn't assemble and shrink-wrap the bundles. Earlier that day, the Hong Kong office had emailed with bad news. The gemstone supplier that Spectra had initially contracted for the job had unexpectedly closed. Several of their workers had developed various forms of lung diseases. A class-action lawsuit had been filed on behalf of the workers, leading to the closure of the supplier.

I Googled *pneumoconiosis* and drew up images of lungs in formaldehyde, lungs that had been X-rayed, lungs shriveled up into morel mushrooms. With the force of the images in front of me, I picked up the phone and called the production editor at New Gate Publishing, based in Atlanta. I took a deep breath and explained the situation.

What's pneumoconiosis? she asked, on the other end of the line.

Pneumoconiosis is an umbrella term for a group of lung diseases, I said. The workers who grind and polish semiprecious stones, they've been breathing in this dust and developing lung diseases, without their knowledge, for months, even years. Apparently, from what Hong Kong is telling me, the lawsuit claims that the workers have been working in rooms without ventilation systems or any sort of respirator equipment.

This doesn't have anything to do with the Shen Fever thing that's been in the news, does it?

This is unrelated, I confirmed. This is a matter of workers' rights and safety. The gemstone granules are tearing up their lungs. That's why it's a particularly urgent matter.

A silence at the other end of the line.

I mean, they're dying, I clarified. The supplier is putting all its contract jobs on hold. Hello?

Finally she spoke, slowly and stiffly. I don't want to sound like we don't care, because obviously we do, but this is disappointing news.

I understand, I conceded, then almost couldn't help myself: But the workers are dying, I repeated, as if I knew.

I mean, the thing is this. There's nothing else like the Gemstone Bible on the market, and we think a title like this is going to do very, very well. So I want you to tell me where we can go from here, as far as the Gemstone Bible is concerned. Can your Hong Kong office find another supplier?

I had to tread gently. We could try, yes, but this is now an industry-wide problem. It's not just one gemstone supplier. This isn't an atypical issue in Guangdong.

Guangdong? Her voice grew incrementally more exasperated.

It's a province in China, where all the gemstone suppliers are centered. This isn't an isolated incident. Almost all suppliers are suffering from the same problems and are also suspending production to evade lawsuits.

Almost all, she repeated.

Yes, almost all, I confirmed, then tried a different tack. We could package the Bible with faux gemstone charms instead. We know a plastic supplier—

I could almost hear her shaking her head. No. No. We're committed to the Gemstone Bible. We placed the order with you guys as the Gemstone Bible. We're not reconceiving this entire project on the basis of one supplier failing. She was speaking very quickly, her words stumbling over one another. Obviously, it doesn't reflect well on Spectra that you guys placed this job with a shoddy supplier.

I'm very sorry, I said mechanically. The working conditions—

I know. She sighed. Everyone says placing jobs in China is a risk. There are no rules, no enforcement. But that's why we used an intermediary like Spectra, because you guys are supposed to eliminate the risk. Otherwise, we could've just dealt directly with the suppliers ourselves.

I started, Let's try—

So what I need you to do, Candace, she continued, is to replace the supplier, find another gemstone source. It can't be that hard. You need to pull every string you can, call in every favor. Because, honestly, if you can't produce this, then we're going to look elsewhere, maybe even in India. Maybe we'll start working directly with suppliers.

She hung up before I could respond.

It took me a second before I put the receiver down. Then I picked it up and put it down, picked it up and put it down, picked it up and threw it, the receiver unleashing a loud, repeating signal in protest. With both hands, I took the phone and yanked its cords out of the wall, dumping the whole thing into the wastebasket. With my heels on, I jammed my foot into the basket, until I heard plastic crack. I took my foot out, assessed the damage. I took the phone back out of the basket, swabbed it with some antibacterial wipes, reassembled it, and plugged it back in.

I picked up the phone and called Hong Kong. It was six in the morning there, but I knew there would be someone who'd come in early to work. There was always someone. I had been to Spectra's Hong Kong office. Through the sweeping windows, you could see the sun rising over the shops along Causeway Bay, the Tian Tan Buddha, the Hong Kong Cricket Club, Victoria Park, so named after the colonizing English queen herself, over the mountains and over the sea, rising and rising, an unstoppable force, bringing in a new day of work.

2

Let us return, then, as we do in times of grief, for the sake of pleasure but mostly for the need for relief, to art. Or whatever. To music, to poetry, to paintings and installations, to TV and the movies.

But mostly TV and the movies.

Has anyone ever see *Torn Curtain*? Bob bellowed. Who's seen *Torn Curtain*? Raise your hands.

Is that the one with Jimmy Stewart? Todd said.

No. Paul Newman. Bob looked around. C'mon, Hitchcock, guys. Film History 101.

When no one said anything, he sighed. I have my work cut out, I see.

We were clustered around the fire, at night. We sat on logs, huddled in coats and blankets, waiting for dinner to cook in the Dutch oven. Somewhere in Pennsylvania.

Bob continued with his *Torn Curtain* rant. Released in 1966, *Torn Curtain* is a Cold War thriller starring Paul Newman and Julie Andrews. Though overlooked as one of Hitchcock's minor works, it is notable for an extended murder scene that shows a man being killed in real time. In the grim struggle, a man is head-locked, stabbed with a knife, struck with a shovel, and gassed in an oven. It is gruesome not for the tactical maneuvers, which are no more or less grisly than other homicidal depictions in movies, but for the scene's painfully protracted duration.

All of this is to say, Bob said, that it takes a long time for a human being to die. You have to do a lot of things, an alternating method of deprivation and attack, a winning combination of pressures and releases, levers and pulleys. A human body accumulates stresses. Killing is more an accumulative effect rather than the result of one definitive action.

But what are you saying? Evan asked.

The point, Bob said. The point I'm making is about the fevered. They aren't really alive. And one way we have of knowing this is that they don't take a long time to die.

It was true, sort of. For the most part, from what we had seen, the fevered were creatures of habit, mimicking old routines and gestures they must have inhabited for years, decades. The lizard brain is a powerful thing. They could operate the mouse of a dead PC, they could drive stick in a jacked sedan, they could run an empty dishwasher, they could water dead houseplants. On the nights when we stalked their houses, we wandered through their spaces, looked at their family albums. They were more nostalgic than we expected, their stuttering brains set to favor the heirloom china, set to arrange and rearrange their aunts' and grandmothers' jars of pickles and preserves in endless patterns of peach, green bean, and cherry, to play records and CDs and cassette tapes they once must have enjoyed. Familiar songs drifted out at us from strange rooms. Bobby Womack, "California Dreamin'." The Righteous Brothers, "Unchained Melody," possibly the most beautiful song I have ever heard, more hymnal than anything. But it was not the emotional content of the songs that they registered, we deduced, only the rhythm, the percussive patterns that had worn grooves inside their brains. Dolly Parton, Kenny Rogers, "Islands in the Stream." Tears streamed down their cheeks. Recognizing their residual humanity, we shot them in the heads but not the faces.

It's like we're in this horror movie, Todd said. Like a zombie or vampire flick.

Bob thought about this, scratching his sling. He frowned. Well, no. Vampire and zombie narratives are completely different.

How are they different? Evan asked, winking at Janelle, who swatted his arm to stop him from egging Bob on.

Bob looked back and forth between the two of them. He smiled benignly. Excellent question, Evan. With vampire narrative, the danger lies in the villain's intentions, his underlying character. There are good vampires, there are bad vampires. Think of *Interview with the Vampire*. Or even *Twilight*. These are character narratives.

Now, on the other hand, he continued, let's think about the zombie narrative. It's not about a specific villain. One zombie can be easily killed, but a hundred zombies is another issue. Only amassed do they really pose a threat. This narrative, then, is not about any individual entity, per se, but about an abstract force: the force of the mob, of mob mentality. Perhaps it's better known these days as the hive mind. You can't see it. You can't forecast it. It strikes at any time, whenever, wherever, like a natural disaster, a hurricane, an earthquake.

Let us apply this, Bob said, to our situation. Let us familiarize ourselves with the fevered.

Wait, I interjected. What are you saying? Because number one, the fevered aren't zombies. They don't attack us or try to eat us. They don't do anything to us. If anything, we do more harm to them.

I surprised myself when I spoke. It was rare that I did. But, having spoken, I felt short of breath, nauseated. Everyone looked at me.

Bob gave me a look. Candace. When you wake up in a fictitious world, your only frame of reference is fiction.

Are you okay? Janelle asked me.

I ran into the woods, where, at the base of a tree, I threw up. The rice and beans we had for dinner, the peanut-butter-and-canned-beet sandwiches we'd had for lunch. Leaning with my hands pressed against its trunk, gasping, I braced myself against another wave of nausea. Whatever was left inside me puckered. The strawberry Nutri-Grain bar we'd had for breakfast, some cold instant coffee. But I didn't stop there. It seemed like I was throwing up a month's worth of food. Like the things I'd eaten in my last days in New York. The slices of hard, old bread that I'd dip into seltzer water to make them more palatable. Powdery mouthfuls of Manischewitz matzo ball mix, spooned out of the box. Tomato soup, made with Heinz ketchup packets and seltzer water. The pallets and pallets of strawberries, dark and spotted with mold, just dumped out on the sidewalk.

Emptied, I wiped my sour, acidic mouth with the palm of my hand and smeared it on the tree bark. I leaned against the trunk for a moment, breathing into the crook of my elbow.

Candace.

I spun around to find Bob walking up behind me. Here, he said. In his hand was a bottle of Pepto-Bismol.

Oh, that's okay, I said, on instinct.

Come on. You need it. Sensing my reticence, he went ahead and opened the new bottle. The plastic shell around the cap crinkled as he tore into and discarded it.

I looked at the plastic piece of litter on the ground.

Littering is only a problem if everyone does it, Bob said wryly.

I accepted the Pepto-Bismol. I could feel him watching me as I took a sip. We didn't know each other. I had been the last out of New York, then absorbed into the group quickly. It had only been a week, a week and a half, since they'd found me.

Is that better? Bob asked, as if the wonders of Pepto worked this swiftly.

Think I'm just tired, I said.

Bob's light gray eyes softened. It's hard for everyone here. Luckily we'll get to where we need to be soon, and we can settle in and not do all this traveling.

A burst of laughter from the campfire cut through the air. Bob waited for it to pass.

But speaking more broadly about this situation we find ourselves in, he continued, my advice is to find some form of spiritual guidance.

I nodded politely. Sure. Like a self-help book or something.

Something like that, he said, pausing. Do you practice any form of religion?

My parents were religious, so I did have that upbringing of, you know, Sunday school. But it's been years. I never went to church after high school.

He was silent for a moment. When he spoke, he said: Before this, I wouldn't consider myself religious at all. But lately, I find the Bible to be very comforting. He cleared his throat. What do you think we all have in common in this group?

I don't know, I said. I guess the most obvious thing is, we're all survivors?

He smiled, professorially. I'd rephrase that to something more nuanced. We're *selected*. The fact that we're immune to something that took out most of the population, that's pretty special. And the fact that you're still here, it means something.

You mean, like natural selection?

I'm talking about divine selection.

I shifted uneasily. Who knew what was true. The sheer density of information and misinformation at the End, encapsulated in news articles and message-board theories and clickbait traps that had propagated hysterically through retweets and shares, had effectively rendered us more ignorant, more helpless, more innocent in our stupidity.

The question that had hung over all of our heads: Why had we not become fevered? Most of us must have been in contact with airborne spores that had fevered others. To Bob, it all boiled down to his religious conviction that we were chosen. That's the story to which the group officially subscribed.

To me (and to Janelle and Ashley and Evan), the fever was arbitrary. The fact that we were alive held no special meaning.

On the few occasions I had been caught alone with Bob, I had managed to avoid his religious talks. Now I felt myself rescinding, emptying of all personality, emotion, and preferences, so that he would know as little of me as possible. My eyes flickered back toward the campsite, the campfire visible through the trees. I could hear laughter. He caught me looking.

Either way, I'm just happy to be here, I said, with a forced laugh.

He pressed, How do you like it here so far, being with us, I mean? Do you think we're the right fit for you?

He asked this in all seriousness, as if I had any other choice.

I like it so far, I managed. It's taken some adjustment. The group dinners are a new experience for me. I'm just not used to doing everything together, the group activities and dinners. I've been—I hesitated—alone for a long time.

He leveled his gaze. I'd like you to be more participatory, if possible. Now that you're one of us, we're counting on you.

Sure, I said.

That Pepto you're holding, he continued, that was harvested on one of our stalks. We make lists of our necessities. We take what we need. We divide up our labor. We organize together to live. We stay together. Do you understand?

I nodded.

Well, we should get back, he said. Everyone's probably waiting for us for dinner.

When we returned to the campsite, I saw that everyone had

dishes in their laps, plated with untouched food. The rule was that we couldn't eat until someone, usually Bob, said grace. They were drinking on empty stomachs, half-full bottles of Amstel Light and Corona.

This is quite a spread, Bob said to Genevieve approvingly.

I sat down on a log, next to Janelle, who handed me a bottle of water. You okay? she asked. What did you talk to Bob about?

I shrugged. I uncapped the water bottle and took a giant swig, swallowing along with the water all the residual bile in my mouth. It was seltzer water, the bubbles biting my gums, my tongue. I capped it as I swallowed.

Genevieve passed me a plate of food, baked beans and peas. I was not hungry.

So are you okay? Janelle asked. Ever since I'd told her about my situation, she asked whether I was okay so often that I was afraid the others would figure it out.

Yes, I finally said. I'm fine.

Bob smiled at me from across the campfire, as if we shared an inside joke. He said, loud enough for everyone to hear: Candace, will you lead us in saying grace tonight?

I looked at him. His expression didn't change.

I bowed my head and began.

I arrived to the city carried by the tides of others. Most of my college friends were moving there, if they hadn't already. It seemed like the inevitable, default place to go. Arriving, we did exactly what we thought we wanted to do. Jobless, we sat outside at sidewalk cafés, donning designer shades, splitting twenty-five-dollar pitchers of spiked Meyer lemonade, and holding tipsy, circulating conversations that lasted well into evening, as rush hour waxed and waned around us. Other people had places to go, but not us. It was the summer of 2006 and the move itself seemed like a slight, inconsequential event in the grand sequence of things. Which was: my mother died, I graduated college, I moved to New York.

My college boyfriend had joined the Peace Corps. When he wasn't digging wells or developing crop rotation systems in outlying South American villages, he was reading postcolonial theory in chambray shirts, sheltered by the cool, gentle shade of indigenous palms. Across weak, spotty reception, we held obligatory sessions of phone sex, more for the novelty of the thing than the thing itself. (You're a fox. I'm a hen. Chicken coop. Go.) He broke up with me via email after the calling card minutes ran out.

All I did that first summer in New York was wander through lower Manhattan, wearing my mother's eighties Contempo Casuals dresses, looking to get picked up by anyone, whomever. The dresses slid on easily in the morning. They slid off easily at night. They were loose-fitting and cool, cut from jersey cotton in prints of florals and Africana. Wearing them, I never failed to get picked up but I usually failed to get anything else—not that I wanted anything else, as I told myself and whomever else. Still, I overstayed my welcome in their beds, wondering what they did for a living as they dressed in the mornings. Where they were going.

I was tying this guy's tie one morning. He wanted a Windsor knot. I tried to follow the step-by-step instructions he gave, blundering on the fifth or sixth step every time.

My wife usually does this, he said apologetically. Ex-wife, he corrected. After his divorce, he'd moved out from Westchester to Williamsburg, into one of those sleek gray high-rises that overlooked the East River and boasted skyline views of Manhattan.

What's the occasion? I asked. For the special knot.

I'm getting remarried, he said, and laughed when I looked up. Just kidding. No, I'm going to be on TV.

Congratulations, I said, trying not to look too impressed. But don't they have their own wardrobe people to help you with this?

It's local cable. He smiled patiently. I'll call you tonight.

Later, I watched the show. It was one of those political debate programs. They were doing a segment about unemployment rates among youth just out of college. I didn't recognize his face right away, not with glasses on, but I recognized the tie I'd helped him pick out and the knot that had taken three tries to get right. The show identified him as Steven Reitman, an economist and author of *You're Not the Boss of Me: Labor Values and Work Ethic Among America's Millennial Youth.*

Steven looked into the camera, sitting against a backdrop of New York skyline. He spoke with authority: The millennial generation has different values from most of America. These kids coming out of college today, they don't *want* jobs, they *expect* trust funds.

The host chimed in. What would you say, Steven, to recent

statistics showing that millennials are the most educated generation of the American workforce? Isn't that an indication that the
new generation is primed for more advanced professions?

Steven nodded. As I've written in my book, the problem isn't
education, it's motivation. It's a mentality issue. What does this
mean for the United States as a leading economic force? We should
be troubled.

He didn't call me that day. A week passed before he summoned
me back to his apartment. We lay in his bed, undressed. He was
trying to go down on me. The sun was only just setting outside his
loft windows, in shades of lavender and pink. Everything felt too
earnest.

He did that thing where he laid me down on my back and
worked his way south, kissing my breasts, my rib cage, my belly. I
found his overtrimmed facial hair alarming. The loose-coiled mattress shifted skittishly underneath me. The only guy I had ever let
go down on me was the college boyfriend, and that was under the
pretense of love.

Hey. I touched his head, his salt-and-pepper hair. I wouldn't
do that. When he seemed not to have heard, I tried again. Maybe
we should have a safe word.

The safe word is *yes*, he bristled.

I lay on my back, looking up at his high ceiling, trying to relax.
I pretended that it was the end of yoga class and I was practicing
corpse pose. But I couldn't do it. I couldn't just lie there.

I'm on my period, I lied.

That's okay. It doesn't bother me.

Really? But, I'm like four days into it. At this point, it kind of
tastes like rust, old dried blood.

He looked up, smiling. Okay, I'll stop.

Like licking a rusty barbed wire, I added.

You don't have to get into it. His smile had vanished.

Yeah, but can I say it anyway?

36

What we ended up doing was something like three-quarters fucking and one-quarter lovemaking—and by lovemaking, I just mean the part that was missionary. That part was in the beginning, when he clasped me, almost tenderly and wistfully, and I shut my eyes against his confused gaze, both paternal and lustful. I didn't want to be part of the meaningful postdivorce narrative he was constructing. Like, Obligatory Sexual Interlude with Inappropriate Twentysomething. If he was looking for newfound meaning, I would be the first to tell him this was nothing. I did this all the time, I would say. And if he left cab fare on the nightstand, I wasn't going to take it. I didn't want anything. I didn't need anything.

Turn over, he said.

I turned over.

In the morning, he left a hundred-dollar bill and I used it for groceries.

Instead of taking a cab, I walked home to the Lower East Side, crossing the Williamsburg Bridge. Halfway across, I realized my dress, or my mother's dress, was on backward, and I took it off and put it back on, in front of the rush-hour traffic, my breasts cold and peaked in the morning air.

When I finally arrived home, my roommate, Jane, was watching TV and eating yogurt.

You got a package, she said, gesturing to a big moving box next to the sofa.

When did this come in?

I saw it when I got back last night.

I opened up the box to discover a strangely curated selection of my mother's belongings. I could smell traces of her scent, a mix of Caress soap and medicinal Clinique. Most of our family belongings had been placed in storage, but likely because of a clerical mix-up, the hospice had shipped the remaining "personal effects" to me instead of to the law firm overseeing my parents' estate. The law firm would have then forwarded this last box to the storage facility that held my family's possessions, from my childhood things to my father's collection of Chinese literature.

Jane knelt down next to me, observing. I unpacked the items slowly. Laid across the scratched wood floor, my mother's belongings looked small, measly, shopworn. There were clothes and jewelry, pictures of ancestral relatives I couldn't name, a silver gooseneck-spouted coffeepot from the silver service we never used, and cooking implements she'd long retired: a brass wire ladle for draining oil, broken sections of a bamboo steamer, small jars of dried star anise and other herbs, and, bundled in a bouquet of tissue paper, a heavy cleaver with a handle made of wood, swollen and split. There was no kitchen in the hospice, and she was definitely not well enough to do any cooking, but these were the items she had chosen to take.

At the bottom of one of the boxes was a plastic Ziploc pint bag filled with what looked like chunks of amber-colored tree resin. I opened up the bag. They were triangular slices, with linear grain and a golden fibrous gleam. Maybe they were hunks of dried shellfish like abalone, the kind you'd find in Asian supermarkets.

What is that, do you think? I asked.

Jane held the bag up to the light. She took out a piece, sniffed. Shark! Shark fins, she pronounced. She smelled again, as if to confirm. For shark fin soup, she added, handing me a fin.

How do you even know this? I asked. I brought a dried husk to my nose. They smelled stale, a tinge of oceanic rust, salt crust.

We should make shark fin soup! Jane said, too excited to answer. Restaurants don't serve this stuff anymore because, you know, animal rights. I read that they cut the fins off and then throw the sharks back in the water.

What happens to the sharks? I smelled them again.

They die, obviously. Slow, painful deaths. That's why it's outlawed, and also! That's why we shouldn't waste these.

Yeah, but shark fin soup is so outdated. It's like banquet-hall food, I said, trying to remember if my mother had ever made shark fin soup. I was pretty sure she hadn't. Could she have been saving them for a special occasion?

Jane smiled. So we'll have an outdated dinner party. I know! She almost burst into flames with glee, scheming. It'll be eighties-decadence themed. Sheath cocktail dresses, gold jewelry. The shark fin soup will be the centerpiece. Three courses. For the first course, something totally passé, like salmon puffs . . .

Because Jane and I were bad at planning things—disorganized, prone to grandiose, unrealistic ideas—the dinner party didn't actually happen for several weeks. In the meanwhile, my college friends slowly found their ways to credible internships and entry-level jobs. The group gatherings at sidewalk cafés continued until there were too few of us to sustain the same festive mood. When rush hour rolled in and people started their evening commutes around us, we reached for our drinks, avoiding one another's eyes. Someone stood up. He had to be out early to paddle down the Gowanus. Another person excused herself because she had to attend a dreamcatcher workshop. No one asked questions.

Instead of wasting time with others, I began to waste time alone. I walked. I had a routine. I woke early, did my stretches, and ate a bowl of granola drenched in milk. I brushed my teeth, I washed my face, foaming up a clear brown bar of Neutrogena soap. I shaved my legs. I shaved my armpits. To shave my pussy, I lowered myself into the tub, crouching like a sumo wrestler pre-bout. Like a champion sumo wrestler. I placed a hand mirror at the bottom of the basin; I liked to be thorough. My body chafed easily in the heat. Afterward, I showered with scaldingly hot water, watching all the hair run down the drain. I put on a Contempo Casuals dress.

I took my purse, a small cross-body that only held a wallet, ChapStick, and a Canon Elph digital camera.

Freshly shaved, freshly showered, freshly dressed, I went outside. The morning air was cool against my skin, still red from the shower. I smelled like Neutrogena and green apple shampoo, fruity and medicinal at the same time. I closed the heavy door behind me and started walking, passing by the familiar sights: the used bookstore with its window display of architecture tomes, the coded graffiti tags, the dollar pizza place, the diner featuring the same people sitting at the same window booths, stirring their coffees with tiny spoons. Then out of the Lower East Side entirely, west to SoHo or north to Union Square.

The sun rose. Humidity levels increased. As the day warmed, my breath steadied. My shoulders browned to a crisp, like an athlete's. Blisters formed on my feet. Midday, heat came off the sidewalks, creating an illusory wave effect, as if I were observing the world through a thick pane of glass. To cool down, I'd skim through the air-conditioned lobby of a hotel or museum or department store, like a swimmer taking a quick, splashy lap, slipping past doormen, salesgirls, concierges, docents, security guards before bursting back outside.

Periodically I'd take pictures. Pictures of ordinary things; of trash bin contents, of doormen yawning, of graffiti splashed across subway cars, of poorly worded advertisements, of pigeon flocks across the sky—all the usual clichés. I used to feel sheepish doing it, fishing around in my purse for the camera discreetly, as if for a lipstick or a compact. But then I would keep the Canon Elph on me openly, dangling from my hand by a wristlet. I preferred if people thought I was a tourist. It looked less weird that way.

I often ended up in Chinatown around lunch. Specifically, the Fujianese side, separated by the Bowery from the tourist-pandering Cantonese part. This part was cheaper, more run-down, less conscious of the Western gaze. You could get a plate of dumplings for two dollars, spiked with black vinegar and julienned ginger on a flimsy, buckling Styrofoam plate. When it felt like my legs would give out, I'd eat pork-cabbage dumplings at a shallow storefront underneath the Manhattan Bridge, then sit outside in its shade and drink an iced milk tea. I could feel the bridge above me rumbling and bouncing with the weight of vehicles. The air was dense with afternoon exhaust and fried foods. Old ladies and hunchbacked men in white wife-beaters fanned themselves with palm leaves, eating chicken hearts impaled on skewers.

In the evenings, as people returned home, I looked into the windows above and imagined the lives of the occupants inside. Their desk lamps, their hanging spider ferns in wicker baskets, calico cats lounging on throw pillows. I could do that indefinitely: roam the streets, look up into windows and imagine myself into other people's lives. Maybe I could be a creepy Peeping Tom and that could just be my life.

When I returned home, I would go through the images on my camera and upload the good ones to NY Ghost. The ghost was me. Walking around aimlessly, without anywhere to go, anything to do, I was just a specter haunting the scene. A wind could blow and knock me to Jersey or Ohio or back to Salt Lake. It seemed appropriate that I kept the blog anonymous. Or maybe the anonymity was because I didn't know whether the photos were any good. What I enjoyed, or at least what I felt compelled to keep doing, was the routine.

I held this walking-and-photographing routine through almost all of that first summer in New York. I did it five days a week, Mondays through Fridays, from ten in the morning to six in the evening. June, July, August. A deep, grim satisfaction buoyed me. The thing was just to keep walking, just keep going, and by some point, the third or fourth hour, the fifth or sixth, my mind drained until empty. Hours blurred together. Traffic blared. Cars honked. A man asked me if I was okay, if I needed anything. What do you think I need? I asked, and something about my face made him look away.

Walking down Central Park South one day, I unwittingly passed by the Helmsley Park Lane. It took a moment to realize why it seemed so familiar: it was the hotel my parents and I stayed the first time we visited New York, as a family. I was maybe nine. It was the first business trip my father ever took, for the first American job he ever landed, an analyst position at an insurance firm.

He was away during most of the day, so my mother and I were left to wander around the city by ourselves. We'd wake up to Central Park and walk down Fifth Avenue for croissants and coffee. We pretended to live there, imagining different lives. She was a divorcée with a massive alimony settlement and I was her spoiled daughter. She was a single Shanghainese socialite and I her little child servant, holding her purse as she paid for leather heels at Ferragamo, where, upon purchase, the saleslady allowed me to use the employee bathroom. It didn't matter what she bought; she just wanted to parade her fancy American luxury wares to her two younger sisters back in Fuzhou.

In the evenings, when my father returned to the hotel room, my parents fought, arguing in Fujianese instead of Mandarin because they thought I couldn't understand. I have always thought of Fujianese as the language of arguments, of fights. And in fact I did understand the language, better known as Hokkien, but never learned to speak it.

It was the same fight every time. My mother wanted to return to China, if not today then eventually, and my father wanted to stay. It would begin as a rational conversation, then disintegrate.

If we moved back, my mother reasoned, you could have any job you want in China.

The only good jobs in China are government jobs, my father

said. I didn't study this hard through university just to sit around and accept bribes.

Your friends back home have government jobs, she fumed. They're happy.

They're happy because they don't have a choice but to be happy. That's the best that they can do. My father raised his voice. If they had the choice to come here like us, you think they'd rather stay in China? he scoffed. You're being naïve.

I have family in Fujian. My mother raised her voice defiantly, matching his.

Right. And how do you think we send money back to your family?

She glared at him in icy silence.

This isn't just about me! He tried a different tack. This is what I'm trying to tell you. There are more opportunities here. Candace can really make something of herself.

Ai-yah! You think she wants to grow up somewhere where she's estranged from her cousins, her grandparents? She only has us. If anything ever happened—

You're being melodramatic. Nothing is going to happen to us.

My mother exploded. A car accident, an illness, an act of God! This is about you being successful at everyone else's expense.

I disagree, he said, his voice suddenly dropping to a calm, measured tone.

My mother was silent, as if ready to drop the argument. But then, in the quiet tone she reserved for only the most scorched-earth malice, she said: Just because your family hates you, doesn't mean I have to leave my family too.

He didn't respond. Which more or less ended the conversation.

Observing from behind the crack in the bathroom door, I waited a few minutes until it seemed okay to come out and pretend that I'd finished taking my shower.

Get dressed! my father snapped. We're going out for dinner.

My mother came over and tousled my dried hair. What do you want to eat? she asked gently. We can eat wherever you want tonight.

Chinese food, I said, because I knew that would please them. All I wanted to eat as a kid was pizza or spaghetti.

We went to a midtown Chinese place called Vega House. It was almost closing time when we arrived, around nine. The place was mostly empty. They seated us in the big corner booth next to the window. Outside, it had just started to rain; droplets streamed down the pane, blurring the scene outside. My skin broke out into goose bumps in the stale air-conditioning.

In a bid to impress my mother, my father ordered Peking duck. It was such a glamorous, high-maintenance dish; it required table-side service. The weary waiter rolled the glazed bird on a cart and lethargically carved it up, knife almost slipping out of his hand. I found the fatty blobs of duck skin off-putting, but I ate it anyway. I was my father's co-conspirator. He was demonstrating that anything she wanted in China, she could get here. Halfway through the meal, my father put his arm around my mother, trying to indicate to her that the fight was over. For now.

The rain had stopped by the time we left the restaurant. The air was warm. Gasoline puddles formed in the streets. Office buildings glittered as if in half-sleep, a scattering of darkened windows. The city was really beautiful. In a few of the fluorescent windows, employees worked late hours, each alone in his or her office. Dressed in collared shirts, they sat at desks littered with thermoses and Chinese takeout cartons, papers piled high. What were they doing? Where were their homes?

Looking at the office workers suspended high above us, I sensed for the first time my father's desire to leave China and to live in a foreign country. It was the anonymity. He wanted to be unknown, unpossessed by others' knowledge of him. That was freedom.

I looked up at my father, his gaze also directed to those office buildings. He glanced down briefly and smiled. Like worker bees, he observed in English.

I remember thinking in that moment that I was going to live in New York one day. That was the extent of my ambitions at age nine, but I felt it deeply. I didn't want to go back to China. When we moved to the U.S., I had wanted to go back home, there was nothing I wanted more, I got on my knees and begged like a dog, but I was six then and stupider and I didn't know anything. I didn't feel that way anymore.

The shark fin dinner party took place on a cold, rainy Saturday night in late August. It marked the end of that strange transitory summer, and the beginning of something else.

The guests consisted of a mix of college friends and Jane's people, coworkers and neighbors. They crowded into our railroad apartment, guys in skinny ties and suits, girls with big Aqua Net hair and acrylic nails. They piled their coats on our beds, rolled a keg up the stairs, brought little hostess gifts. Giorgio Moroder played in the background. Someone came dressed as Ronald Reagan, pelting girls with jelly beans from his suit pocket.

We'd created a makeshift Trump-themed dining table in our living room by arranging collapsible card tables end to end. Over this, Jane had laid a metallic gold tablecloth, weighted by a thrifted brass candelabra, and bouquets of fake plastic flowers she'd spray-painted gold. On the table were ironic predinner canapés: salmon mousse quenelles with dill cream, spinach dip in a bread bowl, Ritz crackers, and a ball of pimento cheese in the shape of Trump's hair.

I navigated through the rooms in another of my mother's loose, billowy Contempo Casuals dresses, this one black with a white burnout Africana print.

In the midst of this fray was Steven Reitman, dressed as if for a Hamptons boating party, standing amongst the secondhand furniture of my bedroom. I had invited him almost as a joke, considering that we hadn't seen each other all summer, so I hadn't actually expected him to come.

Is this a dinner party or a costume party? he asked, pressing his whiskered cheek to mine in an air kiss. The scent of his expensive yuzu aftershave made me suddenly wistful for the few times we'd spent together. I swallowed.

You don't need an eighties costume, I said. You can say you're here for research, observing millennials in their natural habitat. I sat down on the edge of my bed, pushing aside the mountain of jackets.

So you invited me to be the party ethnographer? Should've brought my notebook. He sat down beside me, crossing his legs, exposing ankle sock. The bed sagged.

I shrugged and sipped from my rum and Coke. The dim light from the nightstand lamp dramatized our expressions.

How have you been? Sitting very close, he spoke in a low, conspiratorial tone, intimating an intimacy that we never really shared. I noticed that his sports jacket featured a Liberty floral pocket square that someone else, another girl, I assumed, must've helped him choose. No way would he have chosen it on his own.

How's the postcollege job market looking? he pressed.

I don't know. I've been focusing more on, I guess, personal projects.

Well, the reason I ask is—he reached into his back pocket—I didn't come empty-handed. He opened his wallet. For a moment I was afraid he was going to hand me cash, but it was something else, a business card. It read MICHAEL REITMAN, CEO.

It's my brother's company, Steven explained. There's a position open. Give him a call.

You told your brother about me? I studied the card uncertainly, trying to make out the letters in the low light. What's Spectrum?

Spectra, he corrected. They're a publishing consulting firm that handles book production. It's not art or design, but it's something. They're looking to fill an assistant position. My brother will have more details, if you get in touch.

I studied the card again, avoiding Steven's gaze. I didn't need a job right away, but I needed *something*, a point of entry into another life that wasn't just about milling around, walking. I could feel my parents' disapproval hanging over me. I was embarrassed that Steven had sensed what I needed.

Thank you, I finally said. But you didn't have to.

It's nothing. I just mentioned you. Now he looked embarrassed. I know we're not—

Dinner is ready! Jane clamored through the rooms, gathering guests up.

You go ahead, I told Steven. I'll be right in.

He stood up. Okay, I'll see you in there?

I smiled reassuringly. When he left the room, I closed the door. Then I crawled to the head of my bed, over the mountain of jackets, where I opened the window and climbed out onto the fire escape. The tinny, collapsible structure winced. The air outside was cool and humid. Tiny pinpricks of rain dotted my arms.

The fire escape looked out on the backs of other apartment buildings and a communal garden that all the ground-level tenants shared, its disorganized, uncultivated plots overrun with ghetto palms and riffraff vegetation; a dash of wildflowers here, a fledgling fruit tree there.

I sat down. A full minute lapsed before I started crying. Or more like a shallow, panicky mouth breathing, dry and sobless. I tried to focus my breath, steady it, in and out, like breaststrokes in deep, choppy water.

Hey, you're blocking all the rain.

The voice came from below. I looked down. Through the grating, I saw a guy sitting on his window ledge, reading a book, smoking a cigarette. He was the summer subletter downstairs. I'd seen him at the mailboxes.

Sorry, I said, automatically.

He looked up, smiled impishly. No sorry. Just giving you a hard time.

I'm getting some air, I explained unnecessarily.

Okay. He blew out a lungful of smoke. Fire escape is all yours. Do you mind if I finish this first?

I considered the top of his head. Can I have one?

Sure. Then, after a pause, Should I come up?

I looked into my empty room. I could hear Jane still rallying everyone to the table. I'll just come down.

The fire escape rattled beneath my feet. He helped me down the last steps, where, at the landing, I extended my hand. He had a surprisingly firm grip, given his thin, boyish frame. There was a sadness to his face, dark circles under his blue eyes.

He asked, Do you want to wait here or come inside while I get you one?

I peeked inside his window. Is this your room?

Yes. He hesitated. Would you like to come in?

I climbed in and looked around. He lived in the room directly below mine. It was the same room—our apartments shared the same floor plan—except cleaner, better. My room was messy, cluttered with too many things. His room was clean and ascetic, bare walls dimly lit by a floor lamp. There was something serene about it, a temple emptied of all ceremonial accoutrements and cleared of incense smoke.

I live right above you, I informed him.

I know. I can hear you walking late at night. You pace. He caught himself. Sorry, I don't mean to sound creepy. You just have this skittish way of walking.

A skittish way of walking?

Like, restless. I hear your roommate too. She gets up very early. I can hear her grinding coffee.

Does she not have a skittish way of walking?

He contemplated this. Um, no. Your roommate walks very purposefully, but you, you're more unsettled, unsure. Not an insult, just an observation. He had found his pack of American Spirits and handed one to me, not touching the filter. I liked that consideration.

I rolled it around between my fingers. My roommate gets up early, I allowed. It's a long commute. She has this fashion PR job in Jersey.

Here, sit down. I can't find my light. Let me get one from the kitchen.

I sat down on the edge of the bed. It was a mattress on the floor, carefully dressed with white sheets. There was no chair. Affixed on the walls were two plastic hooks, one for a towel and the other for a jacket, next to the doorframe. In lieu of a dresser, clothes were neatly stacked in three rows on the floor, against the wall: jeans, underwear, and white T-shirts. A small floor lamp was arranged next to a few library books. Rousseau. Foucault.

When he returned, he was holding the largest butane lighter I'd ever seen. May I? he asked.

I nodded, and he attempted to light my cigarette, ridiculously, the gas flame licking my cheek.

Should we go back outside? I don't want to smoke up your room.

No, stay. Smoke up my room. He sat down on the bed. We smoked. He seemed content to say nothing.

So, I said, searching. Tell me about what you do. I regretted it as soon as I asked. It was the question everyone asked everyone else in New York, so careerist, so boring.

What I do for money or what I actually do?

Both, I guess. I exhaled a plume of smoke.

I temp for money, usually copywriting jobs. I freelance a bit too, a few articles and interviews. But what I actually do is write fiction. And you, what about you?

I live off my parents, I said, surprised by the casualness with which I dispensed this information. I didn't elaborate that they were both deceased, and that the family coffers or whatever would last me just long enough—maybe, say, for the next ten, fifteen years—for me to be comfortable with not working, long enough to be useless. The fruits of my immigrant father's lifelong efforts would be gobbled up and squandered by me, his lazy, disaffected daughter.

But I'm looking for a job, I added. I have an interview coming up at this place called Spectra.

What are you interviewing for?

Um, I have no idea.

He smiled, as if to himself. By this point, my cigarette had gone out. I hesitated. There's a party that I'm supposed to be hosting.

What, now? He started.

I nodded. They've probably begun without me. You're invited, if you'd like.

I'll walk you up at least. He came over to me. I thought he was going to pull me up, but instead, he licked his thumb and touched my cheeks. I realized that he was clearing off dried streaks of mascara. I'd forgotten that only moments earlier, I'd been crying.

I'm going to pretend you're not cleaning me with your spit. I closed my eyes. Is it coming off?

No. You might have to use my bathroom.

Can I use your bathroom?

Sure. It's down the— Actually, you know where it is.

I walked to where my bathroom would have been. Unlike our space, the bathroom was also tidy, full of generic Duane Reade products lined up in his medicine cabinet, which I opened to look for prescription pill bottles. There weren't any. I couldn't see his private grievances.

I closed the cabinet and looked at myself in the mirror. My private grievances were all over my face. I looked upset. My skin looked dry and tight; I'd probably forgotten to moisturize. I threw some water on my face.

When I opened the door, he was waiting in the hallway. Together, we entered my apartment the same way I had left it: up the fire escape, through my window, and into my room. We walked into the living room, to a dinner that had just begun. Everyone looked up.

Who's this? Jane asked.

This is um— I turned to him, realizing we'd never introduced ourselves.

Jonathan, he said.

Jonathan, I repeated. He's our downstairs neighbor.

Can I get you something to drink, Jonathan? Jane said. If she was annoyed by our lateness, she didn't show it. We have kamikazes, rum and Cokes, anything.

Just seltzer water if you have any.

I'll get it, I said, walking to the kitchen while Jane pulled up an extra chair for him, clear across the other end of the table, while I was seated next to Steven.

Once we were all seated, we beheld the magnum opus at the center of the table: the shark fin soup was arranged in a crystal punch bowl with a ladle, prom-style. Actually, two punch bowls, one for the original soup, and another for the mysterious vegan version that Jane had made.

Jane served all of us, ladling it out into bowls.

The shark fin had a strange, gelatinous texture. We chewed for a long time, then swished the soup down with red wine.

I should've bought white, Jane said. Better with seafood.

The tannins, someone agreed.

It's not bad, Jonathan said, and really seemed to mean it.

The rest of us forced the soup down our throats. Jane passed around a glass candy dish full of oyster crackers, which guests sprinkled in their bowls. It didn't make the soup any more palatable, any less sour or musty. I wondered if I'd made it wrong. The recipe had called for fresh shark fins. Instead, I had soaked the dried fins in filtered water for a few hours, to reconstitute them, before I'd made the soup. Aside from that, I had followed the recipe precisely.

I guzzled more wine than I could handle. Steven turned to me, his low voice forcing me to lean a little closer. He was saying something about his brother, how his brother was a better man than he because he was a fair man. Or something like that.

And you're not a fair man? I asked Steven.

A *family* man, Steven corrected, slurring. My brother has always been a family man. Whereas I have only performed at it. And badly.

I realized he was addressing his divorce, the emotional repercussions he must have been struggling with. He'd never spoken of his family, and whatever information I'd gleaned was vague and clichéd: the distant wife, the troubled children.

You're fine, I said. You're okay. Nothing bad is happening right now.

He smiled, eyes bloodshot, and spooned his soup.

Suddenly, I felt a bit nauseated. It was so hot and smoky and perfumed inside.

In keeping with the vaguely Orientalist theme, Jane had bought a mah-jongg set that we were all supposed to play after dinner, but no one could figure out the game.

Candace, I thought you knew how to play this, someone yelled at me.

Why, because I'm Asian?

We gave up. We disassembled the card tables that made up our dining table and moved them out into the hallway. The living room was cleared.

Suddenly, the sound of the fire alarm cut through the room. Everyone winced, covered their ears against the shrill, electronic shriek.

What's burning? someone asked. I don't smell anything.

It's all the cigarette smoke, another person yelled.

Shit. Well, crack a window.

Should we stop smoking? a girl asked, her hand frozen, clutching her cigarette.

Jane waved her hand. Guys! Just dismantle the alarm! She climbed a kitchen chair to the smoke alarm on the ceiling, located the battery hatch, and removed it.

The alarm had broken a spell. Afterward, everyone began to relax. We hooked up an iPod to the speakers and took turns DJing. People jumped around in unison, a faux mosh pit, with happy, sunny pop music. In the kitchen, others played a drinking game called Bullshit Pyramid. Someone else had brought Twister, and the mat was laid out in the middle of my room. I wandered from room to room, circulating, playing at everything and losing, laughing hysterically as I scattered the cards, stumbled on the mat, jumped up and down, out of sync.

When other people are happy, I don't have to worry about them. There is room for my happiness. In this happiness, I lost track of Jane. I lost track of Steven. I lost track of Jonathan. I had seen him talking to a bunch of people as they sat around on the floor.

Later still, through a curtain of smoke, I saw him in my room, looking through my bookcase. Those books aren't mine! I wanted to yell, even though that was not true. They were all mine. *My Ántonia. Windowlight. Namedropper. Crime and Punishment*, the one thing I saved from freshman English. *The Metamorphosis*. The Sweet Valley High series, paperbacks of teen horror and sci-fi that I had pilfered from visits back home. Christopher Pike. R. L. Stine. Coming-of-agers. *I Capture the Castle. The Mysteries of Pittsburgh*. A collection of defunct magazines from the nineties, *Index* being my favorite. How long had he been in there? And even later, I glimpsed him in Jane's room, watching some Italian movie on a laptop with a group of people, the loud exclamatory Italian phrases like typewriter keys clacking. *Come stai?!* What was there to do but smile. I smiled and waved. Come join us, he yelled after me, as I went down the hallway to do something else, I forget what. After that, I didn't see him and I figured he had probably gone back downstairs, through the fire escape of my room.

I don't know how many hours passed. I stopped and started. When I was tired, I sprawled out on the rug. When I was hungry, I nibbled on chips in the kitchen. I drank Sprite and wine coolers I found in the fridge. I was like a homeless person in my own house.

I was enjoying myself, but it was an insulated enjoyment. I was alone inside of it.

Around four, the party began to wind down. The sky had begun to lighten outside the window. Guests were gradually leaving, one by one or in groups, peeling themselves off the rug of our living room, where we hovered, drinking and passing a spliff. Jane was sleeping on the floor. The mountain of coats and jackets on my bed diminished until only a few remained. I identified Steven's sports coat, which he had taken off sometime during the night. It was missing its pocket square.

I picked it up and walked through the apartment. Steven? I called.

I found him in the bathroom, gripping the sink. He had sweat through his shirt. He was utterly, swervingly drunk, and with that drunkenness came complete, terrorizing amorousness. But no, he was not just drunk. Something else. He had ingested something, it was so clear that he had ingested something. Maybe he had taken it willingly, or maybe someone had slipped it to him as a joke. My friends could be assholes.

Steven was touching my face, his eyes glassy. You look so sad, he said.

I'm not sad, I replied. Are you having a good time?

You're so beautiful, he said, not answering me. You're really beautiful, he repeated.

Thank you, I said, maturely. Would you like me to call you a cab?

He shook his head vigorously. No. I want to stay.

Okay, you can stay. But why don't you lie down. I led him to the living room, toward the sofa. I was removing his shoes, attempting to unknot his gray leather shoelaces, so fine like mouse whiskers.

No. I want to say something. I want to tell you something, he said urgently.

What's that?

He took my face in his hands and looked at me. I am alone, Steven said. I am without family, I am alone.

You're not alone, I said, though I did not know this to be a fact. And, because I was not close enough to him to tell him the truth, I added, You have people all around you. You're on TV.

I missed you, he persisted.

You have people, I repeated, not knowing what else to say.

No, you're not hearing me. You're not hearing me even though you understand. I *missed* you. All summer, I kept thinking about you.

Is that why you came? I asked, thinking of the times he had deflected my IMs, the times I had deflected his.

He looked at me. You invited me. Why did you invite me?

I didn't answer this. Instead, I said, A lot has changed for me this summer.

Like what? He was grabbing my wrists. How are you different? You look the same. Exactly the same.

He lurched toward me. I pulled back. Undeterred, he lunged again and attempted to kiss me, madly, desperately. When I pulled back again, he came crashing to the floor, dragging me down with him. Jane, lying on the rug a few feet away, didn't stir. With the both of us lying low, he started kissing me. It was like tumbling down a dizzying Escher staircase of beer-tasting embraces and caresses. I kissed him back. Through the yuzu aftershave, I could remember what it was like to kiss him, at the beginning of the summer, when he first took me over to his loft. I went around, looking at his things, his books, the framed art on the walls, his furniture that he'd paid someone to arrange. I opened up his bathroom cabinet and sniffed his collection of aftershaves. I opened up his closet and looked at his wood hangers and shoe trees. He got off on my curiosity. When I kissed him, it was like I was kissing all his things, all the signifiers and trappings of adulthood or success coming at me in a rush. Fucking was just seeing that to its end, a white yacht docking.

Now Steven was the one to disentangle himself. Hold on. Let's go to your room.

We walked to my room, to the very end of the railroad, where I saw Jonathan. He was sitting on the edge of the bed, fully dressed, reading. My heart dropped. As we came into the room, he looked up at Steven and me, putting two and two together. What was there for me to do but smile and try not to look too disgusting.

I was just leaving. Jonathan stood up and went to the window. I followed him, to close the window after him. When he pulled himself out on the fire escape, he turned around, his face half concealed by shadows.

Come downstairs and see me sometime, he said.

I will. Good night, I said, and as I turned away to go, his hand grabbed my arm.

Candace.

I smiled. Jonathan. What?

He leaned over and whispered in my ear. You're making a mistake. Then, before I could react, he licked my ear. With the tip of his tidy, scratchy tongue, he grazed the bottom of the lobe to the tip of the ear, in one stealthy swoop.

I stepped back, grabbing my ear with both hands as if someone had cut it off. It was warm, and wet.

With that, he closed my window and descended the fire escape. I heard the fragile, thin metal clanging as he climbed down. I heard his window opening. Then I heard it close.

4

The sunlit days were for driving toward the Facility, but certain days were different. Certain days, we went stalking. As in: Let's stalk this town. Let's stalk this street. Pick a house, any house. It wasn't just houses that could be stalked. Gas stations could be stalked. Strip malls could be stalked. Gyms. Clothing boutiques. Holistic health centers. Coffee shops. But houses, they were our bread and butter. We basked in their homey feeling, imagining the Saturday breakfasts, the TV evenings. And we were familiar with the range of layouts, the types of products, having grown up in similar homes.

Stalking, Bob liked to say, is an aesthetic experience. It has its rituals and customs. There is prestalking. There is poststalking. Every stalk is different. There are live stalks. There are dead stalks. It isn't just breaking and entering. It isn't just looting. It is envisioning the future. It is building the Facility and all of the things that we want to have with us. He couldn't guarantee what supplies were still available in the Facility, so we stalked everything. Foodstuffs. A library. DVD movies. Office supplies. Throw pillows. Tablecloths, one for every day, one for holidays. Ceramic planters. Soap dishes. Prescription drugs. Toys, though there were no children amongst us.

Anyway. We had arrived. We were going to stalk.

We stood outside on the dry brown lawn of a powder-blue colonial. This was somewhere in Ohio. It was in the afternoon. I had to remind myself of how, in the winter, dark always came early. It was December something.

All right, Bob said. Now let's join hands.

We formed a circle and performed our prestalk rites on the frost-encrusted grass of the front lawn. I stood between Todd and Adam. We took off our shoes and held hands. We began the chant, a long mantra that we recited every time. The fact that it corresponded to the rhythm of the Shins' "New Slang" made it easy to remember, easy to say. You could almost sing it, tumble around on its wistful rhythm. And if we didn't do any part of this prestalk correctly (to Bob's satisfaction), if we stumbled over the chant, if we accidentally broke our handhold, we'd have to do it again.

After the chant, we bowed our heads and closed our eyes, as Bob administered the recitation, part prayer and part affirmation—an ever-changing hokey thing that he improvised on the spot.

As we gather here today, Bob said, speaking slow and loud, we ask that you allow us the fortitude to stalk with circumspection and humility. We don't know what we will find behind these doors, but the Lord provideth. Please allow us to respectfully take what you provide. Please allow us to be fair and merciful toward the previous owners, should we encounter them.

We have come a long way, he continued. The farther we go, the less tenable and certain the path ahead may seem. And while there are those among us who may waver in their faith, I ask that you help us take things one day at a time. For now, for today, may this stalk we are about to embark on be fruitful. And let us receive your fruits not with further demands or expectations, but with humility and grace. His voice trembled. We thank you for the supplies that you are about to give, and which we are proud to receive. Thank you.

At the end, as a sealant to contain the goodwill and luck we had just created, we went around the circle and stated, with solemnity, our full birth certificate names. Bob started first, then we went clockwise.

Robert Eric Reamer.

Janelle Sasha Smith.

Adam Patrick Robinson.

Rachel Sara Aberdeen.

Genevieve Elyse Goodwin.

Evan Drew Marcher.

Ashley Martin Piker.

Todd Henry Gaines.

Candace Chen.

We bowed in unison toward the center of the circle, as if preparing to engage in karate. Then we put our shoes back on.

We considered the colonial in front of us. The doors were framed on either side by skeletal bushes that once bloomed roses. It was one of those prestige new-development homes in middle-class neighborhoods, a heritage property by external appearances but mediocre in quality, all shoddy thin walls and hollow doors inside. It looked easy.

First, the men made their approach, firearms in hand, and opened up the front door, hung with a molting eucalyptus wreath. It took them about half an hour to scope out the situation, check the gas lines, check the electricity, while Janelle, Rachel, Genevieve, Ashley, and I waited outside. If it was a live stalk, the occupants were still alive, but incapacitated by the fever. They were rounded up and herded into rooms. If it was a dead stalk, then Todd and Adam cleared the bodies and put them in the yard before we entered.

Through the large dining room windows, we saw Todd and Adam rounding up the fevered into the dining room.

I guess it's a live stalk, Ashley said.

There was a father, a mother, a son. Or that's what it looked like. It was hard to tell right away because of their skeletal frames. Well, the mother was easy to identify. Her face was a birthday cake, covered in night cream, dripping onto the cable-knit sweater she wore. Todd and Adam left and locked the doors.

The family seated themselves around the cherrywood dining table, decorated with a cream lace runner, anchored with a bowl holding what looked like moldy, decomposed citrus fruits.

The name on the mailbox indicated that they were the Gowers.

As we watched, the mother began to set the table with dishes, white with navy trim, from the matching cherry sideboard, her movements rote and systematic. First she began setting up the dinner plates, then the salad plates on top, then soup bowls on top of that. After place settings were arranged, she distributed the cutlery. She set up four place settings.

When she sat down, they clasped their hands together on the table and bowed their heads. The father opened and closed his mouth.

What are they doing? Ashley asked.

Looks like they're saying grace, Janelle observed.

When the father spoke, he uttered sounds but no words, at least none that I could decipher from our proximity. He could have been speaking in tongues. After a few moments, they opened their eyes and began to have dinner, as a family.

They ran their tongues over the cutlery. They clinked knives and forks to the plates, dashing off chicken cutlet or veal Parmesan. They brought the plates to their lips and licked them, like child actors in Chef Boyardee commercials, as if the plates were redolent of savory spaghetti sauce. A pasta primavera with fresh garden vegetables. A Salisbury steak with canned corn.

Dinner was over when Mrs. Gower stood up again. She circled around the dining room table, gathered up the dishes and cutlery, then stacked them back in the sideboard. As soon as she finished, she began again, unstacking plates and resetting the table. The Gowers were having dinner once more, the second of dozens of dinners they would have that night. They bowed their heads and said grace, although they likely did not speak words but animal mumblings following the same rhythm, the same cadence, like humming a favorite tune. Words are often the first to go when you are fevered.

Hey. Hello? Someone was saying something. It was Rachel. Her nails were digging into my arm. You're blanking out again.

I blinked, coming out of my trance. Sorry, I said.

You could lose yourself this way, watching the most banal activities cycle through on an infinite loop. It is a fever of repetition, of routine. But surprisingly, the routines don't necessarily repeat in the identical manner. If you paid a little attention, you would see variations. Like the order in which she set down the dishes. Or how sometimes she'd go around the table clockwise, other times counterclockwise.

The variations were what got to me.

When I was a kid, I used to watch my mother go through her daily facial routine. She subscribed to the Clinique 3-Step skin-care regimen: Liquid Facial Soap Mild, Clarifying Lotion 2 (because she had dry combination skin, like me), and Dramatically Different Moisturizing Lotion. Every morning and evening, she stood in front of the bathroom mirror, going through this process. It wasn't always the same. Sometimes she'd wash her face in circular clockwise motions, other times counterclockwise. Then there were times when she'd finish with an extra, unsanctioned step: Fujianese face oil, patted onto her face. The oil was a mystery, tinted emerald green, reeking of some chinoiserie, a fussy floral scent, imparting unknown medicinal qualities. It came in a small broad-shouldered glass flask imprinted with the image of a poppy flower. I have looked for that product everywhere, in both Cantonese China-towns, in Fujianese Chinatown, in Sunset Park, in Flushing, and never found it.

During freshman year of college, she would call to stress the accumulative benefits of a proper facial regimen, her Mandarin always sounding like a reprimand.

Are you moisturizing? she asked, her thin voice crackling over the cell reception. You need to moisturize properly because your skin is naturally dry. Your father has the same problem.

Yeah, I'm doing it right now, I answered, as I checked my email, poured myself another coffee. I'm moisturizing as we speak.

Every day. I sent you a set of Clinique. Has it arrived?

Yes, thank you, I responded, though she had done no such thing.

They were having a sale with a free gift. It was a good deal. In your twenties, a skincare regimen is more for preventative mea-sures. Even if you don't see its effects, the aging process will be worse if you don't do this, she said. So you have to do the regimen regularly every day.

Yeah, I said.

Pat the moisturizer in lightly, don't just smear it, she said. Then there was a pause, while she waited for me to do as she said. How does it feel?

Great. It's very light.

What you do every day matters, she'd say, before hanging up.

By that point, she had grown dreamy, her brain flea-bitten by an early onset of Alzheimer's. She was given to strange, sensuous pursuits like rinsing our silver coffeepot under a cold tap faucet for abnormally long periods of time, or ordering fifty entrées of mapo tofu, her favorite thing to eat, for some imaginary dinner party. There was never not a dinner party. My voicemail filled with invites to lavish nonexistent gatherings. Those parties, if they actually happened, would've been kind of amazing, like a cross between a classic Chinese banquet-hall dinner and eighties-era Studio 54. She'd describe the menu she was planning and the guests she'd invited: my dead father, some divorced aunts and uncles, then some other Chinese names of friends or relatives I didn't recognize, just a tangle of gibberish.

They'll be so happy to see you. Don't worry about airfare; I've already bought you a ticket, she'd say.

Thank you, I'd say, though, again, she had done no such thing. I'll be pleased to come.

Todd opened the Gowers' front door. Okay, ready! he yelled.

We put on our face masks and rubber gloves. We went inside, carrying empty boxes and garbage bags.

The door opened up to a large foyer. The walls of the staircase were hung with family photos. The Gower clan included a mother and a father, a son and an older daughter. The father balding and portly, the mother, a bleached blonde, tightly trim with a wan smile, her hands crossed in her lap, displaying a pert French manicure, the manicure of choice among porn actresses and midwestern housewives.

How tragic, Genevieve pronounced.

Let's go, ladies, Todd said. He loved to prod us and make us work.

The men hunted, and the women gathered. Each of us was assigned a division of sorts. Janelle and Ashley worked Craft Services, gathering cooking supplies and shelf-stable products that the moths and pantry rodents hadn't touched. Rachel worked Health, accumulating prescription meds, bandages, aspirins, and skin-care products. Genevieve worked Apparel, rifling through the closets for jackets and coats, but more often for quality linen tunics and silk blouses. I worked Entertainment, a broad category that included DVDs, books, magazines, board games, video games, and consoles.

As usual, I started in the entertainment room. This was in the basement.

Room by room, we amassed boxes. The boxes were placed out in the hallways for Bob to inspect, taking out or adding items as he saw fit. As the rooms emptied and the boxes filled, Adam and Todd and the other guys would take the inspected boxes outside to the supply vans.

For some reason, this process took hours.

Every time we stalked, this feeling would come over me, imperceptible at first. It is hard to describe because it is close to nothing. Gradually, the din of other people's conversations or Todd's heavy footsteps, his ugly, flat gait on the floorboards would fall away. I would forget where I was or why I was there. I would get lost in the taking of inventory, with the categorizing and gathering, the packing of everything into space-efficient arrangements in the same boxes. *Planes, Trains and Automobiles. Vertigo. Halo 2. Seinfeld: The Complete Series. Grand Theft Auto: Chinatown Wars. Scrooged. Tales from the Hood. Blow-Up. Apocalypse Now. Waiting to Exhale. The Conversation. Sex and the City: The Complete Series. The Legend of Zelda: Ocarina of Time. Back to the Future*. It was a trance. It was like burrowing underground, and the deeper I burrowed the warmer it became, and the more the nothing feeling subsumed me, snuffing out any worries and anxieties. It is the feeling I like best about working.

The only sound that would cut through this ebb and flow was Bob. In every house, he would take the muzzle of his firearm, a vintage M1 carbine semi-rifle, and run it along the walls as he walked. We would hear that scraping everywhere, in the floors above us, below us, and know where he had been. It left a mark, a black jagged line across fleur-de-lis wallpaper, sponge-painted designs, bare white walls. The scent of French vanilla drifted through the rooms. Occasionally, the scraping stopped, and we braced ourselves for the shot that would ring out. We never knew what he was shooting at: a bat trapped in an attic, a squirrel chasing leaves through the rain gutters, or nothing, nothing at all.

Finishing up in the entertainment room, I found my way upstairs to the study to collect some books. In the Gowers' house, the study was on the first floor, adjacent to the kitchen. The unusually small doorframe, so low that I had to stoop my head, opened up to an unexpectedly grand room. The walls were lined with built-in bookcases. There was a fireplace, as high as my shoulder. Tall windows looked out on the backyard. The burgundy plaid curtains, so large and heavy that they sank to the floor, were tightly drawn.

I went to the books first.

The shelves were almost all filled with children's books. Only the top shelf held adult titles, vanity set pieces that gestured toward the cultured minds of the homeowners. In this case, it was a Shakespeare anthology, a Jane Austen anthology, the complete collected poems of Walt Whitman, and so on. They looked stiff, dusty, and barely opened. All except for the Bible, at the very end of the shelf.

I took the Bible down. It was the Daily Grace Bible. I had produced it, years ago when I first started at Spectra, and overseen several of its reprintings. It was a comfort to see it again, an artifact from a previous life.

I sat down on the green plaid armchair with the thing in my hands, recalling the production details. The Daily Grace Bible was an everyday Bible for casual use, but Three Crosses Publishing also wanted to imbue the product with the high-value feel of an heirloom. In order to hit the publisher's target cost, substitutions had been made. The cover was made of leatherlike polyurethane instead of leather. The book block edges boasted copper-hued spray edge, duller compared to the more expensive gilding. The ribbon markers were made of sateen instead of silk. Most consumers couldn't really tell the difference between what was mass-produced and what was artisan or handmade. And in fact, real quality heirloom Bibles, with their pungent, heavy leather covers, weren't always preferred. The Daily Grace Bible had sold very well. I'd always felt fond of it, maybe because it was the least ostentatious Bible I'd produced.

For the cover, I'd ordered the polyurethane material from an Italian company that specialized in faux-leather. They also supplied the same material to Forever 21 and H&M, to be made into wallets, coin purses, shoes, other lifestyle accessories. For the specialty Bible paper, I'd calculated the number of rolls to be ordered from the Swiss paper mill, I couldn't remember how many now. But I'd always overorder a bit, accounting for a five percent wastage, because Bible paper was so thin that it often ripped on web presses, fast-spinning and dangerous, the kind of machinery that could slice an arm off. Even before production, I'd have recurring nightmares of Bible paper ripping on web presses, a dream that has never gone away. Swiss Bible paper, famed for its creaminess and opacity despite its thinness, had taken months to be made to order, its slurry stifling nearby rivers, and then shipped to the Hong Kong port, where someone from our Hong Kong office picked the rolls up and delivered them across the mainland China border to Phoenix Sun and Moon Ltd. in Shenzhen.

At Phoenix, it had taken six weeks for the Daily Grace Bible to be printed, assembled, and packed into custom-made boxes. The initial print run had been a hundred thousand copies, the largest of that year. Once completed, the product traveled back through to Hong Kong, where it cleared customs, was stuffed into a forty-foot shipping container, and departed in a freight vessel at the port. After fifteen days at sea, the Bibles arrived at the Long Beach port in California and were transferred to a freight train. The Bibles traveled east until, at some point, the shipping container was transferred to a truck and driven south to the publisher's distribution center in Texas, where they were shipped out to retailers. The Gowers could have bought it at a Barnes & Noble, a Books-A-Million, a Christian bookstore, a gas station Christian shop, a Hallmark kiosk, or a megachurch gift shop.

Opening up the book, I saw, on the inside front cover, written in frilly teen cursive script, the name of its owner. *Property of Paige Marie Gower.*

I enacted an old ritual from product-coordinating days. With my eyes closed, I opened the Daily Grace Bible to a random page and placed my finger on the text. I'd read whatever verse I touched.

And David said unto God, I am in a great strait: let us fall now into the hand of the Lord; for his mercies are great: and let me not fall into the hand of man.

It was then that I heard it, a quiet sound, like paper rustling. I put the book down. I stood up, slowly, and approached the windows, where the sound was coming from. As I approached, I spotted something beneath the curtains. A pair of socked feet, red polka dots on orange.

I drew the curtains back.

It was a girl, twelve or thirteen years old. She was reading, or assuming the act of reading. She turned a page, looked at it for a few seconds, and then turned the page again. It was upside down. I craned my neck. *A Wrinkle in Time*, a vintage pink edition. As she read, she chewed her hair, a strand in her mouth. In fact, she was literally chewing all of her hair off. That was the sound that I was hearing, hair chewing and the turning of pages. The carpet around her was covered with strands of auburn hair.

She was fevered, obviously. She was thin from malnourishment, bruises running down her discolored, impossibly bony legs. Mosquitoes feasted on her open sores. Her bare calves were sticky with some kind of dried liquid. On the windowsill was a glass of possibly orange juice with a whitish mold growing in it. Periodically, she reached up for it and drank the rotted juice.

The sight took me away. I stepped back slowly, still holding the Bible in my hands.

This was probably Paige Marie Gower. Her mother had set out four place settings in the dining room. The fourth seat was probably reserved for her.

I heard the sound of Bob's rifle down the hallway, heading toward the study.

I closed the curtain on Paige and arranged myself in an armchair, pretending to look through the Bible.

How is it coming along? he asked.

I found this Bible, I said, holding it up unnecessarily.

Good. Bob nodded. We'll take it.

There's not much else in here, just a lot of children's books.

We're about to wrap up. Meet us in the dining room for a poststalk. Bob was about to turn away, then stopped. He stood still and looked around.

In my haste, I had not drawn the curtains fully as to obscure Paige Marie Gower entirely. Her socks peeped out from underneath the curtains. I held my breath. I looked elsewhere, at the children's books on the shelves. So many were ones that I had read myself as a kid, when my mother would take me to the library every week. *Anne of Green Gables. The Secret Garden. Matilda.*

The sound of a page turning, quick, like paper ripping.

Bob was now walking around the room, trying to track the sound down. He drew aside the curtains. A long, terrible moment passed.

He turned to me. How did you not see her? he asked, although he already knew. He could read it all over my face.

Come with us to the dining room, he said. He swung his carbine behind him and yelled for Adam. Together, they grabbed Paige Marie Gower and dragged her down the hall and toward the dining room. I scurried behind, dreading what was to come. They were rounding Paige in with the rest of her family, to join in the cycle of endless dinners.

Todd had gathered everyone.

At the end of every live stalk, we had another stalking rite. Everyone had to observe it. We crowded around the doorway of the dining room. Through the window, the sun was setting. In front of us, there was Mrs. Gower, going through the plates with her French-manicured nails, now overgrown, dirtied, and broken. And Mr. Gower and his son, running their tongues over the plates. Paige Gower had sat down at the table.

Bob began. So, I realize now that Candace has gone on a few stalks with us, we should properly explain to her our poststalks. Can someone fill her in?

When it's a live stalk, we kill them at the end, Todd supplied.

No, we don't kill them, we release them, Bob corrected. And why do we do that?

It's the humane thing to do, Genevieve replied. Rather than having them cycle through the same routines, during which they degenerate, we put them out of their misery right away.

Bob removed his bad arm from his sling, which he wore inconsistently. He needed both hands to work the M1 carbine.

This is how Bob shot Mrs. Gower, Mr. Gower, and Gower Jr., one after the other, all in a row. Each sustained a brusque, merciful shot to the head. Like slumbering bears in a fairy tale, one by one they slumped over their dinner plates.

Bob turned to me. Now you go. I've left you one more target. The girl behind the curtains, whom you apparently didn't see.

I flushed and tried to refrain. I'm not really good at shooting.

Let this be a lesson to you to be more observant next time. Here. He put his carbine in my hands. It was heavy, still warm, sticky as if he'd been eating candy all afternoon.

I grasped it halfheartedly, its long, lean shape bundled awkwardly in my arms. I've never done this before, I protested.

It's okay. Here, let me do it, Janelle said. She reached for the carbine, but Bob stopped her.

No, he said. This is for Candace only. She should do it. He turned to the rest of the group. Okay, now let's see Candace shoot.

The first shot blasted through the window, its recoil force ricocheting through my shoulder, searing it with an afterburn that was so deep I almost cried out. The second shot pierced through the chandelier and shards of crystal rained over the dinner table. Paige Gower barely glanced up.

Jesus, someone—was it Todd?—muttered in the background.

Steady, Bob said. Hold it firmly. He adjusted the gun.

The third shot hit a place setting, piercing through the porcelain of a salad plate. Paige Gower did not flinch. The fourth shot hit her in the arm, at which point she registered something. Her eyes widened and she started to get up. The fifth shot hit her in the stomach, and the ensuing cries were weak little bays, attempts at protesting more than actual pleading.

At this point, everyone was beginning to get impatient.

Okay, look, Bob said. He was speaking slowly. You have to put some intent into this. If you do this without intent, it's not going to work. Locate your target. Focus on it.

I let my gaze rest on Paige Gower's face. The target was the forehead. In the moments before we shot them, they looked at us with crocodile eyes, knowing our difference.

She raised her blue eyes and looked at me, as the sixth shot hit her in the cheek, and then the seventh reached the forehead. The eighth shot hit her in the arm, the ninth in the stomach, the tenth in the eye, which spurted. At some point, I lost track of what I was shooting. I just kept shooting, my hands welded to the humming carbine by someone else's sticky candy, every shot pulsing through me like a spark of electricity. She was probably obediently dead by now, but still I was shooting, past the death barrier and into someplace else, I don't know where. Where else is there to go. I kept going.

A cool, light hand touched my back. That's enough, Janelle said.

I stopped. There was a strange rattling sound in the room, a shallow, irregular wheezing. It took me a moment to realize it was the sound of my phlegmy, panicked breath.

Bob broke the silence. Good job, he said.

5

So, tell me a bit about yourself.

I took a breath. Well, I was a Visual Studies major. I studied photography. And I am impressed by—here, I glanced around the office, filled with a swarm of books on the shelves—the book projects that Spectra has produced. I'm familiar with many of the art titles here.

Well, this position isn't about art appreciation, Michael Reitman said. His desktop pinged with another email, and he glanced at the screen briefly, momentarily distracted from my unimpressive answer. He picked up a printout in front of him, skimmed over it. Your résumé doesn't tell me much. Is your interest in being an artist or is your interest in working in book production?

I hesitated. I do dabble in photography. But obviously, that doesn't pay the bills.

Okay. I don't mean to be blunt, he said, leaning back in his chair. We get a lot of aspiring artists and designers applying here, thinking that they're going to be involved in book design or that they're going to be part of the art world. This position is not about that. It's about project management. We work with publishers in New York and printers in Southeast Asia. It's about logistics. It's about making sure the right people have the right information at the right time.

I nodded slowly, realizing how little Steven had told me about the position.

Did my brother tell you what this job entailed? Michael asked, as if reading my mind.

He said it's an assistant position. That's all he mentioned.

Typical, Michael muttered under his breath, which made me wonder how many girls Steven had sent here, that maybe this entire place was staffed with girls who'd once bedded Steven Reitman.

Well, let me backtrack by explaining what this company does, he said. He swiveled around in his chair, plucked a case off the shelves behind him, and set it down in front of me. It was a white coffee table book, with an irregularly pleated jacket cover. I riffled through the pages carefully, recognizing the designs of Rei Kawakubo, Yohji Yamamoto. It was a book on the history of Japanese fashion.

We help publishers produce specialty book projects at printers and suppliers overseas. They contract these projects out to us, we contract them out to the manufacturing plants, typically in Southeast Asia. Now, you'll notice that the books we focus on often require more labor-intensive work. You see this pleated cover?

Yes, it's a beautiful book.

This publisher specifically wanted a pleated feature to recall— I can't remember the designer's name. He's well-known for pleats?

Issey Miyake, I supplied.

Right. Issey Miyake. He smiled for the first time. So this pleated cover requires a certain hand detail work that printers here in the United States and even in Canada just aren't capable of. It's cheaper to produce more labor-intensive book projects like this in Southeast Asia, even factoring in the cost of shipping. To say nothing about the four-color printing.

Four-color printing?

CMYK, which is cyan, magenta, yellow, and black. Essentially, color printing. Almost all of that is done overseas nowadays. But you don't have to worry about color printing, because the position we're looking for is in our Bibles division. What do you know about Bibles?

Well, I grew up going to Sunday school. I had this Precious Moments–themed Bible. It was this powder blue. All the kids had that Bible, either in pink or blue.

Uh-huh.

I hesitated, intimidated by Michael's intricate knowledge. I can't say that I have any Bible production experience, though. Or, really, any book production experience.

No one does, he said gently. What we do here is very specialized. But that's not what's important to me. What's important to me is that you're organized, that you're detailed and meticulous. He lowered his voice confidingly, in a way that reminded me of his brother. Our last production assistant quit. I suspect he found the work too tedious, and he grew bored easily. But this job is only as boring as you make it.

I know I don't have that much work experience, I said, but I am organized and meticulous, as you mention. I worked an office job at a federal home loans bank, mostly filing papers and inputting data. Working with other people's accounts, I had to be very careful and thorough. I think I could do well in this position.

He glanced at my résumé printout again. So when you worked at this bank, it was during a year you took off from college. Why not just finish college first?

It was a family situation. My mother was ill. I liked working in an office. It took my mind off things.

He nodded, appearing to soften. I'm sorry to hear that. That's certainly a priority.

My eyes flickered over the pictures on his desk, showing his wife and two preteen kids. A family man.

He shifted in his chair, looked at me closely. Steven said that you pick things up quick, that you're very detail-oriented. You came on his highest recommendation.

That's nice of him, I replied, thinking of that Windsor knot I tied, the warm silk in my fingers.

He studied me. You say you like working in an office.

I do. I like the routine.

Michael nodded, stood up decisively. Let me get Blythe. She should meet you.

After he left the office, I looked around: a bleached wood desk, a Noguchi coffee table, and a sleek chaise longue. Upholstered in black leather, it would not have looked out of place in a psychiatrist's office. I had seen this model in design magazines. If the walls weren't made of glass, I would have lain down on it to see how it felt. Maybe that's what he did. Maybe that's what power would feel like, napping publicly while everyone in the office scurries on with their tasks around you. I thought of Lenin's tomb, his preserved body on display in Moscow, remembering a photograph from a book my father owned about the rise of communism.

Michael appeared with someone who had to be Blythe. She looked young, maybe only a few years older than me, but infinitely more pulled together.

This is Blythe, product coordinator in our Bibles division. You'll be working closely with her, Michael said.

Wait, so I have the job? I asked, glancing at both of them.

Michael paused. Well, first we'll put you on a three-month trial period. But we're thinking you can start next Monday. HR will review the terms of the position with you.

Blythe smiled and extended her hand. We just need someone quickly, she said in a manner that suggested I should calm down. I'll be making a trip to Shenzhen in another few weeks, to check on a print run. You'll come with me, and I can show you the exciting world of Bible manufacture.

Thank you, I said, trying to cover my surprise at the pace of things. I look forward to it.

Michael looked at me. Do you have a passport?

On every trip to Shenzhen, I always stayed at the Grand Shenzhen Moon Palace Hotel. It is not a hyperbolic name, because the hotel and its expansive grounds, featuring tennis courts, a rolling golf course, and an English-style rose garden, all enclosed by feudal iron gates, are indeed grand and palatial. If there is anything false in the name, it's the *Shenzhen* part, because you wouldn't know from staying there that it is located anywhere remotely in Shenzhen, let alone in China.

But the first time I went to Shenzhen, I shadowed Blythe on her visits to various printers and suppliers. We had flown into the Hong Kong airport. A white van with tinted windows, sent by one of the printers, picked us up and chauffeured us over the mainland border to Shenzhen. The two cities were less than an hour apart, but crossing into mainland China, we had to go through customs a second time. The weather felt more humid on this side.

It was a relief, then, after a twenty-hour journey, to step into the sweeping, aggressively air-conditioned marble lobby of the Grand Shenzhen Moon Palace Hotel. Blythe handed some documents to the Chinese attendant at the check-in counter. Someone came to show us to our rooms and helped us with our bags. The lobby opened up to a grand atrium of several floors. The rooms were seemingly arranged in a maze. My room and Blythe's room were across the hallway from each other.

What do we do now? I asked Blythe.

Now we rest. Even if you're not tired, jet lag catches up to you. Charge whatever you need to your room. She fiddled with her key card at her door.

What about tomorrow? I asked. She had told me our itinerary, but now I felt disoriented and unsure.

Our first appointment is tomorrow morning. We'll meet in the lobby at nine and then head out to the printer. The door clicked open, and she stepped inside. Sensing my disappointment, she assured me: Don't worry, we'll have fun when we're in Hong Kong.

My room at the Grand Shenzhen Moon Palace Hotel was pleasant and nondescript, except for an intricate navy bedspread, embroidered with phoenixes in elaborate plumage rising to the moon. The place smelled like fake, sweet peach candy. The motorized curtains opened to a sweeping view of the estate. Off in the distance, a handful of white businessmen in polo shirts and khakis played golf, cigars hanging out of their mouths.

Feeling restless, I paced around the hotel. The carpeting was so plush and springy that I felt as if I were on another planet, one with weaker gravitational pull. I took the elevator to all the different floors. There were three restaurants of differing cuisines: an upscale European bistro, an Asian tapas lounge, and an Italian trattoria. There were two gift shops, a specialty one that sold silk ties and jade paperweights, and a cheaper one that sold Hong Kong souvenirs, even though we weren't technically in Hong Kong. There was a gym, and on the same floor a swimming pool. A water-aerobics class was in session, a tall Nordic man practicing leg lunges in the shallow end.

I circled back to the lobby and out the front entrance. I meandered down the long, winding driveway to the edge of the estate, looking for something. It didn't feel like I was in China. It didn't feel like I was anywhere.

I had only returned to China once since my parents had immigrated. I'd visited Fuzhou during high school. My father had been sick, and the trip was understood as a peacemaking attempt with his relatives, who had felt abandoned after he'd moved to the States. I saw all of my relatives, many of whom I remembered and some I did not. My grandmother cried upon seeing me. My contact with them has been intermittent at best.

Approaching the end of the driveway, I reached a dirt road with a row of dusty storefronts, some closed with a rolling garage door. The difference between the hotel and its immediate surroundings was acute. At one of the storefronts, an old Chinese man in a wife-beater and plastic sandals sat on a plastic crate, in front of a dusty display of candies. He glared at me and spoke something. His Chinese, either a local dialect or heavily accented Mandarin, was impossible to understand.

I said hello in Mandarin, meekly.

But now he was standing up, speaking angrily. Though I couldn't understand what he was saying, it was clear he didn't think I should be sticking around.

I turned back.

In the morning, another white van pulled up outside the Grand Shenzhen Moon Palace Hotel. Blythe and I waited in the lobby, where she debriefed me on what we were doing. The printer was called Phoenix Sun and Moon Ltd. They were one of Spectra's biggest suppliers, the one we threw many of our largest Bible jobs. She would troubleshoot a cover situation for the Journey Bible, a portable-sized Bible with a printed cover, which was supposed to be made of all-weather, waterproof stock. The stock had trouble absorbing ink; the colors looked too muddy. As an alternative, Phoenix would be running embossing tests. She was there to oversee the tests, and to make a decision on behalf of the client.

I nodded, trying to keep up.

So, here's what's going to happen when we get there, Blythe said. I'm going to observe the embossing tests, and you're going to be given a tour of the printer.

Sounds good, I said. My stomach grumbled. I hadn't eaten any breakfast. The breakfast buffet offered English breakfast, all beans and warm tomatoes and mushrooms and blood sausage. There had been a congee bar, with additives like duck skin and scallions. It'd all looked too rich for this early in the morning.

The lobby was scattered with hotel guests, mostly white businessmen. I recognized one of them, with his big build and bald head, from the golf game I'd glimpsed from my room yesterday. It suddenly occurred to me, though it had been obvious all along, that they too were all here on manufacturing-related business: apparel, cell phones and cell phone accessories, sneakers, toilet brushes, and whatever else. They were doing what we were doing.

A short Chinese man in a polo and aviators walked into the lobby. Blythe stood up, catching his attention.

Phoenix? he asked in accented English as he came forward. Blythe greeted him with familiarity. He had chauffeured her on previous trips.

It was another hot and humid day, but with the AC blasting aggressively, it was like the Arctic inside. The driver merged onto an expressway that cut through the city. Rows of factories and apartment buildings, laundry hanging off the clotheslines outside the windows, white undershirts waving in the wind. Palm trees thrashed, their fronds breaking off and hurtling onto the streets. He swerved crazily, thrashing across lanes, doing unpredictable U-turns. Asian pop music played from the radio. When someone cut him off, he didn't curse or yell, just changed his driving strategy. Blythe seemed unfazed.

When we arrived at Phoenix Sun and Moon Ltd., a receptionist in teetering club heels escorted us into the receiving room. It was an important-looking room, anchored by a mahogany conference table. Blythe checked her phone. I looked at the walls, lined with plaques, commemorative tokens, and industry awards etched with Chinese characters. It was probably the room where all their American and European clients were received.

Two middle-aged Chinese men entered. Blythe greeted them familiarly, shook their hands, and introduced me. There was Edgar, VP of customer relations. Despite the weather, he was dressed in a gray pin-striped suit, like a London banker. Then there was Balthasar, one of the operations directors of the printer, who was dressed more casually, like the driver, in a polo shirt and slacks.

Nice to meet you, Edgar said in perfect English. Sit down, sit down.

The receptionist served us steaming jasmine tea in delicate porcelain teacups.

As we sipped our tea, Blythe made small talk. She was great at it, friendly but professional. She provided introductory anecdotal details about me that made me seem competent and smart. She asked after each of Edgar's and Balthasar's daughters, both of whom were enrolled in a competitive middle school where they only spoke English.

How is their English? she inquired.

Ai-yah. Only so-so. But they should learn English from you! Edgar joked. My English is . . . how do Americans say, rusty.

We laughed politely. Blythe smiled. Your English is excellent. They should learn English from you, she complimented Edgar, reestablishing the equilibrium.

The small talk gradually led to business. Edgar told us about the company's year, which had exceeded expectations. For the upcoming year, they were planning to expand their facilities by twenty percent, focusing specifically on making stationery and gift sets that required manual assembly.

We expect to be fully operational with gifts and stationery very soon, Edgar said.

The market has shifted, Blythe agreed. Whenever I walk into chain bookstores like Barnes & Noble, the gifts and stationery section grows bigger and bigger; all these journals, board games, crafts kits. It makes you wonder if anyone reads anymore.

Nowadays, anyone can download a book on their e-reader, Edgar said.

Bibles are good business. They are always in good style. Balthasar spoke less fluently than Edgar, his words stiff and heavily accented.

We finished our tea. For the first time, Edgar addressed me. Balthasar will give you a tour of the factory now, he announced.

Balthasar stood up and smiled obligingly. I followed him. We walked through the lobby and into the printing facility. The place was enormous, housed in a multilevel brick-walled building with large windows. The equipment was impressive but confusing: a tangled abstraction of levers and pulleys and buttons. The printing facility was hot and humid, loud with the whirring and grinding of machinery. Workers in blue jumpsuits and earplugs looked up curiously from their work.

Balthasar explained that in addition to offset printers and sheet-fed printers, Phoenix owned seven web presses, which were typically used to print newspapers and magazines.

And, of course, your precious Bibles, he added, the snideness of his tone barely perceptible, but the subtext of which could only mean: We manufacture the emblematic text to propagate your country's Christian Euro-American ideologies, and for this, for this important task, you and your clients negotiate aggressively over pennies per unit cost, demand that we deliver early with every printing, and undercut the value of our labor year after year.

Balthasar smiled. Pointing to a web press, a giant roll of paper furiously spinning onto other cylinders, he explained the mechanics of how it worked, the revolutions it spun per second. I tried to write everything down. He explained that only certain printers in China were granted a license to print Bibles, and even then there were rules.

What are the rules? I asked.

If there are—how you say—reference maps in the back of the Bible, Tibet and China must be printed in the same color. Otherwise the officials won't allow the Bibles to ship. Taiwan too. Hong Kong. They must all be printed in the same colors as China. You know, we are all one, he said, letting slip an ironic grin.

So it seems like Chinese authorities aren't as sensitive to religious content as they are to political content?

Balthasar smiled enigmatically.

We walked onward. He showed me the dark, humidity-controlled room where children's board books were kept after they were bound, so that the glue dried without warping the board pages. He opened the door and switched on the lights to reveal row after row of illustrated board books on wooden pallets.

Oh, *The Very Hungry Caterpillar*, I said, locating one stack of board books.

Yes, very popular, he affirmed. We do so many reprints. As we turned to leave, he asked: Why is it so popular in America?

I shrugged. I guess it teaches children counting skills. They practice counting all the apples that the caterpillar eats.

The worm is very greedy, Balthasar said darkly. He eats all the food and doesn't share. What lesson does that teach children? To eat with no—he paused, searching for the word—no conscience?

American kids are very fat, I joked, though I knew that was not what he really meant.

Yes, he agreed, dropping the topic. He switched off the lights in the humidity-controlled room and closed the door.

What I knew about overseas labor came from a college Economics class. First, the U.S. manufacturing jobs went to Mexico, to the maquiladoras that staffed laborers willing to work for cheaper rates than Americans. Duty-free, tariff-free. This was the 1980s and 1990s. Later, a portion of those jobs went to suppliers in China, which offered cheaper labor rates, even cheap enough to offset the shipping costs that coincided with a rise in oil prices. And after this, in another few years, the jobs will go elsewhere, to India or some other country willing to offer even cheaper rates, to produce iPods, Happy Meal toys, skateboards, American flags, sneakers, air conditioners. The American businessmen will come to visit these countries and tour their factories, inspect their manufacturing processes, sample their cuisines, while staying at their nicest hotels built to cater to them.

I was a part of this.

The workers looked up at me with benign expressions as we walked past. My first impulse was to smile, but it seemed condescending. I didn't know them. I didn't know what their jobs were or what their lives were like. I was just passing through. I was just doing my job.

As we walked on, I could see other buildings out of the big-paned windows. There were several nearby buildings that looked like apartment complexes, with air conditioners sticking out of the windows, leaking rust stains, and nightgowns hanging out from clotheslines. I walked closer to the windows. Despite the loudness of the factory, I could hear strains of Chinese pop music and Peking opera, something that my grandmother used to play. The music was coming from the buildings.

What are those? I asked, pointing.

Balthasar followed my gaze. That is where the workers live, he said. Except when they return to their hometowns for Chinese

New Year. The printer shuts down for two weeks. Big holiday. He looked at me carefully, as if seeing me for the first time. Do you celebrate Chinese New Year?

I'll eat a moon cake, I said, purposely evasive. Does that count?

He smiled the same enigmatic smile. Ah, moon cake.

We walked through other rooms. There were areas devoted to bookbinding. He showed me the machines that folded together the page signatures, machines that stitched together page signatures, the machines that glued the book blocks. They were all operated by workers in jumpsuits, who wore earplugs and safety goggles. The air was thick with paper dust.

Can you speak Chinese? Balthasar asked.

Yes, I can speak Mandarin, I replied stiffly, sticking to English. I had been six when I left China, and my Mandarin vocabulary was regressive, simplistic. I used idioms that only small children would use; my language was frozen in time. I could carry on a casual conversation for ten minutes. Any longer, and I was like a shallow-water dog paddler flailing in deeper ocean waters. It had worsened every year. I had only spoken Mandarin to communicate with my parents, and was out of practice.

I added: But it's been a long time since I've spoken Mandarin and I'm a bit rusty.

He looked at me, as if trying to decide whether my response truly indicated the limits of my Chinese-speaking abilities or if I was simply conveying modesty, a very Chinese quality.

Without warning, he switched to Mandarin. He asked if I liked Chinese food.

I took the bait and responded in Mandarin. Yes, I quite rather like Chinese food, I said, proud to know so many qualifiers, the hallmark of a nuanced conversationalist. I like—here, I racked my brain. I was too embarrassed to say General Tso's chicken, an American invention. But I didn't know the names of other dishes, so I named something I never ate at all—Peking duck. I like Peking duck.

Ah, your Chinese is very good! he delightedly exclaimed. Which was an inverted form of what Chinese immigrants would say to me: Your English is very good!

He pressed on. Were you born in the United States?

No, I said. I was born in China but—I scanned my mind for *immigrate* and came up short—I went to America when I was six.

Oh, so young! Our exchange now took on an air of familiarity. Balthasar lowered his voice to confiding tones and told me about his daughter, how he was constantly pressing her to learn English. Because it's good for business, you know? More opportunities.

Yes, there is a lot of business exchange between China and the U.S. these days, I agreed, hoping that the conversation wouldn't veer into economics or international relations or globalization, more complicated issues I probably wouldn't be able to converse in as fluently.

Do you speak Mandarin at home with your parents? Balthasar asked.

Yes, I speak Mandarin with my parents, I answered, thankful that the language does not require tenses distinguishing past, present, and future.

What do your parents do?

My mother doesn't work. She stays at home.

And your father?

My father is a . . . doctor, I said, because I didn't know the words for housing loans risk analyst. Then I added, unnecessarily, The brain.

Ah, a brain surgeon, he said, then hesitated. Or do you mean psychiatrist?

I selected the more Chinese-impressive title. A brain surgeon, I said. I understood the terms as he spoke them, but I couldn't come up with the words on my own.

He looked at me with what seemed like respect. While I hoped that we would stop conversing in Chinese and switch back to English, I sensed that something important rode on my ability to speak fluently in both languages, I wasn't sure what. It was important that I gave the appearance of fluency.

He asked where my family was from, what part of China.

Fuzhou. That's where I was born.

Ah, Fujian province. He nodded knowingly.

I looked at Balthasar uneasily. There was a hierarchy of provinces, and each province carried a stereotype, like the cultural biases associated with different New York neighborhoods. He was probably unimpressed. My knowledge of Fujian consisted of basic encyclopedic details: it is located directly across the strait from traitorous Taiwan; it has been historically separated from the rest of the mainland by a mountain range. With its seafaring traditions, most of the world's Chinese immigrants consist of the Fujianese. They go to other countries and have children and claim citizenship, sending money back home to their families to build empty McMansions, occupied by grandparents. Fujianese was outlier Chinese.

I switched back to English, changed the subject. How did you and Edgar get your names? I asked.

They are not our real names, he said, following suit in English. They are just our business names, when we work with Western clients.

How did you pick Balthasar? It's unusual.

It's from Shakespeare. I choose from the best. He laughed. Then he asked, What is your Chinese name?

I told him.

Ah, very poetic, he said. It reminds me of the poem by Li Bai. It's very famous. All the students in China study it.

I didn't know it. I couldn't bear to ask him the name of the poem. I had no idea what my Chinese name meant, or that I was even named after a poem.

In the packing room, Balthasar showed me a machine that made customized cardboard boxes in which books were packed. He spoke to one of the attending workers, a small, lanky man, in a fast-paced Mandarin I couldn't catch. The worker punched some measurements into a digital screen. His fingertips were yellow. With both hands, he pulled the lever. A weight descended and then lifted.

When he pulls the lever, the machine punches through cardboard, Balthasar explained.

Out came a flattened cardboard, with indents, ready to be folded into a box. Wordlessly, the worker handed it to Balthasar.

He has to pull the lever to make one cardboard box? I asked.

No, no, this machine punches through several cardboard boxes at once. It's only an example.

Turning to the man once again, Balthasar issued requests for different-sized boxes.

The worker, in his late twenties with a goatee, punched in some different measurements and pulled the lever again. Out came a larger stack of cardboard, then a midsized stack. The shipping boxes were the least important part of the book production, I wasn't sure why we were focusing on this so much. But I was mesmerized anyway. It was such a rote, mechanical movement, the punching in of measurements, the pulling of the lever. Cardboard boxes of different sizes and shapes were produced. He did this same thing over and over again, on a loop, until suddenly, he stopped in midaction and unleashed what sounded like a protest.

Balthasar responded calmly, something about how part of his job was to demonstrate the machinery for visiting businessmen, but as the irritated worker grew louder and more insistent, the two men engaged in an argument, speaking too quickly for me to get every word. Something I did hear: Balthasar told the worker he was making a fool of himself in front of the foreigner.

I looked away. On the wall, someone had taped up a titillating photo of a woman, holding an ice cream cone and sucking her finger. It had been ripped from a magazine.

The photo was of Claire Danes, and it had been ripped from a 1996 issue of *Us* magazine. I knew it right away, because, as a kid, I had been obsessed with the Baz Luhrmann production of *Romeo and Juliet,* and had read all the interviews with its stars, collected them in a folder. It was unbelievable to see it here, of all places. The fact of finding a childhood artifact in such a strange place on the other side of the world, years and years later, I couldn't put this sensation into words.

Claire Danes! I love Claire Danes, I exclaimed, to no one in particular.

Balthasar and the worker looked up. They exchanged glances. Something about my behavior, in keeping with a dumb, enthusiastic American, put things into perspective.

Finally, Balthasar spoke. Gesturing to the other man, he said in Mandarin, This is Chengwen. At Balthasar's behest, the worker held out his hand, and so we shook hands. *Ni hao. Ni hao.*

Chengwen is from Fujian province too, Balthasar added.

My family is from Fuzhou, I told him.

Really? he asked, which in Mandarin sounds more like a request for veracity than a benign comment.

Are you from Fuzhou too? I asked, trying to make polite conversation.

Most of us are from villages, he answered. He named the Fujian village he was from, but I didn't quite catch it.

It's a village very close to Fuzhou, Balthasar interjected, adding jovially, Maybe your families even know each other!

Ridiculous as it sounded, I thought to ask Chengwen whether he knew my aunts or uncles. But I realized I didn't actually know the full names of any of my relatives. I always called them by their designation in the family, the first uncle, the second aunt, my grandma. My mother had written their legal names on a list somewhere, though this was in a box in a storage facility in Salt Lake City.

Chengwen smiled at me, politely, then turned back to attend to his work.

Okay. That's the end of the tour, Balthasar announced. Now you've seen all of Phoenix.

That evening, we returned to the Grand Shenzhen Moon Palace Hotel. I swam a few laps in the pool. Then Blythe and I ate dinner in the hotel, at the trattoria that modeled itself after Little Italy, with red tablecloths. On the walls were photos of Italian mobsters, real and fictitious, from Al Capone to Tony Soprano.

Blythe raised her glass and made a little toast. To your first time in Shenzhen, she said. May there be many more returns.

We clinked glasses.

I ordered squid ink spaghetti, the most exotic thing on the menu. It was the first time I'd ever had it. My tongue blackened.

After dinner, we retreated to our rooms. It was pretty late. I had a hard time going to sleep. The events of the day churned in my mind, the blur of whirring web presses, the Claire Danes photo, Chengwen.

After tossing and turning, I gave up on sleeping and checked my work email. There was a new message sent by Balthasar from his Phoenix email earlier that day. The subject line was *Your Name*.

I clicked on it, and the software asked me to download a Chinese translation program that would allow the characters to encrypt properly. I declined, because it was late and I didn't have time to download a whole program.

The email that opened showed gibberish in place of Chinese characters. And yet, when I scrolled down, I found a PDF attachment he had sent. It was a scan of a page from an unidentified book that featured a short poem. It was the English translation of "Thoughts in Night Quiet" by Li Bai. He must've been trying to send me both versions of the poem, in Chinese and English. I read it aloud to myself.

> Seeing moonlight here at my bed
> and thinking it's frost on the ground,
>
> I look up, gaze at the mountain moon,
> then back, dreaming of my old home.

7

I have four uncles.

The first uncle I used to know better than all the others, though we're not related by blood. He lives in Fuzhou, a southern coastal city of Fujian province, aka the armpit of China, aka the Jersey of Asia, where I spent the first six years of my life. He has a slender frame and raffish profile; his upper lip sprouts a ratlike movie-villain mustache. That's the way I remember him, when I was a kid and he let me stay in the wedding suite with him and my aunt, his face lit by the glare of the TV screen.

Fuzhou is so hot and humid all year round; the kind of place, my grandma says, that breeds indolence. Things rot more quickly, everything melts, the local cuisine, rooted in sea and land meats, makes no comestible sense. Crime proliferates, mostly petty thievery; when there is violence, it is of the most astonishing, unimaginable kind. The streets are cleared for weeks, and the hose they use for cleaning is anvil-heavy. It's the kind of climate, my grandma says, in which it's difficult to maintain your character. Not only during the day, but at night too. So you see, she concluded, fanning herself with a dried palm leaf, this oppression is truly inescapable.

A long time passes between our move to the U.S. and when I go back. When I finally do return, in high school, it is to lacquered, air-conditioned rooms of relatives uncrinkling wrappers from hard candy, shelling peanuts and gossiping. Days and days of rooms of relatives.

During the first uncle's bouts of depression, he stops eating, stops speaking, and spends his days online. When he does go out, late at night, creeping past wife and daughter asleep in other rooms, it is to frequent karaoke bars solo and sing Taiwanese pop songs whose lyrics, everyone is surprised to learn, he knows word for word by heart: *I am a nightingale that croons for a love that doesn't exist. / Into the mountains and valley swells my love flees. / Against the northern winds I chase, not far behind. / How ardent my love, how worthless my lover. / Fuck my bitchy bitch bitch.*

Every weekday, when his wife and daughter go out, my grandma walks to his house and cooks him lunch. When she peeks into the bedroom, he is in his usual stance: his back to the door, kneeling in front of the nightstand, clutching the beige phone receiver in one hand as he speaks to someone he declines, has declined over and over again, to identify, this person for whom his voice unfurls slow, drowsy murmurings, like a comb through wet hair.

The second uncle also lives in Fuzhou. I know even less about him than I do about the first. He has a bespectacled, gentlemanly appearance, and carries himself with a demeanor so mild-mannered that it borders on disinterest. Once the tallest of all the uncles, he is now known primarily for his bad health, a spine that, in recent years, has grown so knotted and crooked that he's unable to work, the exertion of sitting at a desk being too great. He spends his days in the apartment, lying on the hard surfaces of the fake wooden floors, fanning himself in the heat.

Only in the evenings during my visit does the second uncle force himself to sit upright, at the dining table, when his wife and daughter come home from their jobs at the bank. The women cook a simple dinner, which they lay out in front of him: cockleshell soup, sautéed bok choy, dumplings slathered in Chinese ketchup. The conversation is light, jovial, laughter ringing out in swells. After dinner, there is more tea. For a time, it seems like the second uncle may stay upright for the rest of the night. Maybe he'll join in playing mah-jongg with the next-door neighbors, who come proffering snacks: pistachios, sliced oranges, dried squid, sweet rice candies. The TV is switched on, blaring music videos and commercials. The room fills with chatter and jokes, cigarette smoke. A window in the corner is opened.

Quietly, so as not to be caught in the act of crawling, he lowers himself again to the floor.

My grandma maintains that of all her daughters, only my mother has married wisely. Of the first and second uncles, she once said: One is weak in the mind, the other is weak in the body. She turned to me meaningfully: But not your father.

The third uncle is the only uncle I'm related to by blood. He is my father's brother. He works as a driver for local government officials. In the concrete courtyard of his apartment complex sits a black Lexus with tinted windows that he washes and shines daily, in the mornings before work. The Lexus is to Chinese communism what the Lincoln Town Car is to American democracy, he would say. Both look nice, but not too nice.

He wears aviator glasses, a polo shirt, and chinos, and misleadingly he affects a stoic expression. When I see him for the first time in ten years at a train station, he sizes me up. The trains get slower every year, he says.

The third uncle doesn't resemble my father in stature or personality. My father is thin and lanky, whereas the third uncle is muscular and heavy. My father is reserved and contemplative, whereas the third uncle is brash and emotional, prone to jagged, drunken bouts, punching through tables, chairs, mirrors, the plastic chandelier that swings above our heads, throwing shadows everywhere. He lunges at my father, yelling so fast and crazy that all his grievances blend together, rendered indecipherable. Everyone rushes to hold him back, their cries drowning out his yells, his own son trying to pry the tiny blade, a paring knife, out of his hands. He is so angry, it is so clear that he is so angry, and if it's not about one thing, then it's about everything. The words come so fast, so accusingly, in a scrambled Fujianese that only the smallest, most childlike part of me understands: You can't just come back. You can't just come back. You can't just come back.

He says, You've been gone for so many years, and now we're supposed to invite you to our homes? More than a decade, the capitalist comes back and he's welcomed like some prodigal son?

My father stands there, as close as he can, daring his brother to come closer, his hands balling into fists at his sides. The low, mechanical hum of the ceiling fan descends over the room.

Think of all your similarities! my grandma interjects. You're brothers—think of everything you share!

Despite their physical differences, there is one feature my father and his brother do share. It is the face, a face so eerily similar they could've been identical twins. They have the same furrowed brow, the same dimples below the mouth, and the same deep, sunken eyes. Beneath the stilled chandelier, as my uncle finally sits down to break into heavy, chafing sobs, I think: So that's what my father looks like when he cries.

There is a fourth uncle, but I don't know much about him. Married to the sole aunt on my father's side, the man has barely said a word to me all my life. Not that I've said anything to him either.

He is balding, with bulbous features and a paunch. He owns a gourmet olive oil store that doubles as a bootleg shop; in the back room he sells American movies and porn.

The important thing about the fourth uncle is his son, Bing Bing, who's my favorite cousin, the only cousin I get along with, though it's generally agreed that he's the failure of the younger generation. No one faults him for it, though. Only my grandma says what everyone else has avoided saying: that Bing Bing is the most intelligent and most sensitive of any of us, but the fourth uncle and the entire family have breathed down his neck his entire life, casting doubts on every decision, disparaging every move, and now what the family has on its hands is a stunted, unmarried thirty-five-year-old man.

A failed doctor, a failed lawyer, a failed entrepreneur, my cousin has a plain face that is neither handsome nor ugly. It's innocuous, forgettable. At times, when neither of his parents is looking, a mischievous grin steals over his face, mouselike, as if he lives with an almost unbearably pleasurable secret, unknowable to anyone. My cousin, my first friend.

We walk the streets of Fuzhou at night, in the one summer when I come back. Streetlights send our elongated shadows tumbling ahead of us, across the neon-tinged storefronts and buzzing lamps. Everyone comes out, the old men in wife-beaters and plastic sandals, the teenagers in fake American Eagle. Senior citizen ladies roll out before bedtime in pajama pants printed with SpongeBob or fake Chanel logos. There is a Mickey D's and a KFC, street dumpling stands, bootleg shops, karaoke bars. Everything is open late, midnight or even later. There are places to get a full-body massage, an eight ball, a happy ending. If you stay on these streets long enough, it's possible you could get everything you want, have ever wanted. Because I misremember everything, because I watch a lot of China travel shows when I am alone at night in New York, because TV mixes with my dreams mixes with my memories, we walk along the concourse that runs alongside the river even though there is no river, we turn down boulevards punctuated by palm-tree clusters even though those belong in Singapore, we smoke cigarettes openly even though it's unseemly for women, especially in my family, to smoke in public. But the feeling, the feeling of being in Fuzhou at night, remains the same.

When I was a kid, I named this feeling Fuzhou Nighttime Feeling. It is not a cohesive thing, this feeling, it reaches out and bludgeons everything. It is excitement tinged by despair. It is despair heightened by glee. It is partly sexual in nature, though it precedes sexual knowledge. If Fuzhou Nighttime Feeling were a sound, it would be early/mid-nineties R&B. If it were a flavor, it would be the ice-cold Pepsi we drink as we turn down tiny alleyways where little kids defecate wildly. It is the feeling of drowning in a big hot open gutter, of crawling inside an undressed, unstanched wound that has never been cauterized.

Bing Bing, his face half-submerged in shadow, tells me, One day you'll want to return permanently.

That would be terrible, I say, laughing. I would be henpecked to death by all of my uncles. I begin imagining it:

The first uncle would say, When are you getting married?

The second uncle would say, What are you looking for in a man?

The third uncle would say, Work on your appearance. He hesitates. Especially the chin and calves.

The fourth uncle wouldn't say anything; he would just think it.

In my imagining, I return from New York. I do whatever my uncles say. I relearn Mandarin. I relearn Fujianese. I get married to another Fujianese. I live here, in beautiful, sunny, tropical Fuzhou, Fujian, fenced in by towering mountains and bounded by a boundless sea through which everyone leaves, where the palm trees sway and the nights run so late. I am so happy.

8

The Shenzhen factory trips were typically two-pronged: work in Shenzhen, then leisure in Hong Kong. After days of supplier visits and factory checks, we traveled south across the border, before returning to New York. This was the itinerary I would follow on all subsequent Shenzhen trips, whether with Blythe or alone.

Blythe liked to say the only things you can really do in Hong Kong are shop and eat. It is a city that distills life down to its bare essentials.

She took me around Causeway Bay, Harbor City, Kowloon East and West. We went to boutiques and malls, which were just like the malls in the States, except more expensive and grandiose. She liked to shop, I kind of liked to shop, and we shopped so much that I thought I was losing my mind. I bought Banana Yoshimoto novels at Page One. Blythe bought an Issey Miyake makeup bag. I bought two Arnold Palmer satchels, the licensed accessories brand of the American golfer inexplicably popular with Asian teens. Blythe bought a silk blouse and a T-shirt at A.P.C. I bought a winter coat lined with fake shearling at Izzue. We both bought scarves at Uniqlo. There was an insatiable frenzy to shopping in Hong Kong, to using a foreign currency that felt like play money. There was no guilt. I couldn't calculate the exchange rate fast enough.

The shopping wasn't all that different from shopping in New York. I probably could have found the same merchandise back home or ordered it all online. What surprised me in Hong Kong, however, was how many iterations of the same thing were available. Take a Louis Vuitton bag, for example. You could buy the actual bag, a prototype of the actual bag from the factory that produced it, or an imitation. And if an imitation, what kind of imitation? An expensive, detailed, hand-worked imitation, a cheap imitation made of polyurethane, or something in between? Nowhere else was there such an elaborate gradient between the real and the fake. Nowhere else did the boundaries of real and fake seem so porous.

We were standing on a crowded street, waiting to cross, when a middle-aged woman, in a visor and a fanny pack, came up and shoved a flyer in my hands. You like? she asked.

I looked down. The flyer, color printed on quality paper, showed dozens of various designer bags: Fendi clutches, Louis Vuitton satchels, and Coach tote bags. They weren't just logo-heavy generic knockoffs you always found in Chinatown, but looked like the latest, of-the-season models I had seen in magazines.

Are these real? Blythe asked.

She nodded vigorously. Real! Prototype.

Blythe turned to me. A lot of the designer brands contract the factories out here. Often the factories produce an overrun of prototypes and sell them illicitly. So it is basically the real thing. She gestured to the flyer. See anything you like?

I thought designer handbags were all made in Italy or something, I said.

She smirked. Maybe Hermès is still made in Europe. Turning back to the woman, she returned the flyer. Thank you. Maybe next time.

At the beauty counter of another mall, I bought Shu Uemura

Cleansing Beauty Oil, which the saleslady informed me was calibrated specifically for dry skin. She was in her late forties, with
beautiful skin and sparing use of makeup. She spoke English
perfectly.

Now pay attention. She demonstrated the product by applying it on the back of my hand and rubbing it off with cleansing
wipes.

Now, she said, feel your right hand compared to your left hand.
Do you feel how soft and supple the skin is?

I nodded, seduced. I've always been told my skin is too dry.

In a sudden, intimate gesture, she leaned over the counter,
took my face in her hands, and spoke with care. You have beautiful skin, it is just uncomfortable right now. Her hands were thin
and cool. Her perfume was powdery and floral.

And I remembered, in a sudden jolt of recall, that my mother
had traveled to Hong Kong alone, one winter, when I was a teenager. The city was renowned among the Chinese-American communities for expert, cheap cosmetic procedures, and she was
there to get the moles and beauty marks removed from her face.
Her sisters used to call her a spotted leopard. When she returned,
however, there were white spots on her face where the moles
had been. She was still marked in the places she desired to be
unmarked.

I took out my credit card and paid for the cleanser, along with
other products that completed the regimen, Phyto-Black Lift
Radiance Boosting Lotion and the Phyto-Black Lift Smoothing
Anti-Wrinkle Emulsion. I didn't have wrinkles, the saleslady clarified, but it was a preventative regimen.

Ringing up my purchases, she asked: Do you come to Hong
Kong often?

It's my first time here.

She raised her eyebrows. Business or pleasure?

Business. I just started at my job.

Congratulations, she said, wrapping everything in tissue paper and putting the items in a bag. Come back soon.

On our last night in Hong Kong, I was left to my own devices. Blythe was spending the night with her on-off boyfriend, some mystery man whom she took a ferry to Macau to meet. The concierge at the hotel—the name of it escapes me now—hailed me a cab. My plan was simple: I would ride around Hong Kong and take in the sights.

Where? the cabdriver asked.

Is there a good neighborhood for walking?

Shopping? He smiled knowingly. Ah! I know the place.

I could have clarified, but he seemed so enthusiastic that I didn't correct him. We coursed through Hong Kong smoothly, guided by his confident, fast navigation. It was pleasurable to sit back and look outside, ensconced in the darkness and silence of the cab. I hadn't seen Hong Kong this way at night; it almost seemed like a different city from earlier that day. The view became an aching stream of billboards and advertisements. They were advertising Japanese whiskeys, Macau casino-resorts, and skin-whitening creams for women. A Eurasian-looking model with black hair and blue eyes delicately stroked her cheek in a paean of self-care.

The driver exited the highway. He announced our arrival with, Okay, shopping!

I emerged onto the hot, humid street. It was a night market, a neon blur of stalls selling jade bracelets, scarves, fortune-telling services, massages, animals, assorted tchotchkes, crowded with locals and tourists. It smelled like sugar and charred meat. You could get a foot massage. You could get your name whittled into a piece of jade to use as a signature stamp. You could eat dumplings, candied crab apples, raw sugarcane, stir-fries, whole crabs, whole grilled squids on a stick.

The nostalgia of it hit me all at once. I couldn't think straight. As a kid, I used to eat sugarcane, the juicy fibers unsplit from the cane casing.

Across the street, a 7-Eleven magically miraged in front of me, a beacon of American summer, and I ducked inside for reprieve. In its cooling, life-affirming fluorescence, I paced up and down the tidy aisles, stocked with American products in Asian flavors. Squid-flavored potato chips. Cherry-blossom Kit Kats. From among the orderly rows of lychee juice cans and soy-milk cartons and neon aloe vera juice bottles with floating pulp, I selected a Pepsi.

Thank you, come again, the cashier deadpanned in English.

On the street, the familiarity hit me again, but this time, it was a bit more palatable. I sipped my Pepsi, which I hadn't had in forever, and the jittery caffeinated high brought me back. I was four when my parents had left for the States and six when I too immigrated. In those interim years in Fuzhou, my first uncle and my aunt would take me down streets just like this in the evenings. It was the same feeling, the thrill of being out on city streets like this. We crossed the pedestrian bridge, arched over the street, into fluorescently lit shopping malls. Bins of printed pajama sets wrapped in plastic.

I wandered around for a bit, trying to absorb the sights and stopping in at various stalls. One of the larger stalls smelled heavily of incense and featured what looked like shrines. It took me a second to identify what they were selling: accoutrements of mourning and/or ancestral worship. Spirit money, yellow bills imprinted with gold foil, was tied with red string and shrink-wrapped in thick stacks. When I lived in China, my grandmother used to burn it. Once broken down into ashes, she had explained, the money would transfer into the possession of our ancestral spirits. They would use it to buy things or to bargain with others or to bribe afterlife officials for favors. The afterlife, with its bureaucratic echelons and hierarchies, functioned similarly to the government. Nothing turned your way unless you took matters into your own hands.

I thought of my mother and my father, unhoused and hungry, against a backdrop of hellfire.

Some spirit bills were intricately printed to look like U.S. dollars, Chinese yuan, Thai baht, and Vietnamese dong. The spirit world accepted a variety of international currencies. And not only spirit money, but other afterlife luxuries. There were diamond necklaces and cell phones and Mercedes convertibles, all made of cardboard to be easily burned. There were paper Gucci wallets and Fendi handbags, so that the ancestors could organize and store all that spirit money. There were even paper facsimiles of iPods and MacBook Pros. On top shelves were dollhouse-sized cardboard constructions of homes, printed with elaborate, intricate details and furnished with paper furniture.

That night, I bought a stack of spirit money. In U.S. currency, of course. I would make it rain Franklins in the spirit world.

When I returned to New York, I did exactly that. Out on the fire escape, in a large ceramic bowl, I took a lighter to a stack of the fake bills, feeding them to the fire a couple at a time. The flimsy paper burned pretty fast. The fire cast a warm glow, sputtered, and then quickly subsided.

It didn't feel like an adequate-enough offering, for all the time that had passed that I hadn't burned tribute. I wanted to give them more.

Underneath the coffee table in our living room were all of Jane's magazines. She subscribed to all the aspirational lifestyle publications: *Vogue, Bon Appétit, Elle Decor, Architectural Digest,* a bunch of others. Most of them she had read and hadn't bothered to throw out, so she wouldn't mind if I destroyed them.

For my father, I burned a Jos. A. Bank suit, and Salvatore Ferragamo wing tips to match. For more casual needs, I burned him a bunch of J.Crew clothes. I burned him some Eddie Bauer fleece jackets. Then, thinking maybe it was already too hot in the afterlife, I burned him several sweat-wicking Nike workout shirts. I burned him the latest releases in books. And, ripped from *Architectural Digest*, a study full of leather wingback chairs to read the books in. I burned him the latest BlackBerry and a Verizon plan. I burned him a silver Jaguar XJ. I burned him a plate of fried chicken from *Bon Appétit*. He loved fried chicken. It was almost all we would eat when my mother was on one of her extended trips back to Fuzhou. I burned him some Tylenol for his migraines, the afternoons when he'd lie down for hours.

The magazine paper, laden with laminates and acids, probably printed on web presses, produced a stink that clouded up my nose and throat.

For my mother, I burned a Louis Vuitton suitcase and a Fendi handbag. And should she be wandering around unclothed, I burned her a stash of apparel, some Gap basics and some Talbots dresses, favoring her preferred shades of cream or beige. She'd always wanted a Burberry trench, so I burned her one of those too. I burned her a Coach satchel. She loved Coach; she liked most classic American brands, their clean lines. I burned her some Ralph Lauren slacks. As the pièce de résistance, I burned her some Clinique Dramatically Different Moisturizing Lotion. Clinique anything, I burned. Clinique Moisture Surge, Clinique Youth Surge, Clinique Repairwear Laser Focus. After that I burned her a shrimp cocktail. She loved a good shrimp cocktail, the shrimp arranged on the rim of some crystal-cut glass coupe that held the red sauce. She thought it was classy, in a really American kind of way.

I watched the last luxury images burn and extinguish into ash, entering some other, metaphysical realm where my parents feasted. As the fire subsided and the embers dimmed, I imagined them combing through the mountain of items, dumbstruck by the dizzying abundance. I imagined that it would be more than they would ever need, more than they knew what to do with, even in eternity.

9

It was late. The rest had long gone to sleep, sealed inside their tents. But, like on every night, Ashley, Evan, and Janelle were still awake, sipping beers outside around the dying fire. Many nights I had fallen asleep to their conversation, punctuated by the gentle crackle of embers. Their voices, rising and falling, have drifted into my dreams.

Ashley, Evan, and Janelle were the closest I had to friends in the group. Every day, we drove together in a champagne-colored Nissan Maxima, the only sedan in a caravan of utility vehicles, all running on gas siphoned from the stilled, unused cars that littered the roads and parking lots. We listened to music and smoked weed (except me) and blasted the heat. The group road trip toward the Facility proceeded at a snail's pace. Without GPS, Bob relied on outdated Fodor's road maps. Sometimes he made miscalculations. The highway routes were often clogged with deserted cars, so under Bob's directions, we took whatever routes were cleared, meandering through back roads. We got lost often and backtracked.

Given these circumstances, I came to know Ashley, Evan, and Janelle pretty quickly. We liked the same types of music and we were all insomniacs. We knew one another's life stories, or at least the basics.

In the half-dozen times I woke up that night, I'd see their flickering shadows against my tent. There was nothing preventing me from unzipping my tent and joining them. I could lay claim to a log and make bad jokes, contribute gossip, wax and wane about group politics. But a part of me always felt like I was interrupting. It had to do with their closeness, so apparent in the way they laughed at their inside jokes, the rhythm of their rapid-fire rapport, despite the bickering. Even the way they reinforced one another when someone said or did something stupid.

They were talking about the Facility.

How far do you guys think we are from the Facility? Janelle asked.

Bob says we're less than a week away, Ashley said. We're almost to Indiana.

Yeah, but didn't he say that *last* week? Evan said. Do you think the Facility even exists?

Of course it exists! Ashley was indignant. He talks about it all the time, in detail.

Are his details consistent though? Do they add up? Evan took special pleasure in teasing Ashley, the way a schoolboy might make fun of a girl he crushed on.

Stop trying to stir things up, Janelle said to Evan.

Ashley was the baby of our driving clique. She had been a fashion student at Parsons. She was from Ohio and had only lived in New York for two years when the End hit. She had never really taken to fashion school. Teachers and students alike moved in hierarchical herds. Her sweet, feminine, midwestern designs, stitched together from workman fabrics like calico and flannel, contrasted unfavorably with the reigning Goth-lite urban aesthetic.

What do you think about the Facility? Evan asked Janelle.

It doesn't seem unreasonable, Janelle said cautiously. I'm not looking forward to living in the suburbs, but it makes sense, logistically. We'd be close to all those retail outlets and big-box stores, most of which are still stocked, most likely, with an endless amount of food and supplies. We would have access to everything we could ever need for the foreseeable future.

If I could live anywhere, I'd just go home, Ashley said. I'd live in my own house.

Of all of us, Ashley was the most homesick. An only child, she spoke often of her parents, gazing delicately off in the distance.

If I could live anywhere, Janelle said, I'd go somewhere completely new. I'd head south, toward the equator. I'd like to live near a beach. Personally, I've never lived in the Chicago area, but I'm not looking forward to the cold. And with winter coming up soon . . .

Yeah, but cold is good, Ashley said. Everyone knows that the fever spreads more easily in warmer weather.

No one could argue with that. The spread of the fever was slower in cold weather, why cold-climate countries like Finland and Iceland were still baseline functioning, at least the last that we had heard. They had also been among the first countries to cut off all imports from Asia, had imposed a travel ban.

I'd rather move to Scandinavia if I'm going to live in the cold, Janelle said.

Yeah, good luck getting through their customs, Evan dismissed.

Good luck learning how to sail a boat across the ocean, Ashley added.

Thanks for all the support, guys.

Look, I think we should make a pact, Evan said. If we don't like the Facility, we should all go off somewhere together.

Let's toast to it! Ashley exclaimed, drunk.

They clinked bottles together, running all kinds of exaltations.

And Candace too, Janelle added. She can be part of our pact.

Evan snorted. She'd probably just want to go back to New York.

I shifted uncomfortably in my tent.

There were people in New York at the End, Janelle said. Didn't you ever read NY Ghost?

As media outlets closed, NY Ghost was the de facto news source of New York throughout the fall. Readers wrote in asking for pictures and dispatches from their old neighborhoods, their friends' apartments, nostalgic sites. NY Ghost complied. Eventually, as the fever spread across the country, the queries dried up and not long after that, the blog came to a standstill.

I hadn't told anyone in the group that I was NY Ghost. I guess I wanted something that was still mine.

Evan was thinking aloud: In those NY Ghost photos, if I'm remembering right, the city did not look habitable. It looked almost empty, except for some security guards and some random fevered. Then even the guards left. I don't know why someone would stay as long as Candace.

Guys, Janelle reprimanded. One day, Candace is going to tell us about what it was like. But leave the girl alone. She's only been with us for, what, two weeks? The problem with this group is that we all like gossip too much.

Yeah, Ashley echoed. Then she laughed.

Okay. Evan changed the subject. He started talking about how he wished it was summer. The thing he liked most about summer was the night sound of cicadas, chirping in sync, like the hum of an electric power generator. It reminded him of growing up in Michigan, the nights he and his friends would climb the water tower to tag it or when they would hang out by the railroad tracks, rickety and rotting, drinking and bullshitting. The smell of old railroad wood, of deep blueberry bushes, of cheap Schlitz beer. When was that? Ashley asked, and he took a moment to answer. It was before art school in Baltimore, before the boring, pretentious magazine internship in New York, which led to the industrial design gig. He worked on toothpaste boxes and tampon wrappers, the sides of cereal boxes. It was artless and inane, and he was glad it was over now. Not that he didn't do it to himself, he said. Not that he didn't make those decisions himself.

From Evan's wistful, beer-induced narrative, I began to drowse in a free-floating half-sleep. This drowsing was interrupted by a sharp hiss, the sound of the fire being hastily, sloppily put out with water. They whispered in hushed, urgent tones, amid a whirlwind of flurrying and scuttling, nylon whining, dry leaves and branches cracking under their feet.

I sat up.

Then, in the distance, the sound of a motor turning, by the side of the back road where all our vehicles were parallel parked. The sound of the engine receded as the car pulled out onto the road, slowly and deliberately. They waited until they had reached a certain distance to turn on the headlights, but in the total darkness, it was still visible. Did anyone else hear this? I waited. Silence. No one in the camp seemed to stir.

It was none of my business, but the fear that maybe they were running away permanently, and were leaving me behind without telling me, filled me with panic.

I unzipped my tent and stealthily crawled over to Janelle's tent, pitched next to mine. By the light of the dying embers, I could glean that all her personal belongings were still inside; her sleeping bag, her ChapStick, her journal with a pen tucked inside. She wouldn't have left these if she was running away.

I crept back to my tent, my panic dissipating. But if they weren't running away, then where were they going in the middle of the night? I zipped myself back into my sleeping bag and crossed my arms behind my head. If I drew attention to their leaving, they would get in trouble. There was nothing to be done but lie back and wait, try to sleep.

As the sky began to lighten, I heard, once again in the distance, the sound of the motor sputtering. They were coming back. I heard the sound of their tents being slowly unzipped. Within minutes, everything was silent.

It was not until then that I drifted off to sleep.

Two or three nights had passed without incident before it happened again. I had begun to think that the excursion, or whatever it had been, had been imagined. The days had begun to seem simpler, easy. The sky was cloudless, a full, heavy orange moon shone low, weighing atop the boughs of trees. We were so close. We had crossed into Indiana earlier that afternoon, marking the penultimate leg of our road trip. The next state was Illinois. That meant we were not too far away from the Facility. To celebrate, not that we needed a reason to celebrate, we broke out the last of our beer rations, clinked the lukewarm bottles together next to the roaring fire, and toasted ourselves, our good fortune, our collective future. We drank to keep warm.

Genevieve had made her dulce de leche as a special treat. She had been boiling cans of condensed milk in a Dutch oven, because if you boiled this stuff long enough, it turned into a nutty brown, tooth-numbingly sweet caramel taffy. We dipped saltine crackers into it. Around the fire, our tipsy thoughts cast large shadows.

Candace, Bob announced, standing up. I'd like to give you something. Smiling, he passed a book to Adam, who passed it on to me. It was just a Bible.

Would you like me to read something aloud from this? I asked, knitting my brows in confusion. He's already given me a Bible. Everyone in the group has their own copy.

Open it, he implored.

Opening the front cover, I saw that it was a trick Bible, one of those with a hollow cut into the pages. The hollow didn't hold a whiskey flask or a gun as I've seen in the movies, it held a smartphone. It was my iPhone, the one I had in New York.

I looked at Bob in amazement. Where did you find this?

It was in the cab when we found you, Adam said, beside me. It was in the passenger's seat.

I was quiet for a moment. I had always thought my iPhone had been lost, during the chaos of fleeing New York. But Bob had simply, for whatever reason, kept it this whole time. I clasped my fingers around it, feeling the familiar scratches and nicks in its smooth surface, an old relic, and was suddenly flooded with a bittersweet happiness of what I had back. I could access my old photos. I could read my old emails. Maybe I could use it to take photos again.

Thank you, I said to Bob, sincere in my gratitude. My eyes met his across the fire. I turned the iPhone around in my hands. There was a giant crack in the screen that hadn't been there before. I attempted to turn it on, but no Apple logo appeared. The screen remained blank.

Consider this a gift, Bob said, watching me. Let it serve as a reminder of your former self, an artifact from long ago. I truly believe a person should be reconciled with their past before they can move forward into the future.

I think the battery might be dead. Do you think I could find a charger? I asked Bob.

It's not supposed to work, Adam informed me. We broke it.

Bob continued smiling at me. Like I said, Candace, this is just an object. It serves as a reminder of who you used to be, but accessing all your old data is not helpful to you in moving forward. It is a symbol of how far you have come.

I looked at Janelle, who shook her head, warning me not to

pursue it. Okay, great, thanks, I repeated again, to no one in particular. I slid the iPhone into my coat pocket, wanting instead to
throw it into the fire—or better yet, to throw it at Bob.

Bob's proselytizing continued, except that it was directed at
the group now. His enthusiastic gusts of rhetoric swept through
the campground. What exactly is the internet? he boomed, and
our heads snapped back to attention. How do you make it begin
again? How do you bring back something that's in the ether?

Ashley rolled her eyes. We took long, generous pulls from our
soapy, sudsy beers.

Bob tried again. How old is the internet? he bellowed.

It was invented in the 1990s, Todd offered, between bites.

No, it was commercialized in the 1990s, Evan corrected. It
was invented earlier.

How do you know? Todd said.

I do something called reading.

Bob cleared his throat, and we quieted. I bring up the internet
because I'd like us to think about exactly what the internet is. It's
dead, but what exactly have we lost?

In response to his own question, he set down his beer, punched
up his glasses, and sermonized:

The internet is the flattening of time. It is the place where the
past and the present exist on one single plane. But proportion-
ally, because the present calcifies into the past, even now, even as
we speak, perhaps it is more accurate to say that the internet
almost wholly consists of the past. It is the place we go to commune
with the past.

I guess that's true, Evan agreed. All those archives of news
articles.

Or like when we follow the Facebook profiles of our exes, Rachel said. We're broken up but we never really break up. I never
totally forget the past because I'm seeing it on my Facebook wall

every day. You can never reinvent yourself because your social media identity is set.

Bob continued: Our eyes have become nearsighted with nostalgia, staring at our computer screen. Because being online is equivalent to living in the past. And, while we can agree that the internet has many uses, one of its significant side effects is that we all live too much in the past. But!—here, he looked around at all of us inclusively—there is a bright side. This loss of the internet presents an opportunity. We are more free to live in the present, and more free to envision our future.

I'm saying all this tonight, Bob continued, because we will arrive at the Facility very soon.

Todd instigated a slow clap, and soon most everyone was clapping. The sound filled the air, like a flock of birds scattering from a shuddering treetop.

Evan changed the subject with another question, aimed at Bob: Can you give us an ETA on the Facility? Like, how many days is it going to be?

He sighed, exasperated by our shifting conversation. Well, that all depends on the roads. If the roads are decent, I'd say—here, he squinted into the distance, apparently intuiting the future—two or three days.

That soon? Evan asked.

Not if we keep staying up this late every night, Bob said. He looked around and made an announcement. Tonight, we should go to sleep earlier so we can wake up early tomorrow. Now that we're so close to our destination, let's get a head start.

We all nodded in unison. Then there was a flurry of dishes being cleaned, of trash being collected, sleeping bags unfurled. In less than an hour, we had nearly all retreated back to our tents or the cars, preparing to bed down.

I also returned to my tent and changed into my plaid flannel pajamas. The only people who remained were Evan, Janelle, and Ashley, who, as usual, stayed talking around the fire.

I lay on my back, treading a thin, shallow sleep.

When I next opened my eyes, I saw shadows flickering across the nylon membrane of my tent, wavering by the fire. There was the sound of hissing, the fire being extinguished quickly with water.

Then I heard Janelle speak. Let's go.

Without hesitation, I got up and unzipped my tent.

They all turned to look at me, frozen, as I came out. They were fully dressed, in jeans and boots and coats.

Where are you going? I asked automatically.

Oh my god, keep your voice down, Evan said.

Janelle came over. She took me by the shoulders and said, like a mother gently shooing a child, Go back to sleep. You never saw this.

I shot her a look. Where are you guys going? I repeated, this time in a whisper.

She hesitated.

C'mon, Janelle.

We're gonna stalk. Relax. We do this all the time. They're not like full-fledged stalks. They're more like baby stalks. We don't empty anyone's house, we just get drugs. Where do you think our weed supply comes from?

Does Bob know?

She looked at me impatiently. Do you think Bob knows?

How long have you guys been doing this? I kept asking questions, trying not to feel hurt that they'd never included me.

Maybe five times so far, she said, and as if reading my mind, she added in a whisper, I would've asked you, but given your condition, it's better if you get rest. You need to be taking care of yourself.

I glanced at Evan and Ashley, yards away near the extinguished bonfire, wondering if Janelle had told them about my condition. They hung back, oblivious.

Where are you guys going tonight? I looked around. We were surrounded by trees, trees and road and darkness.

Janelle hesitated. Tonight is a little different. We're going to find Ashley's house.

Ashley lives here?

Close enough. If it were your house that was so close by, wouldn't you want to go see it?

I looked at Janelle's, Ashley's, and Evan's faces. Can I come?

10

Officially, the baby stalk to Ashley's house was for getting weed. We didn't take the car. We went on foot by the side of the road instead. It was only a mile away, Ashley said. Maybe a mile and a half. Back into Ohio. She pointed out into the darkness, gesturing. We could barely see past her wrists, her fingers disappearing as if behind heavy stage curtains. Like, if we just go about a mile, less than a mile, down the highway, then we'll be on my street and you guys can see the house where I grew up.

The house where I grew up. I shivered. Like most of us, Ashley had understood her family to have succumbed to Shen Fever. I wasn't sure why she would want to return. What if she saw things she didn't want to see?

You lead the way, Evan told Ashley.

We were moving backward, reversing over the state line into Ohio again. The interstate was our lifeline. As long as we stuck to it, it would lead us to Ashley's house, and it would lead us back.

Ashley led the way, holding the main flashlight. As we stumbled along behind, she began reminiscing. It was a small ranch house, she said, and most of the rooms were covered in wood paneling. Once, when she was a teen, she decided she couldn't stand the fake wood anymore. Without telling anyone, one night she painted her room carnation pink, first a whitewash and then two coats of the pink. She had planned everything, everything except the fact that it was winter. And it was in the middle of the night. And partway through, she'd had to open the windows to let all the paint fumes out. She painted in her winter coat, piling on her parents' coats as it got colder and colder. All night she shivered and painted. But she'd finished the job.

Ashley perked up. You guys are going to see my room! It's pretty embarrassing. Don't judge, guys. It was my—she searched for the words—my former self.

The important question is where did you keep the weed? Evan said, half joking.

There's like a whole ounce, in a shoe box under my bed. My parents never went into my room. It's probably in pristine condition.

Awesome. When we get back, we're gonna make it rain with kush!

Janelle was more skeptical. Yeah, but we need to be careful.

Bob confiscated whatever weed we found during the stalks; he didn't want anyone driving while high, citing the high levels of THC in engineered weed. But we needed it. It helped blunt the uncertainty and stress we felt. I didn't let myself smoke, but I wasn't against it. Whatever I consumed was secondhand when we hotboxed the car. It helped with my nausea.

So we'll make it rain inconspicuously with kush! Evan said, undeterred. Someone has to deal with the boredom in our group, and obviously that person isn't Bob.

I turned to Ashley, changed the subject. What about your parents? I asked. Like, were you in touch with them when the fever hit?

Janelle answered protectively for Ashley: It's different for every family.

Sorry, I wasn't trying to pry.

It's okay. I have a strange relationship with my parents, Ashley said carefully. I come from a, I guess, a blue-collar background. My mom was a waitress at Perkins and my dad was a truck driver. They were pretty mad that I moved to New York to study fashion. They thought I was just racking up student debt for nothing. We hadn't kept in touch for a long time—and by the time the fever hit, I couldn't get in touch with them.

A lot of people lose contact with their families, I offered.

Ashley kept her gaze on the road ahead. Yeah, but I should have come back earlier, she said, as if to herself. She flicked her flashlight beam across a sign in front of us. It read JORDANWOOD, OHIO. Hey guys. This is it.

The exit ramp was just to the front of us. We turned down the strip in silence. I wondered what would happen if I myself returned home, to Salt Lake, I mean. I wouldn't know where to go. The house my parents owned had been sold and, I later heard, drastically renovated by a couple who were prominent Mormon officials. Maybe I would go to the church that my parents fastidiously attended. But I'd always disliked that place, the claustrophobic mildewed basement of Sunday school lessons. Maybe I would go to the storage facility that held the remaining family possessions. But it was just a storage unit, a cold box. If I ever found myself in the vicinity of Salt Lake one day, I would probably keep on driving. It is too depressing, too soul-crushingly sad, to reminisce. The past is a black hole, cut into the present day like a wound, and if you come too close, you can get sucked in. You have to keep moving.

How much of this had Ashley actually thought through?

At the base of the ramp, we turned left, onto a commercial street full of gas stations and fast-food chains. Jordanwood, it looked like, was basically a rest stop for truck drivers to take a leak before they continued on toward wherever they were going. I took out my key-chain flashlight and played it over the scene: McDonald's, a Shell station, a BP station, Wendy's, Subway, a Kum & Go, a Motel 6, and a Comfort Inn.

God, I want a burger, Evan said. Those square burgers at Wendy's. Plus some fries, a Coke . . .

It's not a big town, Ashley said. She sounded almost apologetic. It's not even a town, it's just technically a hamlet.

Janelle squeezed Ashley's arm kindly. Thanks for bringing us here.

The walk to Ashley's house was not quite as easy and streamlined as Ashley had made it out to sound. She became quieter as we advanced closer and closer. We walked down a stretch of the commercial street before turning onto another street, a residential white-collar lane that emptied out into a cul-de-sac. Our flashlights played over the overgrown lawns, the broken windows, the empty driveways.

Here it is, Ashley said.

Abruptly, we stopped and glanced up. The house was a small, boxy ranch with blue aluminum siding, stained with rust along the sides. An old station wagon sat in the gravel driveway, which was studded with weeds and dandelions.

Let's just go in, she said, the anticipation in her voice unmistakable as she started up the driveway.

No, wait. Evan stopped her. Just wait. Let's do this right, like the other times.

We gathered on the weedy, overgrown front lawn, riddled, I imagined, with insects. We took off our shoes. It was cold, the frozen brown grass against my clammy, sweaty soles. The edges of everything looked sharper, more brittle. We joined our sweaty hands and chanted the "New Slang"–like chant. Then, to my surprise, we bowed our heads and closed our eyes for Evan's recitation. I didn't expect that we would follow the prestalk protocol so closely, but I knew Evan's recitation wouldn't be anything like Bob's. He wasn't going to locate us within some triumphant trajectory of a victory narrative.

As we gather here today before these doors, Evan said, we

hope that you'll help us find a copious amount of pot so that tomorrow morning, we can make it rain with kush and quell the boredom of our road trip. May the pot we find help make things more bearable and help us figure out why the hell we're doing all of this. He paused. What the point even is. Thank you.

We listed out our names. Our voices, hoarse from talking all night long, sounded tinny and weak, thrown to the wind.

Evan Drew Marcher.

Ashley Martin Piker.

Janelle Sasha Smith.

Candace Chen.

We put our shoes back on and approached the house slowly. The front door was locked, but it looked weak; it gave off a hollow sound when I knocked on it. The rusty knob was jiggly and weak, didn't have much give.

Stand back, Evan said. He reversed a few paces, ready to charge toward the door.

Actually, Evan, I have a key, Ashley said, reaching into her jeans pocket.

The door opened to a hideous smell. I brought my collar to my nose. The air was stale cigarettes and mildew, fecund rot, and the industrial odor of too much air-conditioning. There was the sound of scuttling, like rodents or mice.

Once, in sixth-grade history, we watched a documentary on King Tut. When the archaeologists first opened his tomb, they heard a loud tearing sound, like a knife gashing through cloth. It was the sound of all the textiles inside the tomb, the imperial fabrics, ripping at the sudden exposure to fresh air.

We switched on our mini flashlights and played their beams over the wood-paneled walls. It was not a palatial tomb. The small living room was furnished with a cushy chenille sofa, a coffee table, an old boxy television, and a La-Z-Boy recliner. Above the sofa hung a pair of grimacing stag heads. On the carpeted floor, disarray: dinner plates and saucers filled with gnawed chicken bones, cigarette butts and ashes, assorted liquids. Fried-chicken buckets, pizza delivery boxes. And bottles, bottles and bottles of vodkas and tequilas, glinting in the flashlight. Shattered glass crunched underfoot. The smell of alcohol.

Sorry, Ashley said, embarrassed.

Yikes, Janelle said. She grabbed my arm, gestured to the La-Z-Boy chair. We observed the silhouetted figure slumped inside it. It was motionless. It neither took in air nor breathed it back out. We didn't need to aim our flashlights to know that this was going to be a dead stalk.

It's probably my dad, Ashley said, her voice flat and unemotional. She aimed her flashlight beam in his direction but I grabbed her arm. As if expecting someone to stop her anyway, she lowered it easily.

C'mon, I'll escort you to your room, Evan said, gently. Let's get the weed and get out of here. Lead the way.

Ashley didn't protest.

Janelle and I were left by ourselves with the father. On a normal dead stalk, Todd or Adam or someone would have already removed the bodies before the women swept the house for supplies. I tried not to look even as I looked. It was unmistakably a person, saggy and deflated, as if someone had let out all its air. Something glowed in its hand, resting down on the armchair. It was a remote control with glow-in-the-dark buttons. Then a flicker of movement.

I hit it with my beam: an insect crawling on the volume buttons. It took me a second to figure out, as I spotted another one and another, that these were maggots. I followed the trail of maggots with my flashlight, first up the man's arm to his shoulders, and then to his maggoted face, all of his features obscured by a bustling hive of maggots. They dripped from his chin down to his threadbare T-shirt, onto his belly. Flying maggots, larvae maggots, maggoty maggots, maggoted maggots, dancing their maggot mating dance all over his maggoted face.

I staggered back, dropping the flashlight.

Janelle grabbed my arm and dragged me into the kitchenette at the far end of the living room. It was hard to take deep breaths in the foul air, so I just stood, choking, over the counter, not wanting to touch anything, wanting to only keep my hands to myself, from now on and forever. Even Janelle, when she tried to help, yelling instructions to breathe, all I could think about was how disgusting she was, not her but her embodiment, her physicality; her breath, hysterically teeming with bacteria, spewing micromaggots toward me, the grit under her nails, the sweat that glistened on her arms and collarbone, that clung to her hair, ready to drip down all over me. I turned away, fighting nausea. There was not one clean thing, not one clean place. If there were no cells dying and procreating all over the place, in this room, in other rooms. If there were just not cells at all. If I could just find one clean thing here, one thing to please just anchor me. A cold, crisp, starched hospital sheet. A piece of ice lodged in my throat.

Candace? Janelle was shaking me. Her breath was in my face, a hot subway grate of soured condensed milk. Are you okay?

She rustled around in the cupboards for a glass. When she turned on the faucet, it rumbled like the sink was going to explode. The entire house groaned in solidarity. She drew me a glass, not listening to my pleas as the stream of rusty water cleared.

We're not supposed to be here. Let's go. Let's just go. Something feels wrong. I kept saying this, repeating the same sentences in different variations, just repeating, repeating.

Calm down, Janelle said, rubbing my shoulder. We'll get the weed, we'll go.

We shouldn't be stalking our own homes.

Ten minutes, Janelle said, handing me the glass of water. I shook my head, waving it away.

It's not that, I said. It's something else, it feels wrong. It feels wrong that we're stalking our former, old . . . I mean, would you go back?

I trailed off when I saw Evan. He had emerged, red-faced and panting, from the hallway. His expression was unreadable, but on cue, by some unspoken understanding, Janelle dropped everything and followed him. I also followed, from the kitchenette down the wood-paneled hallway, tripping on pizza boxes that littered the carpets, passing closed doors.

Ashley's room looked as if it belonged to a different house, so tidy and orderly. Though small: it was a little candy box, no larger than a walk-in closet. That the room existed as she'd said, that the walls were in fact painted a carnation pink, comforted me. On the pink walls, costume jewelry, bracelets and necklaces, hung from nails, from largest to smallest. The bed was a cornucopia of stuffed animals, also arranged from largest to smallest. Cluttering the floor were shoe boxes that Evan and Ashley must've searched through, the shoes now mismatched and tossed all over the floor; grimy New Balances, outdated Candie's platforms, scuffed heels in a range of colors.

Ashley was going through her shallow closet, engrossed in the seemingly endless array of dresses in all colors and fabrics, satins and tulles and canvases. Wearing only shoes and underwear, she replaced one dress on the hanger and lifted a black dress off the next hanger. She put it on. Turning around, she modeled in front of the full-length mirror. Her neutral expression registered no opinion on her outfit, neither pleasure nor displeasure, but her body went through all the motions of posing. She sucked in her stomach. She pushed out her ass. She puckered her lips into duck face.

I looked away. There was something unbearably private about this, watching her rehearse her sexuality, informed by the most obvious movies and women's magazines, with embarrassingly practiced fluency.

The posing went on for a while. At some point she winked at herself, her eyes blank but her features contorted to willfully suggest playfulness. Then, after a certain number of poses, she took the dress off, placed it back on its original hanger, and reached for the next dress in the closet.

Janelle made her no-nonsense approach. Assssssshley, she hissed. We don't have time for this.

Evan tried to explain. She won't—

I don't care. She yanked the dress out of Ashley's hands. Undeterred, Ashley took another dress out of the closet, and Janelle snatched it out of her reach again. It seemed that there was a methodical way Ashley was choosing the dresses. She was going in the order from which they hung in her closet, left to right. The next dress Ashley selected was an electric-blue bandage dress, and this time Janelle didn't stop her. She was starting to figure it out.

The dress was too tight on Ashley, and as she squeezed her body through, the stitching on the sides began to rip.

Janelle stood in front of the mirror, blocking the reflection. Ashley, she said loudly, enunciating, you can take as many of these dresses as you want. Just come with us, please. She grabbed Ashley's shoulders. Snap out of it. We need to go.

Janelle, I said.

Janelle, Evan said, a little louder. Janelle! I already tried that.

She turned to Evan. How did this happen?

We were trying to find the weed under her bed, Evan explained. It was stashed in one of those shoe boxes but she didn't remember which one. When we were opening up the boxes, she also started trying on some shoes.

So? Janelle said accusingly.

Well, then she started trying on old clothes. Evan gestured toward Ashley. Just like what you see now. I told her that we didn't have time but she said she wanted to take a few things. She said it was her only chance, and I was too busy going through the shoe boxes to notice.

Did you find the weed? I asked.

Well, I found this. From his back pocket, Evan handed me a Ziploc bag. It was barely anything, just a tiny nugget riddled with twigs and seeds. The plastic of the bag was warm and moist from his pocket. You could make one joint, if that even.

Evan turned to Janelle, continued speaking. And she was just lost in this thing. I tried to snap her out of it. I even said we could come back and do a real stalk on this place in the morning, with Bob and everyone. It was like she couldn't hear me.

We all looked at Ashley.

The next dress that she tried on was the biggest of them all. Reaching in the back of the closet, she brought out what looked like a prom dress, in the style of Jessica McClintock, a beaded, jeweled white bodice anchored by a ridiculously fluffy tulle skirt, a dinner-bell silhouette. Her hair caught in the zipper as she zipped herself up in it, but she didn't flinch, and the strands of hair stayed stuck in the zipper.

It's almost light out, Evan said. They're going to wake up any moment and find us missing. Look, I say, let's go get Bob. We'll come back here with everyone, and we'll get Ashley. We'll figure this out.

Janelle raised her eyes and looked straight ahead in the mirror, at Evan, sizing up his reflection, his manners. When she spoke, it was cold and quiet. And what, we tell Bob that Ashley is maybe fevered? Bob is just going to leave her here—or worse.

He took a breath. I don't know what to do, Janelle.

Well, we can't just leave her here. She paused for a moment, studying Ashley. You know what, guys, we're going to carry her. Evan, help me. She was already attempting to hoist one of Ashley's arms over her shoulder, but it slid off.

Help me, Janelle repeated, grabbing Ashley again by the arm. Candace, hold the flashlight.

With Janelle and Evan on either side of Ashley, buffered by an unwieldy cloud of tulle, they managed to hoist her successfully. I followed behind them, holding up the flashlight to light their way, still clutching the weed in my other hand, down the hallway through the kitchenette. Ashley's head was rolled back.

I looked at her eyes, upside down. They were open but unfocused. They didn't register me. The pupils didn't move. The closest approximation for this gaze is when someone is looking at their computer screen, or checking their phone.

Then she sneezed. She sneezed all over my face, and I clutched my mouth. I ran into the kitchen and splashed cold water on my face—an instinctive reaction.

Candace, Janelle hissed. We need your help.

They had carried Ashley as far as the living room when, suddenly, her arms and legs went slack. Her whole body went slack, in fact, and it was all Evan could do to slide her down to the floor gracefully. They set her down carefully on her back.

Ashley's eyes were now closed, as if she were in a deep slumber. She lay absolutely still, a sleeping beauty, the soft, submissive center of some fairy tale, a piece of linty candy left on the floor in her princess dress. Janelle and Evan argued about what to do, but we just stood there helplessly.

She opened her eyes. She opened her mouth.

It took me a second to understand that there was sound coming out of Ashley's mouth. It was a sound of pain, but resigned; flattened into monotony. I had never heard anything like it before. The closest approximation is a hum, but stronger and fresher; sticky and electric and rhythmic like a pestilence of parched cicadas on the deepest summer night. It is a sound that you can feel, that enters your body like bass pumping from an SUV on the street below, outside the window. The SUV is waiting at the red stoplight. The track is Rihanna, and it was the only thing I'd heard that weekend. It was a few nights after Jonathan had left. Summer nights in my Bushwick studio, when it was so hot with no air-conditioning, and I'd put cold water on dishrags and stick them leechlike all across my body. Across my legs and thighs, my forehead. I'd put ice in a Ziploc bag and stuff it in my pillowcase before I went to sleep. All the lights were off, and I just lay there, trying to pass the hours before I had to get up and go to work, which was impossible when the night was so loud. My neighbor's electric air conditioner, the bass pumping from other people's cars. They were all converging together to say one thing: You are alone. You are alone. You are alone. You are truly and really alone.

Such a sound is mesmerizing. It comes into your body. Your breath syncs up with its rhythm. You can feel cells struggling, breaking down, or otherwise proliferating with overcompensating energy, engaging in mitosis and dividing and dividing. Stop, I wanted to say to my body, just stop it. Stop. The feeling of these cells overreacting is one of pins and needles, like what happens when your foot falls asleep, except all over my entire body. It started in the back of my head, then spread from there. The pins and needles pulsated, squeezed me like a fist, performed the Heimlich, issued lashings of pain, masticated me, palpitated me, pummeling me with crashing waves of nausea. My body was falling asleep. I needed to wake it up, I needed to wake my body up.

I ran through the living room, out the front door, onto Ashley's street, and when I reached the end of that street, I ran onto the main drag, past its vacant storefronts and fast-food joints, retracing, not consciously, the route that Ashley had led us down. I just ran. I was just running. I was running back to where I came from. I was running clean into the night, except that it wasn't night anymore. It was almost morning. Light was breaking over the horizon, just barely. I could hear the sound of birds chirping, trees swaying. Ashley's town that I was running down was filled with shaggy, overgrown trees. I slowed down at the exit ramp, heart exploding.

Candace!

It was Evan, following behind me, red-faced, panting.

Where's Janelle? I asked, when I had regained my breath.

She's— He gulped, still panting. She's still behind.

We can't go back, I said.

I know.

We can't go back, I said again, as if we were arguing.

I know, he repeated.

We kept running, even though no one was chasing us. The sky was lightening so quickly. On the freeway, pines and bare branches brushed against us noncommittally. Everywhere we ran, we were touched. We couldn't not be touched, even if we preferred it that way. The world just felt unbelievably full and dense, bursting.

Running and running, we returned to camp, where Bob was waiting.

11

After the shark fin dinner party, all the tenants in our East Village building, including Jane and me, received notice that our leases would not be renewed; our apartments were being converted into single-family condos. In less than six months, they would be knocking down walls, installing dishwashers and marble countertops. We were given the option to buy our units, but they were going for millions. Jane decided to move in with her boyfriend, a trader who lived in Murray Hill. Most everyone else was moving to the boroughs, outer Brooklyn or Queens.

In the last few weeks of living in the apartment, I spent most of my free time at home. With Jane out at her boyfriend's most weekends, I had the whole place to myself. Rarely did I go on long, meandering walks like I used to. It was either office or home, home or office. My habits on the weekends were sedentary. I did some household chores, ate sandwiches, watched TV, read books and magazines, tunneling deeper in solitude. I didn't see anyone, not Jane or Steven or any of my college friends. I'd once read about how animals go off by themselves into the forest to rest for several days or weeks, without moving.

Occasionally I saw Jonathan, in the form of casual, inadvertent encounters. He would come up to return a misplaced piece of mail addressed to me, or ask to borrow eggs, or to bring me a bottle of iced tea, unbidden, from the corner bodega. After each neighborly act, we'd smoke a cigarette out on the fire escape, circling around each other. Twenty minutes would pass, at which point he would politely excuse himself and tromp downstairs. He seemed to respect my space. He seemed to intuit the threshold of my ability to be social. He never asked me out, never asked me to do things with him. Except once.

One Saturday morning, I was sitting by the window, reading, when I heard his voice. Hey.

I glanced out at the fire escape and saw Jonathan, halfway up the stairs.

Hey, I said, and opened the window to let him in.

How's that going for you? he asked, gesturing toward my book, *The Death and Life of Great American Cities* by Jane Jacobs.

It's kind of amazing. You actually recommended this one, I said. Sometimes, while I was away at work, he'd stick Post-it notes of book or movie recommendations on my windowpane. He said it was because it was too cumbersome to text on his flip phone.

It's kind of timely, considering we're getting priced out. He paused. I actually came up here to ask you something. What are your moving plans?

I'm moving to Bushwick.

I meant, *how* are you moving?

I haven't really figured that out yet. It's not until the end of the month though, right? So I'll probably figure out something last minute.

I rented a U-Haul. And I'm moving to Greenpoint, which is pretty close to Bushwick. I can help you move.

Oh, that's okay.

No, seriously. I don't have a lot of stuff. I bet all of our belongings can fit into one van and we can just make one trip.

I hesitated. Are you sure?

Yeah, it's not a problem at all. He said this so casually that I knew he was serious. It's a date. With that, he stood up and descended.

Weeks later, I waited for Jonathan outside the Spectra office. As I glimpsed the U-Haul coming down the street, I couldn't help feeling nervous and excited.

Jonathan opened the door for me, looking very much like a nervous prom date. It's my first time driving in New York, he explained. Let me apologize in advance for any really bad driving you're going to witness.

I've never driven in New York before either, I said, you don't have to worry. I have zero expectations. Just don't, you know, kill us.

I fiddled around with the air vents, I adjusted the window, I turned on the radio to something from the eighties, skittish guitar and a deep male voice.

Hey, Joy Division, Jonathan said. I love this song.

He made a wrong turn and, suddenly, we were caught in Times Square. There was a traffic jam, and it was like being ensnared in the center of a spiderweb. Horns trumpeted and cabbies yelled, angry, belligerent. Maybe there had been an accident. I could smell exhaust and hot dogs and candied nuts. I could feel the aggressive blasts of air-conditioning from all the stores and theaters. Ian Curtis crooned, in his heavy voice, about how love was going to tear everyone apart. Suspended in that chaos, he was so calm, gently drumming his fingers on the steering wheel to the radio, as if we had all the time in the world. I reclined in my seat. The track ended, a new one played, and then another. "Sweet Dreams," "Tainted Love," "I'm on Fire," "99 Luftballoons."

The radio trilled, *It's Eighties Night!*

The sun was setting, and as the sky dimmed, the billboards and advertisements and flagship stores around us gradually became brighter, unnoticeable at first and then completely blindsiding us in their brilliance as the traffic began to move and we crawled, inch by inch, out of Times Square. An entire office building sat vacant, leased out as a supporting platform for billboards. It was a dream space, a collision of brand worlds, floating in a vacuum. Sitting in the passenger's seat, with that hypnotic red Coca-Cola sign winking at us, I knew that I was going to be with Jonathan.

We drove back to our apartment building, loaded up the van with my belongings and furnishings, and drove to Bushwick. As it turned out, he had already moved his things into Greenpoint earlier that day, so we just had my stuff to move. We shared the weight of the mattress and boxes of books up the three flights of stairs. It took several trips, and my efforts fell off as his doubled. He took most of the heavy boxes, as I dragged my feet carrying a small ficus or a handful of smaller boxes.

In my new studio, we took a break. There was nothing to drink, so we opened the boxes of mismatched dishes and had some tap water. The former tenant had left ice in the freezer.

We crawled out onto the fire escape. My new neighborhood spread out before us: single-family row houses, the pizza joint that sold knuckle-hard garlic knots, some factories, a Gold's Gym in a converted warehouse, and pretty much nothing else. The neighborhood was still quiet, not yet gentrified despite people like me taking up residence. Nothing was open twenty-four hours, and you could still hear the buzzing of streetlights.

Next to me, Jonathan lit up cigarettes for us. He studied me. You know, you told me you studied art, but I never asked you about your work.

I take photographs sometimes, I said, at first reticently. I don't do as much anymore. Back in college, my honors project was this landscape series on postindustrial towns in the Rust Belt. I'd go to those old steel towns, like Braddock and Youngstown.

Will you show me?

I took out my MacBook and clicked around until I found the folder. It took me a while. They were color shots of decaying steel mills, Saturday nights at polka halls, bocce games in the back of Italian restaurants. Looking at them again, I remembered how engrossed I was in that project. I used to drive by myself from campus after class on Fridays and spend whole weekends in those towns.

He studied the images. These are really good.

The photos were printed large-scale, Thomas Struth dimensions, I explained, warming up. At our department show, someone actually bought one, the father of one of my classmates. I heard he's an oil tycoon. It's weird to think that my photo is hanging in his dining room, somewhere in Texas.

That's not surprising. It all ends up in these upper echelons of the rich, Jonathan said, scrolling through the images until he reached the end. Do you have any other work you can show me?

That's pretty much it, I said, taking my laptop back and closing it.

The Rust Belt series was supposed to be the first of several on declining industries in America. I had planned to do another series on coal mining in Appalachia, including about the effects of strip mining. I never managed to apply for the grant that would fund the project. I moved back home to take care of my mother. Everything seemed pretty irrelevant afterward. And there was that nagging sense that, though I was taking photos that were supposed to say something about these communities living in the aftermath of folded industries, I didn't really know what it was like to live there. One night, at a bar in Youngstown, this grizzled old man came up, looked at me coldly, and said, Go back to where you came from. I had retorted, politely, Where's that, sir? He'd responded, Korea, Vietnam. I don't give a shit. You don't belong here. You don't know us.

I changed the subject. What's your fiction like?

He took a puff of his cigarette. I'm working on a novel about this family in small-town southern Illinois. It's inspired by my family. Well, we're all from there, generations and generations living in this same place. No one ever leaves.

Except you, right?

He nodded. I left when I was eighteen. I moved to Chicago, lived there for years. Then I decided I needed to get even farther away, put more distance between myself and my family. That's when I ended up in New York.

What did you do in Chicago? I asked.

He told me the story of his first job. Right after college, he worked as an assistant editor at a magazine in Chicago. It was a storied indie culture publication, started in the eighties, that had, at the time, recently been acquired by a giant media company.

It's the first and only time I've ever held down an office job, he said.

I have a hard time picturing you in a tie. How long did you work there?

Three years, believe it or not. He continued. By the end of his first year, the corporate owners made changes to the vacation benefits policy: Instead of allowing for unlimited rollover vacation days, they would only roll over a maximum of ten from that year to the next. In response, some of the older employees, many of whom had been there since the eighties, took early retirement in order to capitalize on the months' worth of vacation days they'd amassed before the policy could go into effect. It was essentially a forced retirement of senior employees with higher salaries. The magazine founders also left.

By the end of his second year, corporate announced that policy regarding severance packages would be changed. Severance would no longer be scaled according to the number of years that employees had worked, but the company would provide a flat fee for all employees who had worked there for fewer than ten years.

Within the following year, almost all of the senior staff had been laid off, given their diminished severance payouts. The editor who'd hired him was also let go.

By the end of that third year, the magazine was run almost entirely by twentysomethings. They were paid entry-level salaries. Jonathan was promoted to Senior Editor and he was tasked with managing others, but it was a promotion in title only. The budget for freelance writers was severely slashed, so everyone started staying late at night. Anyone who didn't was considered disposable. The quality of the publication diminished.

Jonathan lit a second cigarette. If you are an individual employed by a corporation or an institution, he said, then the odds are leveraged against you. The larger party always wins. It can't see you, but it can crush you. And if that's the working world, then I don't want to be a part of it.

In Chicago, he told me, he lived in an apartment on Milwaukee Avenue, above a laundromat. And he took the 56 bus, which stopped right outside his apartment, downtown. Sometimes it felt like he only lived on one street, just shuffling to and from work. During nights and weekends, he would write. Then he would go to work.

One day, he just stood up from his desk and walked off. He never went back.

I've never worked a full-time job again, Jonathan said. He exhaled a plume of smoke. I work enough to get by, doing part-time or freelance gigs. Most of all, I want my time and my efforts to be my own.

I took a sip of water. The ice had almost completely melted. I have to get up early to get to work in the morning, I said.

We laughed, awkwardly.

Before I thought about it too much, Jonathan picked up my hand and held it to his face, as if examining it. Then, without warning, he bit the back of my hand, like it was an apple.

Ouch, I said, feeling the sting of his teeth. His eyes were on me, waiting to see what I was going to do. It was dark enough that he couldn't see me blush. So I bit him back, on the soft spot where his neck met his shoulder. And then he bit me again, this time on the soft inside of my arm, close enough to the ticklish pit that I burst out laughing. Then I bit him again. Everything hurt, but nothing broke skin. It continued this way.

The mattress hadn't been dressed with a liner and proper sheets. The surface was itchy against my skin as he attempted to take off my pants. Wait, I told him, and peeled them off cleanly, as he unzipped his jeans and took out his Schwarzenegger dick and plowed into me, harder and more aggressive than circumstances of introductory sex usually dictate, the raw mattress surface chafing our skin pink. The sex we were having was not romantic. It was matter-of-fact sex, sex that was trying to do something, to stake a claim, to mark territory.

I felt my whole body pulsating through the night, skin raw and bruise-blooming, an electric wire left askew.

In the morning, Jonathan drove me to work in the U-Haul. My office was en route to the rental site, somewhere on Eleventh Avenue. We ordered coffee at a drive-through. He took the slow, scenic route from Brooklyn to Manhattan, through Battery Park and Wall Street and past the 9/11 Memorial. It all looked desolate early in the morning, though it was only an hour or so before the working day officially began.

I worked the usual hours and then I took the train back to his new apartment in Greenpoint, retracing my steps. I could feel a gravitational force inside me, a near dread, a stomachache, dragging me toward him. It wasn't even a choice.

In that first year of working at Spectra, I would spend many nights at Jonathan's apartment. Lying in his bed, I would have this recurring dream:

I'm at a Bible Sales Expo in a large, glass exhibition space that looks like the Javits Center. The place is a labyrinth of Bible sales-men in identical suits, pacing in front of their expensive, classy exhibit booths. In each booth are prototype displays of their latest and newest Bibles, most of which I've spec'd or produced. There's the Outdoors Bible, housed in a lightweight steel case that opens with a clasp, for the adventurous types. There's the Alternative Bible, featuring a blank cover and packaged with Sharpie markers, for the alt-Christian teens to decorate however they want. Then, in the center booth, there's the showstopper, the Bible Handbag, a portable Bible enveloped in the customized front compartment of a Coach-like satchel, for the housewives to show off at study groups and prayer circles.

I walk past the exhibit booths, fronted by all these white guys in suits. They know and I know that they are all selling the same thing, year after year, in different translations and with different packaging. I'm too smart for them. I see through everything. They can't touch me. I go up one escalator, then another. Rooms open into other rooms, unlocked with keys, security codes, secret pass-words that I magically possess. Though I know how to open these doors, I don't know what it is that I'm actually looking for. Finally, I end up in an empty room where it looks like there are no other doors. I can hear the din of voices, balloons popping, laughter scattering wildly like dice across tile. The sounds seem to emanate from one wall. At the foot of that wall is a tiny doorway, fit for a cartoon mouse. I get on the ground and squeeze myself through, but my hips don't fit.

Half-in, half-out, I look around at an enormous red ballroom, decorated with gold bows, balloons, and banners, and crowded with people sitting around round tables, piled mountainously high with pig offal and Peking ducks and KFC buckets, toasting one another and smoking cigarettes. In one corner, a bunch of Chinese children crowd around a giant TV screen that plays movies with-out sound, only captions. It's playing *Jaws*. On the opposite wall, there is a karaoke stage where Bryan Ferry sings languorously to his own songs, stumbling confusedly on the lyrics. He's singing "Avalon." My father loved that album, and Roxy Music, and most British New Wave.

At floor height, I see people I recognize, but it takes a moment because they are all dressed in formal evening wear, their makeup done, their permed hair souffléd into intricate styles. My grandmother and my grandfather. The other grandmother and grandfather. My great-great-aunt, eyes blinded, world-weary. My mother's two younger, slimmer sisters, mischievously confiding in each other. My four uncles, dressed in tuxedos, patting one another on the back and smoking so hard like it's still the eighties. My father, sitting next to them, peeling an orange with his bare hands.

Then I spot my mother. She's the only one not in a dress, but a navy skirt suit she used to wear to church. She sees me at the same time that I see her. Coming over, she bends down and pulls me through the mouse door, my hips squeezing through with a pop. I stand up, dust myself off.

Have you eaten yet? she asks.

In this dream, I can't speak. I try to open my lips, but I have none. I have no mouth, and even if I did, I have no language. I have deep emanations though, indigestive blubberings coming out of my stomach. My mother seems to understand.

You're hungry, she tells me. Sit down, you look tired.

I sit down. She sets a bowl of shark fin soup in front of me. The smell is so delicious, unbelievably rich, that I understand why sharks have to die to make it. I open my mouth.

I wake up.

As soon as we had left the scene of the past behind, we were revisiting it. Bob was driving us back again in his SUV. We sweated on his leather upholstery as he drove us toward Ashley's house, cautiously creeping down the shoulders of the freeway. Adam and Todd followed in another vehicle, close behind.

From the backseat, I tried to give instruction of the route. The whole landscape looked different, unremarkable and ordinary, from the night before. I looked to Evan next to me, waiting for him to chime in or to correct me on the directions. But he just looked quietly out the window.

Bob was quiet too. He had listened attentively but hadn't spoken much since our return. His face, hidden by a pair of Ray-Bans, appeared willingly neutral. He drove smoothly and patiently, as if we were just out running errands on a Saturday, making a bank deposit, filling up on gas. When I said, Get on the freeway, he got on the freeway. When I said, Turn left, he turned left.

The Jordanwood sign appeared in front of us.

Go right when you get to the exit ramp, I said.

Bob nodded.

As we drove in silence, I became aware of the body odor, emanating from both Evan and me, in Bob's car. It was a strong funk, sour and astringent, amped up by what must have been our bodies' response to stress.

Sorry about the BO, I said.

There are more pertinent things to apologize for, Bob said. He took the exit, and shortly, after a few turns, he slowed to a stop, engine idling. Is this the place? he asked.

It took me a moment to recognize it. We had arrived so quickly, in mere minutes. It wasn't a blue house. It was gray. There were rust stains going down its sides. Yet I recognized it. The door was ajar. We must've left it like that running out. It looked even smaller than it had the night before.

Yes, Evan confirmed, the first time he had spoken. This is the place.

Okay, hold on, Bob said, before launching into the most impressive parallel-parking job I'd ever seen, a three-point turn into an impossibly tight space between two rusty sedans. Behind us, Todd shut the engine off in the middle of the street.

Nice parking, I said. When I reached for the door handle, the lock clicked. All the door locks clicked.

No, Bob said. Stay here. Keep warm. Drink some water. He gestured to something in my hands.

I looked down. In my hand was a bottle of Poland Spring water, its crinkled plastic slightly crushed from my tight grip. There was a heavy woolly blanket over my lap, its bristly fibers scratching my legs.

I turned around to look at Evan. He also had a blanket on his lap. A full bottle of Poland Spring lay on the seat beside him. They thought we were in shock, I realized. They were treating us as if we were in shock. Then: We *were* in shock. Probably. This must be shock.

I uncapped the Poland Spring bottle and took a sip.

Bob walked around to the hatch of the car. He opened it, pulled out his M1 carbine, then closed it. The whoosh of air as he slammed the trunk closed.

How are you feeling? I asked Evan, once Bob was out of earshot.

Bad, Evan said. Worried. How are you feeling?

We're in shock, I informed him.

I know exactly what I'm in. I'm in trouble. He corrected: We're in trouble.

Drink some water, I said, shaking my Poland Spring at him.

He shook his head.

We've been awake all night, I said, as if that explained every-thing.

Actually, I have something else, he said, and from his jacket he revealed a Ziploc bag holding a ridiculous number of white pills.

What are those?

Xanax. I'm taking one. Do you want one?

No, thanks.

You sure? I've been saving them on our stalks. There's at least sixty. They say a person only needs six Xanax to overdose.

Don't overdose, Evan. I uncapped the bottle and took another sip. And then another. I tried to observe this feeling of shock, to observe its difference, but in fact I couldn't detect any difference from all the other days that blurred together on this road trip. I couldn't point to any deviation from the routine, everyday feeling, which was nothing. I didn't feel anything.

Why do you think Ashley became fevered? I asked.

Candace. Let's not talk about it right now, he said, but took the bait anyway: She had probably contracted the fever earlier, he said slowly, thinking aloud. It had been incubating inside of her for weeks, latent.

Don't you think it's strange Ashley became fevered in her childhood house? It's like nostalgia has something to do with it.

Shen Fever is caused by breathing in fungal spores. I'm pretty sure it's not because of memories.

I'm not saying it's the cause. I'm saying, what if nostalgia triggers it?

He shook his head. Are you sure you don't want a Xanax? You're shaking.

I can't take one because I don't know how it'll affect the baby.

He paused. What are you talking about?

I'm pregnant.

Wait, what? Are you serious?

I've been hiding it.

Evan hesitated. If you don't mind me asking, is it your boyfriend's? John's?

Jonathan, I corrected. And yes.

So I guess that's why you don't drink with us, he said, piecing it together. And why you've been throwing up. Does anyone else know?

Only Janelle.

Well, congratulations, he said emptily. I'm sorry that we—well, that I've been so clueless.

Thank you. But it's not your fault.

Outside the window, all three of them—Bob, Todd, and Adam, holding their greasy weapons—were standing, talking, on the front lawn. I squinted my eyes. The opened door was like a grin. I could make out the carpet, and the scattered bits of glass glinting. As was his custom, Bob gave a cursory knock on the opened door. They didn't wait for a response as they entered Ashley's house and closed the door behind them.

How do you keep a baby alive in this world? I asked Evan.

Honestly, I would just tell Bob. I would get on his good side. He'll probably read some symbolic meaning into it, see it as an auspicious sign for our future, et cetera. He would help you, get you what you need.

But I don't want Bob to find out. I want to leave. I want to leave with you and Janelle and Ashley. I want to be in on your pact.

What pact?

Yeah, the pact you and Ashley and Janelle made to go off together. Let me go with you guys.

I'm not sure that's happening anymore, Candace.

I turned back to the window, straining to see something; a shadow, a flicker of movement. Nothing. A few minutes passed. I looked back at Evan. He squeezed his eyes closed.

Evan? I pressed.

He put his hands to his ears.

What are you—

A blast ripped through the air. Then another. Another, and then another.

I ducked my head down and shut my eyes tightly. It took a moment before I felt something wet dripping all over my stomach, my crotch, my legs.

I've been shot, I thought. I'm bleeding.

Are you okay? Evan said.

I've been shot, I said. I'm bleeding.

I looked down. I had squeezed the water bottle so hard that it had exploded. The water was seeping all over my blanket, all over my shirt. The punctured plastic had gashed my finger.

Here. He reached over, took the bottle out of my hands. You're not bleeding. You're going to be okay. You need to keep warm. You need to think about yourself now.

I nodded. I felt cold all over. Things—the dashboard, the wrong time of day—in my vision were stuttering, as if trying to convey messages. This was because I was shaking. Can I have some water? I asked Evan.

Evan took his blanket and put it over my shoulders. He uncapped his bottle and gave it to me. I took a sip.

The back hatch opened. It was Bob, placing his carbine back

145

in the car. His hand bulged with purple and blue veins. He closed the hatch door and came around. His neck too was bursting with veins, his whole body straining to keep the blood circulating.

Behind us, Todd started the engine. He and Adam left quickly.

Bob opened the driver's door and sat down. He was taking his sweet time. He looked straight ahead through the windshield, his hands on ten and two, his face calm. Then he began to speak.

You may not understand everything that's happening right now, he said, his voice slow and deliberate. You must be, I imagine, extremely sleep-deprived. But I just want to say, I appreciate you telling me what you guys did this morning, and what happened last night. It's not easy to confess, or to own up to your mistakes.

You're wel—

Candace, Evan interjected, just let him say what he has to say.

Thank you, Evan. What I was going to say was, don't think that I'm not sympathetic to what you're going through. But also—and here, Bob swiveled his head to look at us in the backseat—don't think that what happened in there, what we were forced to do, wasn't a direct consequence of what you two did last night.

But what did you do in there? I asked. As he faced forward, I raised my voice. Bob, what did you do?

Bob paused, unhooking the keys from his belt. Then he pivoted back and looked at me, tearing the sunglasses off his face. His red-veined gray eyes were a shock to see. You really want to know, Candace?

They were my friends, I pressed. Our friends.

Okay, he said blankly. Well, Ashley was fevered. She was that way when we came into the house. You know what we do with the fevered. It's the merciful thing to do, rather than allow them to loop indefinitely.

Was Janelle fevered too?

No. No, she wasn't, he said.

So what happened to Janelle? I said, only aware that my voice was rising when Evan put a hand on my arm.

Evan addressed Bob: Janelle probably tried to stop you from shooting Ashley.

She threw herself in front of Ashley, Bob confirmed. I had just pulled the trigger. There wasn't enough time.

That is crazy. That's fucking insane! I exploded, as Evan touched my arm again. He was telling me to shut up, just shut up.

I don't want to talk about this again, Bob said firmly. He turned around. He began to put the key in the ignition, stopped and looked at us in the rearview mirror. And Candace, Evan. One more thing. Don't think that there aren't consequences for your actions, either. Candace, I am especially disappointed in you.

At least that's what I thought he said.

As he had predicted, we arrived at the Facility within days.

SHEN FEVER FAQ

What is it?

Shen Fever is a newly discovered fungal infection. The "fever" is contracted by breathing in microscopic fungal spores. Once inhaled, they spread from the lungs and nasal area to other organs, most commonly to the brain. Although fungal diseases have long existed in the United States, these milder forms are often contained by the immune system. Shen Fever is a particularly aggressive strain, as its fungal spores disseminate through the body quickly.

The first case of Shen Fever was reported in Shenzhen, China, in May 2011. There are now 174 documented cases in the United States, 41 of which were reported in New York.

Symptoms

In its initial stages, Shen Fever is difficult to detect. Early symptoms include memory lapse, headaches, disorientation, shortness of breath, and fatigue. Because these symptoms are often mistaken for the common cold, patients are often unaware they have contracted Shen Fever. They may appear functional and are still able to execute rote, everyday tasks. However, these initial symptoms will worsen.

Later-stage symptoms include signs of malnourishment, lapse of hygiene, bruising on the skin, and impaired motor coordination. Patients' physical movements may appear more effortful and clumsy. Eventually, Shen Fever results in a fatal loss of consciousness. From the moment of contraction, symptoms may develop over the course of one to four weeks, based on the strength of the patient's immune system.

Transmission

Shen Fever is contracted by breathing in microscopic spores in the air. Because these spores are undetectable, it is difficult to prevent exposure in areas where it is in the environment. However, the infection is not contagious between people. Transmission through bodily fluids is rare.

Certain precautions may be taken. The Centers for Disease Control and Prevention advocate a preventative approach. Avoid dusty areas and breathing in large amounts of dust. Use air filtration measures indoors. An N95 respirator may be worn to reduce the chance of transmission. See cdc.gov for more details.

14

Five years pass working for the same company. I worked the same job, albeit under a new title and with an increased salary.

I got up. I went to work in the morning. I went home in the evening. I repeated the routine. I lived in Bushwick, in the same studio. I was still in a relationship with Jonathan, who still lived in the same Greenpoint apartment. We still watched movies together, projected against his wall. We watched *Manhattan*. That scene when Woody Allen's character, depressed and lovelorn, lay on the sofa, listing all the things that still made life worth living. Like: Louis Armstrong. Cézanne pears and apples. Swedish cinema.

A morning cup of coffee, bought at the street cart outside the Spectra building. The feeling of walking outside in the summer with just-washed hair. Bodega snacks, like those Sponch marshmallow cookies, with their tiny white and pink marshmallows clustered atop a biscuit. Watching movies with Jonathan and talking late into the night.

He led me down the basement steps to the place where he lived. It was a room with a mattress on the floor. There was a drain in the middle of it. I stayed for years. Coming and going. We watched Antonioni, Hitchcock, Almodóvar movies, footsteps on the sidewalk above us. We emerged at night, wandering through convenience stores, drifting past Fujianese food factories whose loading docks were in perpetual states of shipping and receiving, whose chimneys unfurled smoke in the service of dumplings and wontons. When I was at my poorest, when I first moved to New York, that's what I ate almost every night, sipping the water they were boiled in for added nutritive value, like soup, like my Chinese mother used to.

New York has a way of forgetting you.

Listen to me, Jonathan had said. Look at me. I have something to tell you.

I had stopped seeing him after that night. I stopped talking to him, stopped taking his calls or responding to his texts. I wasn't going to move with him. I wanted to quit him cold turkey. I emptied myself, lost myself in the work. I got up. I went to work in the morning. I went home in the evening. I repeated the routine.

Things at the office proceeded along the same path. Through some finagling, the Hong Kong office found an alternate, smaller gemstone supplier for the Gemstone Bible. The printed Bibles were shrink-wrapped with teardrop-shaped amethysts, opals, and rose quartz on silver chains. Prepped for Christmas season, they were then packed into boxes, the boxes were palleted, and the whole shipment was loaded onto a boat in the Hong Kong port, along with other export commodities. Once the shipment hit the water, the gemstone supplier folded, due to the workers' health issues with pneumoconiosis.

I was just doing my job.

I got up. I went to work in the morning. The first thing I did at my desk was surf the news. A flock of dead seagulls was found washed up on Brighton Beach, dredged up with seaweed. Various sources reported an unexplained aroma, sweet and warm like chocolate-chip cookies, that inundated the Upper West Side and Morningside Heights. The best soup dumplings in New York were located in a tiny restaurant in Flushing, according to a prominent restaurant critic. Controversy ensued when kitchen photos emerged showing the dumplings being folded in unsanitary conditions. The number of Shen Fever victims was on the uptick. A baby was left on the front steps of an American Apparel in Williamsburg and found by an employee in the morning. It was quickly dubbed Hipster Baby by a neighborhood blog and became an internet meme.

It was still summer. I wanted to party.

With the Art Girls, we went barhopping after work and nibbled at small plates at tapas lounges. One night, I ended up at Lane's SoHo loft. I was standing at the window, wineglass in hand, feeling the cool pane of glass at my forehead. I had directed strangers to this forehead all night. Feel this, I slurred, leaning against the bar. Am I sick? Do I have a fever? I wanted them to be complicit in agreeing that I was indeed sick, that I should have stayed home that day. Because I felt unhealthy, not myself, nauseated. But they had all laughed. You're fine, one guy assured me. A million palms had touched my forehead, now the dirtiest, most bacterial part of me.

Now, at Lane's loft, some people were coming over; "party favors" had been procured and I guess we were going to do things. Behind me, Lane and Blythe donned their respirator masks, making jokes about "epidemic fashion." Whatever that meant, they were giggling hysterically. It was only a few drinks into the night, but sounds had started blurring together. The sound of obscure hip-hop from the stereo system, the sound of water falling from the Zen serenity fountain in the corner, the sound of keys jangling somewhere far off.

On the street below, a lone taxicab found its way down the cobblestone street, its headlights on full beam.

I had never been to Lane's apartment before, on the fifth floor of a loft building. We consoled ourselves with the fact that Lane came from wealth—her father dealt high-end Miami real estate or something—and thus augmented her Spectra salary with her trust fund. We had gone from room to room, Lane flipping on the lights to expose an explosion of exposed brick and midcentury furnishings, beautiful in an obvious way, tits and ass, marble countertops and chrome fixtures. The loft was only a few blocks away, she pointed out, not with insignificant pride, from the building where Heath Ledger had died. The living room, with its high ceilings, was furnished with Eames chairs and a white shag rug, dirtied with kitty litter tracked around by a cat that was nowhere to be seen.

Suki! Lane called out periodically. Suki! Then she would turn to one of us. Suki's shy, she'd say. So I call her Sulky.

Suki! I called, breaking into bouquets of giggles. I thought I could hear her cat, or at least a metallic sound, a kitty tag tinkling.

I had to be somewhere. I couldn't be alone. All day, my cell had filled with texts from Jonathan, messages that he'd spent forever typing out on his flip phone. I hadn't read them, but if I went home, I would open them, pace, overthink, and call him back. He would come over maybe or, worst-case scenario, I would go over to his place, descending those basement steps once again, on some endless loop. This wasn't the first time we'd broken up, but it was the first time that it felt irrevocable.

Lane and Blythe took off their face masks. Blythe said, Should we just tell her?

I turned around. Tell me what?

It's good news, don't worry, Lane said.

Blythe opened up another bottle of wine, averted her eyes. There's a new position opening up. This one's in Art.

Okay. I nodded and obediently took a sip of my wine.

Senior Product Coordinator, Lane added. They're posting it next week. Just thought you'd like to know.

Blythe chimed in. It's kind of like what you're doing now, but in Art. And we know you want to get out of Bibles. She caught herself. I mean, who wouldn't?

Wow, I said, swallowing. Exciting.

So you should put your name in, Blythe prodded.

Lane smiled at me meaningfully. At least you get to work on challenging projects in Art. It's not like Bibles, where you work on the exact same thing over and over again. Her phone pinged with a text. Delilah's on her way, she announced.

Suddenly, I understood why Blythe had invited me. They were trying me out, auditioning me, as a possible addition to their clique. I looked at myself. In my office outfit, I felt wilted in comparison to their glossy day-to-night sheath dresses.

If you did get it, Blythe started, we'd start you off with the reprints first, just until you get the hang of things. I mean, you'd probably be perfect for this.

Yes. I took a sip from the wineglass. It tasted bloody. I wanted to tell them that they had made a mistake. I wasn't like them. I didn't want the same things that they wanted, and they should know this. They should know my difference, they should sense my unfathomable fucking depths. All of these distinctions, of course, belied the fact that I very much wanted to work in Art. I wanted to be an Art Girl.

Or, at least, I couldn't work in Bibles forever. I'd go crazy. I couldn't keep having nightmares of thin Bible paper ripping on web presses, I couldn't keep explaining to clients the working conditions of Chinese laborers, things that I didn't understand myself, I couldn't keep converting yuan to dollars, the exchange rates wildly fluctuating, flailing like a drowning swimmer.

Things were different in Art. The clients weren't so fixated on the bottom line. They wanted the product to be beautiful. They cared about the printing, color reproduction, the durability of a good sewn binding, and they were willing to pay more for it, alter their publication schedule for it. They donated to nonprofits that advocated against low-wage factories in South Asian countries, even as they made use of them, a move that showed a sophisticated grasp of global economics.

Who should I talk to? I asked, smoothing out my skirt.

They looked at each other before Blythe spoke. You should see HR first thing on Monday. I think Michael is doing the hiring, but it's taken up through HR.

We'll put in a good word for you, Lane added.

Thanks, I said, wondering whether to be more effusive in my gratitude.

Lane patted the seat next to her. Sit down!

I obeyed, my skirt riding up my stomach. The music had stopped some time ago, I realized. No one replaced it with anything new. They were both checking their phones as they coordinated the get-together, pings and vibrations filling up the silence. Someone's keys jangled.

Where's this sound coming from? I asked. Someone's keys?

That's my neighbor, Lane said. She's this old woman who always has trouble getting her keys in the doorknob. I used to offer to help, but she never let me.

I opened the front door. Across the hall was a petite middle-aged lady. She was dressed strangely, in a buttoned-up wool cardigan and linen pants, as if her torso and her legs experienced two different seasons. And she kept doing the same thing over and over. She would try to place the key into the knob, and, fumbling at the knob, she would drop the keys on the floor. She'd pick them up and would try again. There was something mechanical, jerky, in her movements.

I walked across the hall and took the keys out of her hands. Here, let me help you, I said, gently. There were at least a dozen keys on her chain. I tried most of them. The last key looked similar to Lane's apartment key, and it didn't take much jingling before the door finally opened.

There you go, I said, holding the door for her to pass through. Then I saw her face. It was so ancient it was cadaverous. Her lipstick was all over her chin, her eye shadow was in her eyebrows. It was marked with bruises and scratches, the thin, delicate neck too. Dried flecks of product in her congealed hair, as if she hadn't bothered to rinse out the shampoo. The cardigan she wore was buttoned up wrong, in a mismatched fashion. Her linen pants had been put on inside out. Without looking at me, she walked straight inside, where she plunked down on the sofa, in front of the blaring television.

And me, I was inside her apartment. Blythe was calling after me. It was so bright, noisy. Every single light was on, every appliance. From the sour, acidic smell, I could tell the coffee had been burning in the pot for days. Alongside the window were placed a row of plants, so overwatered they had drowned, stains in rings around the pots. It took me a while to understand that the floor in the doorway was wet, that water was seeping into my office flats, that water had soaked into the darkened rugs and the doormats, water was pooling in around the electrical wires. I walked over to the kitchen sink, filled with dirtied, broken dishes and decaying food, and turned the faucet off.

From the sofa, the woman issued a laugh, like the laugh track from a sitcom. She was watching, I saw as I walked over, the ten o'clock news, which was running a segment on the widening income gap. She laughed. Remote in hand, she changed the channels periodically. T-Mobile was offering a new no-strings-attached carrier plan. She laughed. Neutrogena Blackhead Eliminating Cleanser, blasting blackheads all over your face. She laughed. The new Lincoln Town Car. French's mustard. The latest MacBook. She laughed. The channel switched to another news broadcast. They were interviewing the head of neurology at Columbia University Medical Center. He was talking about the virus. He said that the cases of Shen Fever must be underreported because there were many who lived alone. She laughed.

I edged back toward the door, my body aflame with goose bumps. I opened it and stepped back out into the hallway.

After the ambulance arrived, Lane tried to answer questions as Blythe and I stood by helplessly.

How long has she been fevered? the paramedic asked.

I don't know, Lane responded. We were only neighbors.

Did you notice any odd behavior? he pressed. Or anything off about her appearance that suggested diminishing cognizance? Like if she wore winter coats in the middle of summer, that kind of thing?

If I detected anything earlier, I would have called.

Do you know how we may reach her family or next of kin?

Lane shook her head. Again, I didn't know her that well. She kept to herself.

All throughout Monday, I was distracted and unproductive, and so I stayed late at the office. I couldn't go to Jonathan's anymore, and I didn't want to be greeted by my own sad, foodless empty apartment.

Nights like this, I only noticed that I needed to leave when the cleaning ladies came in. They emptied our wastebaskets, replenished the paper towels and toilet paper rolls. They smiled at me amiably; if they were irritated by my presence, they didn't show it. Then they began to vacuum, wielding high-energy, heavy industrial cleaners that rang through the halls like drills. It was my cue to go.

Before I left, I printed out and filled out the request form for my transfer to Art, slid it underneath the door of Carole's empty office, too tired to fully grasp how myopic and ridiculous and low-priority the request now seemed, after the Shen Fever–related incident. I collected my things and took the elevator downstairs.

Manny looked up in surprise when I exited the elevator in the lobby. They let you leave! he said.

Yeah. They chain me to my desk all day.

He smiled. Any exciting plans tonight?

You know it, I said, as I walked through the revolving doors.

The crush of Times Square greeted me. The city was so big. It lulled you into thinking that there were so many options, but most of the options had to do with buying things: dinner entrées, cocktails, the cover charge to a nightclub. Then there was the shopping, big chain stores open late, up and down the streets, throbbing with bass-heavy music and lighting. In the Garment District, diminished to a limited span of blocks after apparel manufacture moved overseas, wholesale shops sold fabrics and trinkets imported from China, India, Pakistan.

In Jonathan's apartment, we used to watch single-woman-in-Manhattan movies, a subgenre of New York movies. There was *Picture Perfect, An Unmarried Woman, Sex and the City*. The single heroine, usually white, romantic in her solitude. In those movies, there is almost always this power-walk shot, in which she is shown striding down some Manhattan street, possibly leaving work during rush hour at dusk, the traffic blaring all around and the buildings rising around her. The city was empowering. Even if a woman doesn't have anything, the movies seemed to say, at least there is the city. The city was posited as the ultimate consolation.

Tonight, Times Square seemed dim.

I walked a few blocks to Duane Reade. It was closed, which was odd. And wandering farther, I saw that so was the CVS. The sign said they had new hours, which were more curtailed. Finally, I found a random general store in Koreatown, where I bought an off-brand Korean pregnancy test. I bought two, just to make sure.

I took the N and transferred to the J at Canal. I took the J train all the way back to Bushwick. I was home before I knew it. In my bathroom, I tried to read the test instructions. They were in Korean, but the diagrams made it pretty clear. Two lines meant positive, and one line meant negative. It took three minutes in each case for the results to come back. I stood over the sink as I waited, looking at myself in the mirror. I waited five minutes to be sure. Seven minutes. I had to look.

Two lines, two lines.

Shit, I said. In the mirror, I didn't look pregnant, whatever that meant. I didn't look different. But my period had skipped this month. And I had felt moody, angry one moment, despairing the next. Case in point: I burst out crying. The sobs heaved out almost euphorically, like air bubbles in seltzer water, that first crisp sip, as I gripped the sides of the sink, doubling over. My face touched ceramic. I wanted to disappear down the drain.

I didn't know what to do, so I pushed it to the farthest corner of my mind. I went to sleep. Then I got up. I went to work in the morning. I went home in the evening. I repeated the routine.

15

Memories beget memories. Shen Fever being a disease of remembering, the fevered are trapped indefinitely in their memories. But what is the difference between the fevered and us? Because I remember too, I remember perfectly. My memories replay, unprompted, on repeat. And our days, like theirs, continue in an infinite loop. We drive, we sleep, we drive some more.

After two more days of driving, one loop ended. We had arrived at the Facility.

Todd pulled into the parking lot, following the snakelike caravan of vehicles into the sprawling, debris-littered parking lot. Evan and I watched from the backseat. Everyone was parking, painstakingly, carefully executing their most fastidious parking maneuvers. We were all on our best behavior. Todd parked in the handicapped spot and we stepped out of the car gingerly.

We were standing in front of Deer Oaks Mall, a beige complex with signs boasting a Macy's, a Sears, and an AMC movie theater with eight screens. This was supposed to be the Facility?

Well, it is huge. He didn't lie about that, Evan said.

All afternoon we had driven through the deserted canyons of the Chicagoland suburbs, crawling by deadened Olive Gardens, IHOPs, Kmarts, the H Mart with the parking lot littered with exploded jars of kimchi. And now this. On our road trip, we had passed so many other places. Many other places would have worked. Why here?

I glanced at everyone else to gauge their reactions.

He brought us to a mall? Genevieve said to Rachel incredulously.

It's weird, I chimed in.

They pretended like they hadn't heard me, turning away and lowering their voices. No one really spoke to us—Evan or me— since the events at Ashley's house. Our interactions were cursory, perfunctory, functional.

Bob was the last out of his car. He had parked up close, in the handicapped spot, and he disembarked alone from the SUV. For a moment, he stood staring at the Facility as if in disbelief himself. Finally, he tore his gaze away and looked around at everyone. When he got to me, he looked right through me, as if I wasn't even there. In fact, we hadn't spoken since we'd left Ashley's house two days ago.

Well, we made it, he said, his face breaking into a grin.

Cheers erupted from the group. I cast a dubious glance at Evan, but he was actually clapping, smiling with the rest of them.

So, congratulations to everyone, Bob continued. We have arrived, as they say. We had a few hiccups in our journey—here, Bob's gaze darted toward Evan and me—but in the bigger picture, we got to where we needed to go.

A smaller wave of clapping began. I glanced at Evan. He continued clapping, his eyes straight forward, unblinking.

Bob's grin disappeared. We don't have a lot of time before it gets dark. So let's get started. We need to stalk this thing before it gets too late.

We paused. Wait, we're still stalking this thing? Todd asked. Isn't this, like, a secure location?

Precautionary measure, Bob answered.

But we're staying here, right? he pressed.

Of course.

It was late afternoon already, the sun low in the sky. I thought about the long stretch of unpacking and moving and cleaning before us. I didn't want to do it.

Bob looked at us expectantly. Let's circle around, he said.

I glanced at everyone else. They had to be skeptical too, but no one wanted to be the first to express their doubts. It would break the mood to say, This is just a mall. Did we have to come all the way to the Midwest for this?

Adam began to take off his shoes. We looked at one another, in slight disbelief. Todd followed in taking off his shoes, then Rachel and Genevieve. Then Evan. Finally, I cast off my sneakers too, wondering whether my pregnant bulge showed through my baggy sweatshirt.

We made a circle and held hands. Bob began the recitation, his voice low. We spoke our full names. I kept thinking, Ashley Martin Piker. Janelle Sasha Smith.

As always, Todd and Adam went in first, with Bob close behind. The revolving door was blocked with trash, but Todd and Adam jiggled around with the locks of the double glass doors, which cracked open. We watched them enter the Facility, one by one subsumed into the darkness.

Five minutes passed, then ten. Fifteen.

In order to really stalk, Bob once said, you have to engage your memory. Before you go inside, visualize it. Visualize what's inside. Visualize opening the door and walking in, the sound of your footsteps clattering across tile, or muffled by thick carpeting. Ghost from room to room, from store to store. You know what's here. You've been here before, if not this exact place, then variations of it. The mall directories mounted on those upright, lit-up billboards, the plastic trays at the food court, the mannequin display at Express, each one modeling this season's new office trousers. The hours of roaming around, waiting for your mother to finish trying on cardigan twinsets at Talbots. The chemical smell of Sephora, with its walls of perfumes and colognes, arranged with tester bottles and paper strips. The kiosks selling cell phone covers or beauty products made from Dead Sea–sourced mud. The Orange Julius and the Auntie Anne's, next to each other. The feeling of walking into a mall before you've spent any money, the sense of promise that always diminishes gradually, as you go into the same stores, looking at the same merchandise.

You are not accumulating new knowledge. You are remembering, even though you have not set foot in a mall since you were a teenager. And whether the memories source from some collective memory (enshrined in movies, books, magazines, blogs, shopping catalogs) or from personal memory, try to see as much as you can. Try to remember as much as you can. And because memories beget more memories, you always remember more than you think is even there. The ones that are hidden from ourselves are the most revealing, give you the most information. Let your feelings fall away from you. A stalk should never be personal. It is about envisioning.

At least half an hour had passed.

The double entrance doors opened again. To everyone's relief, Bob, Todd, and Adam emerged. Adam drew his thumb across his neck, conveying that this was a dead stalk.

Okay! Adam yelled. You guys can come in now!

Passing through the entrance, we walked carefully on the cracked beige tiled floor. The mall consisted of two levels of shops. There was a large skylight cut into the ceiling, but the glass was grimy, casting the light with a grayish tint, the perpetual feel of a rainy day. A swampy scent, as if of a zoo or a greenhouse, hung in the air. Here and there were still-green potted trees that, upon closer investigation, were just silky simulations of ficus and maples.

Todd and Adam both turned on their flashlights, leading the way. We turned on our key-chain flashlights.

Welcome to the Facility, Bob said.

We walked past an empty fountain. At the bottom was a dried copper crust of pennies for all the wishes made. The sound of our footsteps on the tile echoed through the place. We looked around at all the familiar stores. There was Aldo, Bath and Body Works, Journeys, all boasting desperate sale signs typical of the End. Everything was 50 PERCENT OFF, BUY ONE GET ONE FREE, CLEARANCE. The mall must have remained functional up until the End. Though there were vacant storefronts, the other shops were still full of merchandise, covered in dust.

Everything we want is here, in these stores, Bob said, gesturing to the stores as if he owned them. We have endless supplies.

Bob, how much does a mall like this go for? I asked.

A trillion dollars, he answered facetiously. I'm part owner.

So how much did that come to for you?

Bob shrugged. My friend was one of the developers. He got me a good deal. It was a business opportunity.

As we walked on, it occurred to me that maybe the only reason we had come all the way out here was because Bob part-owned this place. Did he think owning this place still mattered?

The first floor led to the food court, its signs once ablaze with TACO BELL, CHICK-FIL-A, WENDY'S, FALAFEL GRILL, TOKYO PALACE. Brown liquid seeped out of defunct freezers. They would have to be cleaned later. The Formica tables remained, but no chairs could be found. We came across a two-tier platform of gum-ball machines, still filled with an assortment of candies and mini party-favor toys.

No one had any quarters, or any money for that matter, but Todd ran back to the wishing fountain we'd passed earlier and returned with a handful of calcified silver coins. The first machine he tried yielded a blue gum ball. He popped it into his mouth and chewed.

Gross. Genevieve made a face. How old are those? They probably haven't been changed in over six months.

Still good. Todd grinned, chewing. They're shelf stable.

That was all it took. The tension broke. We swarmed around the machines. There were so many candy options: marbled jawbreakers, Bananaramas, Skittles, M&M's, Wicked Watermelons, Hot Chews, Hot Tamales, Reese's Pieces, Good & Plentys. Then there were the toys: little alien figurines, temporary tattoos, sticky hands, neon bouncy balls. The best part was in choosing, in deciding what to get. We sent Todd back to get more quarters. Buoyed by the sugar rush, the mood brightened. We could all feel it, even me. I hadn't had candy like this in forever.

Todd hurtled fistfuls of bouncy balls at the columns and walls around us, and we ducked, laughing, trying not to get hit as they bounced back, hitting us from all sides.

Okay, let's keep going, Bob said. It's getting late. We should think about how to allocate this space.

We quieted down, murmured consent as we followed Bob up the stilled escalator.

The general idea, Bob continued, is for the department stores on the first floor to serve as communal spaces. And the smaller boutiques on the second floor here could serve as personal rooms. Why don't you each pick your rooms?

Dibs! I call dibs! Genevieve yelled as soon as we got to the top. She indicated the J.Crew, a corner store at our right. Inside, the store boasted blond-wood floorboards and built-in shelving, displaying shoes and handbags. The studio lights no longer worked.

Now we couldn't help ourselves. Everyone ran around the second floor, calling dibs on our rooms. Rachel went with the Gap. With its white walls and beechwood floors, it reminded her of a beach house. Todd picked Abercrombie and Fitch, which resembled a dim club. Adam went with the Apple Store, with its clean, modern interior and glass doors. Evan got Journeys. Bob selected Hot Topic, with its cavernous black interior and faux-iron doors.

I chose L'Occitane, one of the smaller spaces. It seemed cozier than the others, with faux-wood-lined walls and red tiled floors. Advertisements hung in the display windows; lavender fields in Provence. It was quaint and old-fashioned; perhaps that was what helped it sell skin care. I knew that I wouldn't be staying there for very long. I would find a way to leave soon, with or without Evan.

We went out to the parking lot and moved the packed boxes inside. In the expanse of Deer Oaks Mall, our pilfered belongings seemed meager and junky, kitschy. We took only what we needed for the night, including electric generators and space heaters and LED lamps. Todd and Adam went from store to store with manual bicycle pumps to inflate each air mattress. We unpacked pillows and sheets and comforters.

In L'Occitane, I was packing away the merchandise on the shelves, clearing the way for my own stuff, when Bob came in. Hi, Candace, he said, casually.

Hi, Bob. I also tried to sound casual.

He put down his carbine and leaned against the shelves. I just wanted to take a moment with you, he began, now that we've arrived at the Facility, to talk about how we can make this new arrangement work for us.

What do you mean?

He leveled his gaze. Evan tells me that you're pregnant.

Evan? I repeated in disbelief.

How far along are you?

I didn't say anything because I didn't know if it was a sure thing, I lied. I'm maybe five months?

It seems like a sure thing at this point, he said flatly, then softened. First of all, let me congratulate you. I just wish I had known earlier, is what I'm saying. Because this is a blessing.

After everything that's happened, I didn't think it would take.

That's my point. It's miraculous. The fact that you're pregnant, it means something for our group. Maybe you don't know it, but it does. It makes us feel hopeful. I know everyone will be happy to hear about it.

Thank you, I allowed.

I glanced at the doorway, where Todd and Adam had suddenly materialized. How long had they been standing there? Bob turned toward them and said, Back up for a moment, will you, guys?

He turned to me again. But I didn't come here to talk about this. I came in here to present you with my dilemma. Which is this: I can't have you leaving.

I forced a laugh. I'm not going to leave, Bob. Where would I go, at this point?

His expression was stark, severe. But you intend to leave. You told Evan. And now that you're with child . . . He trailed off, before catching the thread again. The point is, right now I can't trust you. And Candace, honestly, it's for your own good that we keep you in here. It's very dangerous out there.

My breath caught. Keep me in here? I repeated.

Starting tonight, he confirmed. And don't worry about anything. We'll take care of you, provide for you. You'll carry your baby to term.

How long do you plan on locking me in for? I asked, and as soon as I asked, I knew it was going to happen, I was going to get locked in. Asking acknowledged his authority to do this to me.

Like I said, until you carry your baby to term. And starting tonight we'll keep watch over you.

Right, I said, and proceeded to walk out of L'Occitane, my heart pounding. Todd and Adam both grabbed my arms, their grip firm and intentioned.

Don't hurt her, Bob instructed them, as they walked me back into the store.

So you're saying that I don't even have a choice, I said, trying to keep cool, to play along.

Bob's voice escalated, betrayed anger for the first time. Everyone has a choice, Candace. Ashley had a choice. Janelle had a choice. You all had a choice when you decided to go on your little road trip that night. And all those other nights when you guys did stalks without telling anyone. He took a breath. Look, you've shown that you had no problem breaking the rules of the group.

It took me a moment to find my tack. Arguing only seemed to make him angrier. Better to appear meek and fearful, better to assure him of his power. I began this way: I'm sorry that—

So starting tonight, he interrupted, you'll stay here. For the duration of this confinement, you should work on showing me that you can follow the rules.

Adam and Todd were unhooking something in the entrance. They tugged at a metal-link gate that slid down from the top of the frame.

You're imprisoning me, I said in disbelief.

Try not to look at it that way, Bob said. You're safe. You're healthy. You're going to be a mother. As soon as this baby comes, we're going to celebrate it.

With that, he spun around and walked out. He passed Todd and Adam at the entrance. Then they pulled down the metal grating, sliding it from the top of the doorway to the floor. They took a combination lock and snapped it closed.

They had locked me in.

Bob looked through the gate. It won't be as bad as you think, Candace, he said. You'll see.

So passed my first night in the Facility.

16

In February 1846, the members of the Church of Jesus Christ of Latter-day Saints embarked on an exodus. They fled their hometown of Nauvoo, Illinois, where, in acts of religious persecution, their homes had been burned and their leader, Joseph Smith, had been killed by a mob of nonbelievers. There was nothing else to do but go. Led by a new leader, Brigham Young, sixteen hundred members loaded up their belongings in wagons and headed west. They trekked across the frozen Mississippi River, the ice cracking underneath, in search of a different future they could not yet envision.

With an unknown destination, the exodus turned into a wandering. It would last for months. Like any venture into the unknown, such a mission required blind faith amongst its constituents, faith in a story line. They referred to themselves as the Camp of Israel, like the Jews wandering the desert after leaving Egypt; they referred to Brigham Young as the American Moses. Temporarily, they sought refuge in Sugar Creek, Iowa, from where Brigham Young sent envoys to scope out the territories ahead. Campfires burned day and night. The envoys returned and confirmed the openness of the westward path. They packed everything up and forded the Des Moines River. Spring brought thunderstorms and muddy embankments. They forged farther westward.

It was summer when they arrived at Salt Lake Valley. The beauty of the land, surrounded by vast mountains and pines and lakes, entranced Brigham Young. The canyon rocks, large and cathedral-like, were patterned with streams of white where water once coursed. In early settler photographs of the West, all streams of water—rivers, brooks, waterfalls—looked like milk. Between the motion of the water and the long exposure times of early cameras, the land once looked as if it were lactating.

Upon his first glimpse of the Salt Lake Valley, Brigham Young proclaimed: This is the place.

When Zhigang Chen and his wife, Ruifang Yang, arrived in Salt Lake City, the mountains in the distance looked brown and ugly from the plane window. This was the winter of 1988. The sky was overcast. Patches of dirty snow melted on sidewalks and parking lots. It had been a long journey since they left Fuzhou, but now, nearing its end, they found themselves more excited than tired. They gazed out the window as the plane descended, as America crystalized from an abstraction (ice cream sundaes, Disney cartoons, blond hair) into a reality (snow-littered mountains, highways, municipal buildings).

This must be the place, Zhigang said, before the plane dropped its wheels and skidded down on the cold asphalt.

He had been granted the opportunity to study in America through a scholarship from the University of Utah, which had offered him full funding to pursue his PhD in Economics. He was the first graduate student from China to be admitted into the department. Due to the rarity of such an opportunity—the doors between China and the United States were tentatively opening through scholarly exchanges—the Chinese government picked up the cost of his airfare, and in the months leading up to the trip, the couple had scrimped to purchase a ticket for Ruifang too.

A Russian exchange student had been delegated by the university to chauffeur the couple to their new home. He took them on a scenic route through Salt Lake, narrating the downtown sights in his thick Slavic accent. He slowed down at all the historic landmarks: the palace-like Temple, the Visitors Center, and the historic house of Brigham Young and his many wives. As the two men conversed in their clipped, accented English, Ruifang gazed outside at the dark, empty streets. Though Christmas had long passed, the streetlamps were still strewn with decorative wreaths and strings of lights.

The Russian told them an anecdote about the film director Andrei Tarkovsky. Upon seeing Utah for the first time, Tarkovsky remarked that now he knew Americans were vulgar because they filmed westerns in a place that should only serve as backdrop to films about God.

Their new home, a whiteboard house in a residential, middle-class neighborhood of tall, shady trees, initially appeared promising. They knocked on the front door, and the old man who owned the house, an absent-minded English professor, came out to lead them down the basement steps, where they would stay: the beige carpets stank of cigarette smoke and the sweet-sourness of mildew. The place came furnished with odd, heavy wooden furniture: a chair carved to look like a gnome, a sofa upholstered in marigold-printed velveteen, a pair of plastic Adirondack chairs masquerading as indoor furniture.

That first night, in their efforts to find something to eat, they walked to the nearby grocery store, about a mile away. Their breath came out like fog in the cold, obscuring their vision, so that when the supermarket first appeared, it seemed like a mirage: enormous, lit up like a sports stadium, surrounded by a vast parking lot. If they needed confirmation they were in America, this was it. There were no grocery stores like this in Fuzhou. They walked toward the light. The glass doors automatically slid open, and in those initial, dizzying moments as they wandered the miles of fluorescent product aisles, their skin breaking out in gooseflesh in the frozen section, it did not occur to them that they were allowed to handle any of the goods. Observing the other customers, they realized that you weren't supposed to wait at a counter while a clerk retrieved the products. You didn't have to pay first, as was custom in Fuzhou.

The supermarket was called Smith's.

They didn't know what to buy, so they bought a gallon of whole milk, plucked randomly from a variety of brands and types. In Fuzhou, milk was rare, reserved for children, so an entire gallon seemed incredibly decadent, incredibly American. When they returned to the basement apartment, they each drank a glass and fell asleep.

Thus passed their first night in America.

In the beginning, they socialized and circulated. They went to grad school parties. Ruifang tried to make new friends while her husband wallflowered, gingerly sipping at his Pepsi on some forlorn armchair. When she opened her mouth to speak her faulty, broken English, her throat constricted. She pressed her lips together, feeling the wax of her new lipstick, Revlon Cherries in the Snow. In their thirties, they were already older than most everyone there. Ruifang wore a navy shirt dress that had seemed chic in Fuzhou but now seemed completely conservative in the sea of denim miniskirts and spaghetti-strap dresses.

If she were fluent, if she could've overcome her shyness, her hesitancy, she would have liked to convey how far she had come. How in Fuzhou, she had been a certified accountant, and she counted among her clients various city and regional government officials. That her job had been deemed important enough for her to remain in Fuzhou during the Cultural Revolution, while her sisters, along with other youths, had been banished to menial labor in the countryside for years.

The Cultural Revolution had shut down all universities for several years. It was only when they reopened, accepting only a few students, that her husband gained admission. By then, he was already twenty-five and had worked as a foreman at an auto-parts factory. He had aspirations of becoming a literature professor, but he had the misfortune of scoring highest in math on the entrance exams—and was thus assigned Statistics as his major. In those years he had studied so hard that he had developed ulcers and lay in bed for days. After that period, he was plagued with afternoon migraines that, for the rest of his life, never completely abated.

They were relative newlyweds, after an elopement so quick and discreet that relatives wondered whether it hadn't been a shotgun marriage. And in fact, it had been—though she would never admit this detail to anyone. She was already pregnant by the time they eloped. In moving to the U.S., they had left a daughter in Fuzhou. She lived with her grandparents while they were here, saving money for airfare to bring her over.

They left every party early, and soon, they stopped attending such gatherings at all.

Instead of trying to find new friends, Ruifang ignored her loneliness. She focused her efforts on finding a job. The options were limited given her lack of fluency with English and her lack of a work visa, but there were options.

For the first year, Ruifang assembled wigs for a wig company. Every Monday, she went to the offices to pick up the artificial scalp and a bag of hair, ready to be made into glossy chestnut manes, dowdy pageboys, blond Farrah Fawcett–style poufs. She went home, where she sat on the marigold-printed sofa in front of the TV, playing *One Life to Live*, as she hooked each individual strand of hair into a synthetic scalp. It took thirty to forty hours to assemble an entire wig. Each wig paid eighty dollars in under-the-table cash.

She began every morning with renewed vigor to hook hair, every strand bringing her closer to saving the airfare money to bring their child to America. But by the afternoon, her vision blurred and her fingers ached. The afternoons were when the depression would settle in, and with the depression, there was a sense of anger. If she wasn't careful, she would begin tallying her grievances, and assigning blame: Her husband for bringing her here. Her sisters in Fuzhou for being secretly pleased at her misfortunes, despite the Clinique products she sent them. The dingy apartment that resisted her cleaning attempts; the strands of synthetic hair that embedded in the carpet fibers no matter how frequently she vacuumed.

Her thoughts were interrupted by a knock at the door. Probably Mormon missionaries. They came every month or so, Christ this, Christ that, zealously plying her with brochures. Sank you, she replied, by default. They didn't understand her thick accent when she'd ask them to take their shoes off before stepping inside. She'd long stopped answering the door.

She turned the TV volume down and pretended as if no one was home. The knocking grew more insistent, almost rude.

Ruifang! someone yelled. It was just her husband.

What happened to your keys? she asked upon opening the door.

I forgot them in the car, he replied breathlessly. He looked excited, wild-eyed. But that's not important. Did you hear the news?

Before she could answer, he brushed past her inside. Take off your shoes! she exclaimed, but he didn't seem to hear. He furiously clicked the remote, sailing through the TV channels until he settled on a news broadcast.

They were playing grainy footage of what appeared to be a night protest. The shaky handheld camera documented a chaotic swarm of civilians, military tanks, smoke. Gunfire rang out. The crowds chanted, Fascists, fascists! She understood, suddenly, that the protest was taking place in China.

Where is this? she asked.

Tiananmen Square, he answered.

The footage switched from the protest to chaotic scenes in a hospital. An old woman held a bloody towel to her head as on-lookers rushed her through hospital corridors. She could understand the cries of the civilians, but not the voice-over narration. A concerned-looking news anchor came on, speaking in English.

What's he saying? What's happening?

They're saying that there was a big protest last night in Tiananmen Square, Zhigang said. There were up to a million people there at one point, a lot of students and older citizens.

What were they protesting for? she prompted.

He looked at her. Democracy.

She remembered the late nights at his university dorm, the salons that she and her husband would attend. Everyone would drink beer, shell peanuts and peel tangerines, hold forth on politics. Some were outspoken in criticizing the Communist regime, the same friends who later got jobs working for that same regime. Though her husband had kept his opinions to himself, one night he had spoken passionately about democracy. Every system has its problems, he argued. But any government that granted its people freedom of speech, freedom of protest, showed respect for its citizens. It was the most idealistic she had ever seen him.

Zhigang remained silent, transfixed by the broadcast.

What else is happening? she prompted him again.

He didn't take his eyes off the screen. They're saying that the military are just shooting into the crowds. The protests are peaceful. He looked at her, stunned.

Are you sure that's right? We're watching American news.

His eyes flashed. Look! he said incredulously, pointing at the screen. It's all students and older citizens. They're shooting people randomly.

All she could see on the screen was smoke and crowds; she

could hear some occasional gunshots. A woman in the emergency room of a hospital, blood streaming from her head. The same footage played again, in an endless loop.

Well, we don't know all the facts, she maintained.

The facts are on the screen, he scoffed. Looking back at the television, he muttered under his breath.

At least speak up if you're going to criticize your wife, she responded hotly.

I wasn't criticizing you, he said, his eyes averted.

Then what did you just say?

He muttered again, a little louder this time but still barely audible.

What? She raised her voice.

Finally he looked at her and repeated his words, loud enough that they echoed through the basement apartment, decorated by the owners with dusty bowls of cranberry-spice potpourri and Precious Moments figurines and paintings of autumnal New England landscapes and Utah Jazz sports memorabilia and Michael Crichton paperbacks and pastel seashell-shaped guest soaps and other tchotchkes that did not belong to them, that they did not know or understand within any cultural context and did not find beautiful.

We are never going back, he said. And, in case she didn't hear, he repeated it once more, louder this time: We are never going back.

You brought me here to trap me, Ruifang told her husband.

Accordingly, for the next few months she fashioned her lifestyle in protest. As if to spite her husband, she made no efforts at learning English seriously, beyond conversational banter. She made no friends, not even with the other exchange students at the university. She lived an ascetic lifestyle, taking cold showers in the morning, eating only vegetables and rice at all meals.

If she remained on this path, Zhigang feared, he would probably lose her. She could easily return to Fuzhou and resume her accountant's job, which she had left in good standing. If she couldn't adapt to this new place, then the solution, he decided, might be to highlight the advantages of living in America, to placate her with all of its convenience, amenities, comfort, and prosperity.

So they did things they didn't normally do, American things. They got driver's licenses. They bought a car, a used beige Hyundai Excel. They pursued leisure activities like sightseeing. They drove to Zion National Park, and Mirror Lake, Yosemite. They toured the Visitors Center of the Salt Lake Temple, puzzling at the significance of the white Christ statue, his incandescent arms outstretched to receive them, his voice playing through the speakers on a loop. They ate lunch at Chuck-A-Rama, a pioneer-themed restaurant where they learned what a buffet was. They went to the ZCMI mall, where Ruifang had her ears pierced at one of the kiosks. All this she did as much for her relatives as for herself, snapping photos, at every instance, to mail back to Fuzhou. She bought a Clinique skin cream, which qualified her for a free gift of a makeup bag with several samples.

Her homesickness eased in department stores, supermarkets, wholesale clubs, superstores, places of unparalleled abundance. The solution was shopping, Zhigang observed. He was not trying to be reductive.

For a whole week, they took baths every day. It was almost enough to forget how, in Fuzhou, most everyone lived without bathrooms. At night, you just wet a hand towel with hot water from the kettle and washed your delicate parts as you watched the evening news.

He also tried to find ways to bring the trappings of her previous life to her. Asking around the university about the Chinese community in Salt Lake, he learned of the Chinese Christian Community Church. Neither Ruifang nor Zhigang were religious, but if this was where the Chinese community congregated, then this was where they would go.

That Sunday, Zhigang and Ruifang drove twenty minutes through the outskirts of Salt Lake to a beige brick steeple surrounded by a parking lot and a weedy lawn, and shyly took their seats in the back pews. Following the congregation's lead, they opened the hymnals and stood up and mouthed the lyrics. The traditional hymns were sung in English. They sat down when the sermon began, delivered, to their immense relief, in Chinese. The pastor, a wild-haired middle-aged man in a formal Hong Kong–tailored suit, grabbed the microphone.

Why do we deserve this? he bellowed in an impeccable Beijing accent. To what do we owe any of this?

The theme of that Sunday's sermon was second chances, the responsibility that comes with a second chance. After escaping Egypt, the children of Israel embarked on an exodus that, as the years passed, began to feel more like an aimless wandering. They lost faith, one by one, in their own ways. As Moses conferred with God on Mount Sinai, in his absence they melted down their earrings and created a golden calf to worship. Bonfires raged. They partied. In the desert, hundreds of miles away from civilization, it felt like the right thing. It felt like a relief. The golden calf gleamed, this tangible thing.

Now, upon finding out this sin, this transgression of idolatry, God was infuriated. He said to Moses, *Now therefore let me alone, that my wrath may wax hot against them, and that I may consume them.* But Moses pleaded, and only because of this did God exercise compassion in exacting a punishment.

The God we know is the God of second chances, the pastor

said. But it is also a responsibility to accept and shoulder the second chance that God gives you. A second chance doesn't mean that you're in the clear. In many ways, it is the more difficult thing. Because a second chance means that you have to try harder. You must rise to the challenge without the blind optimism of ignorance.

He looked around at the congregation. Now we are all, in this congregation, first- and second-generation immigrants. Some of us have been in America longer than others, but we remember where we came from, and certainly we all miss the place where we came from. He paused. But you must understand in immigrating to a new country, this is a second chance. And it comes with difficulty. Being here is not always easy. Too often, it feels like we don't belong. Too often, we may wonder whether we're just wandering aimlessly by living here. But it is a second chance. You must have faith.

The congregation stood up and applauded.

Following the service, Zhigang and Ruifang followed the other congregation members downstairs to the musty, wood-paneled basement, where lunch was served. It was Chinese food, thankfully. They said a group grace and mingled with other church members. The congregation of CCCC consisted mostly of immigrants from southern China. They were doctors, real estate agents, restaurant owners. One member owned all the Taco Bell franchises in the greater Salt Lake area.

Zhigang and Ruifang returned the following week, and the week after that.

Among the other wives, Ruifang flourished. She joined the ladies' committee and helped plan out every Sunday lunch. They organized Bible study groups on Friday nights. Whenever a Chinese holiday approached, the committee prepared big, extravagant celebrations, using the church space to worship and to celebrate at the same time. To teach their children how to read and write

Mandarin, they created an after-church Chinese language program, taking up a Sunday collection to buy pinyin guidebooks and teaching materials. When her daughter arrived, Ruifang thought, she could join this school too. And then she wouldn't lose the language.

There is mystery to how faith takes root and flourishes, how need transforms into belief. Suffice to say, Zhigang and Ruifang came to know the customs and traditions of Protestant Christianity. They learned biblical stories and verses. They learned the hymns by heart. But the thing that Ruifang found most comforting about this religion was prayer. She prayed, at first imitating others during group prayers, and then eventually on her own, alone in the basement apartment. It was during the afternoons, her vision blurry and fingers stiff and fatigued from hooking wigs, that she sat down at the kitchen table and clasped her hands. It would become an important ritual, the one routine that granted her a sense of control. She practically invented her own life in America by praying, she liked to say.

Her prayers began as requests, sometimes bargains. She prayed to be swiftly reunited with her daughter. She prayed that the phone bill, during one particularly rough month when she kept calling her sisters and her mother, wouldn't be too high. She prayed that her husband might find gainful employment after graduating. She prayed for a grocery store that stocked Chinese items, like rice cooking wine and dried mini shrimp for seasoning. Lastly, she prayed that God would deem fit for her and her entire family to move back to Fuzhou. It was the one request that she always made, without fail, in her looping, repetitive afternoon prayers—no matter how improved her circumstances.

They say that if God hates your guts, he grants you your deepest wish. But God in this case, as in most cases, was by and large impartial. In the course of her life, Ruifang's wish of returning permanently to Fuzhou was never granted. God did, however, grant her several opportunities to visit. No matter the frequency of her trips, she never regained the same power or inspired the same awe among her sisters, who had long ago ascended to business jobs in the booming Chinese economy, a country that was said, in the 1990s and 2000s, to be progressing at one hundred times the scale and ten times the speed of the Industrial Revolution. The middle sister became a bank manager, the younger sister was a sales executive at a phone company.

In lieu of a permanent return to Fuzhou, God granted Ruifang's other wishes.

He granted her husband, a few months after graduation, a plum risk analysis position in the federal home loans division of the greater Salt Lake area. He granted her daughter's safe arrival to the States, and her quick, almost effortless assimilation to this new country, new language. He granted them a champagne-colored Toyota Lexus, which replaced the rusted Hyundai Excel. He granted the family a lovely blue split-level house, financed on a fifteen-year mortgage, with a backyard large enough to accommodate a koi pond and several fruit-bearing trees.

It was this house in which Ruifang hosted numerous CCCC Bible study groups and dinner parties, in which she entertained her sisters and other Chinese relatives when they visited, in which she prayed at the dining table every day, in which she heard the news of her husband's fatal hit-and-run, in which her health quickly declined after his death.

It was this house in which I took care of my mother in her last months. When she told stories, I tried to record them, though it was not always me to whom she thought she was speaking. I sat next to her bed, listening and, more often than not, deciphering, as her wandering, tangled narratives flowed in a garble of different languages: Mandarin, Fujianese, Chinglish.

We moved her bed down to the dining room on the first floor. She liked the morning light there; the trees in the backyard provided seclusion. Her face, slabbed on a down pillow, looked big and plumped from constant, coerced rest. From this face, the spurting of stories continued with unstanched flow, as if from a main artery, whether I was there or not, whether she had visitors or not. I was afraid of what would happen should the stories begin to ebb. I braced myself, then eventually lost myself in her telling.

And her remembering elicited my remembering.

I remembered the earliest days I spent with my mother, when I was two, three, and four, which were the years right before she left with my father to move to the U.S. They say you're not able to remember that far back, that memories don't form when you're that young. But I did remember. We lived in Fuzhou. Every morning when I woke up, she explained the day's itinerary, often the same as the previous day's. First, we would have breakfast. Next, we would go to the markets. She spoke to me in a way that assumed my intelligence, even though I didn't have the vocabulary to respond. We ate a breakfast of congee with pickled mustard, and fried dough sticks on the side. I had to drink a cup of warm milk. We rode to the street markets and bought cockleshells and long beans and bok choy. The streets were dense with bicycles; I rode on the handlebars of hers. In the crowd, two men carried the opposite ends of a large stick, from which hung an enormous dead pig by its bound feet.

We lived in an apartment complex that housed other university students and their families. In the evenings, in the courtyard, they played badminton and volleyball. They drank beer and shelled peanuts. She allowed me to do things for myself, and only helped me when I asked. Some nights I could climb into the tall bed beside her, and some nights I could not. She'd lift me up just high enough for me to scramble up to the top. If she said to go to sleep, then I would lie quietly until I went under.

I was calm and obedient in my earliest years; even my mother attested to this. I could sit by myself with a book for an hour, going through the pages over and over. I seemed to lack all neurosis or anxiety. I didn't even cry very often. She thought that maybe that serenity was inherited from my father, but it was actually, I wanted to say, a quality owed entirely to her. It had to do with the way she managed our days, so steady and constant and regulated. I have looked for that constancy everywhere.

Then she was gone, moved to America, and I was transported to live in another part of Fuzhou, with my grandmother and grandfather, who, despite their best intentions, alternately coddled and neglected me. We lived on the middle floor of a three-story concrete apartment building that, like most homes, had no plumbing. I was fed and cleaned and allowed to watch soap operas; for the rest of the time, I was left to my own devices. The days were devoid of order or meaning. I played ninja with a plastic sword on the concrete balcony, often the only place where I was allowed outside. The willow trees draped their branches over me, my mother combing my hair with her fingers.

Once, when I was five, I managed to wander outside on my own. I attempted to befriend a young pretty neighbor, the wife of a train conductor, who smoked her daily cigarette next to the trash bins. She seemed friendly and solicitous until she grabbed my wrist and gashed a scratch down the length of my forearm with her long, dirty nails. It broke skin, a hint of red. Hearing my cries, neighbors came out on their stoops and balconies, and subsequently, the whole neighborhood erupted, indignant, against her, an explosion of insults and accusations that turned personal. How she drank too much, how her husband had a gambling addiction, how she spent so much money on clothes and makeup, but so little on making her home. It was like a public stoning.

It's fine, it's fine! my grandmother insisted, trying to quell the scene. But their yelling only ceased when the woman's husband came home and dragged her back inside.

The world beyond the balcony was hysterical, uncontrollable. My grandparents, in response, further submerged me inside their apartment. My grandmother invented ripped-from-the-headlines cautionary tales of kidnappings of children and told them as bedtime stories. The plot template: A child wanders off from his or her grandparents, gets taken by strangers, and never comes back. The moral: Don't stray from your family. Don't talk to strangers. Stay inside. Be good.

The tantrums began during this period. In the middle of the night, I would wake up gasping, as if struck in my sleep by some unknown force, and kick my legs and shriek. This would last anywhere from a few minutes to a full hour. These tantrums happened once a week or so; my grandparents would hold my legs down, cajoling me, bribing me. Even as they happened, I wished they would stop, but I couldn't stop; the anger was overwhelming. As I grew older, they occurred with decreasing frequency but didn't stop altogether, embarrassingly, until my late teens.

When I moved to the U.S. at six, I was unrecognizable to my mother. I was angry, chronically dissatisfied, bratty. On my second day in America, she ran out of the room in tears after I angrily demanded that she buy me a pack of colored pencils. You're not you! she sputtered between sobs, which brought me to a standstill. She couldn't recognize me. That's what she told me later, that this was not the daughter she had last seen. Being too young, I didn't know enough to ask: But what did you expect? Who am I supposed to be to you?

But if I was unrecognizable to her, she was also unrecognizable to me. In this new country, she was disciplinarian, restrictive, prone to angry outbursts, easily frustrated, so fascist with arbitrary rules that struck me, even as a six-year-old, as unreasonable. For most of my childhood and adolescence, my mother was my antagonist.

Whenever she'd get mad, she'd take her index finger out and

poke me in the forehead. You you you you you, she'd say, as if accusing me of being me. She was quick to blame me for the slightest infractions, a spilled glass, a way of sitting while eating, my future ambitions (farmer or teacher), the way I dressed, what I ate, even the way I practiced English words in the car (Thank you! I yelled. Scissors! I screamed). She was the one to deny me: the extra dollar added to my allowance; an extra hour to my curfew; the money to buy my friends' birthday presents, so that I was forced to gift them, no matter what the season, leftover Halloween candy. In those early days, we lived so frugally that we even washed, alongside the dishes in the sink, used sheets of cling wrap for reuse.

She was the one to punish me, sending me to kneel in the bathtub of the darkened bathroom, carrying my father's Casio watch with an alarm setting to account for when time was up. Yet it was I who would kneel for even longer, going further and further, taking more punishment just to spite her, just to show that it meant nothing. I could take more. The sun moved across the bathroom floor, from the window to the door.

The first time I was forced to kneel was when I was seven, after she caught me playing Homeless instead of House. Playing Homeless was what it sounded like; I pretended that I was homeless. My parents had just bought a new refrigerator, and I salvaged the cardboard box it came in and filled it with stuffed animals. We pretended we lived in the box, on the street of some big, metropolitan city. We shook a tambourine and asked imaginary passersby for change.

She grabbed my arm and led me down the hallway of our tiny apartment, and into the bathroom. In the bathroom, she ordered me to kneel, fully clothed, at the head of the bathtub, the drain between my knees. She said that such a self-nullifying act of pretending to be homeless could only be punished by another self-nullifying act. I would have to be nullified twice over. She set the timer on my father's watch for fifteen minutes. She switched the lights off and left. I was alone.

When the watch alarm sounded its harmless little cry, the door opened. My mother came in and sat on the toilet seat.

I turned to look at her. She had been crying.

Turn around, she said. You have no business looking at me.

When I averted my gaze, she continued. We didn't come to America so you could be homeless. We came for better opportunities, more opportunities. For you, for your father.

And for you, I said, trying to complete her thoughts.

She shook her head. No, not for me. For you. We brought you here to study hard, grow up, get a job, she continued. So you have no business being homeless. Do you understand?

I nodded.

I can't hear you.

Hao.

You're not in Fuzhou. Say it in English, she said in Chinese.

Yes, I said. I understand.

Yet when years later I was accepted into colleges, it was she who did not want to pay the tuition to send me to my first choice, despite the scholarship that would have offset a good amount of it. In the end, my father insisted. Your only child, he appealed to her. He was my permissive parent. He could not deny me. And because he had spoken with my mother before the car accident, the summer before senior year of high school, she had allowed it. I always felt that she held it against me in the four years before she too passed.

Sitting by her bed in the last days of her life, I didn't mention any of this. A part of me wanted to remonstrate with her, to list out all her infractions in a final accounting, but the last days are for relief, not for truth. Besides, even if I spoke the truth, would she understand it, as I pecked through sentences in my garbled Chinese? Sometimes she didn't even know it was me, confusing me with her sisters, her mother, or a distant relative I'd never heard of. She referred to me by their Chinese names, it was all a scramble.

Sometimes, she just talked to herself in English. It actually wasn't that strange. Both of my parents talked to themselves in English routinely, reenacting conversations with American acquaintances, colleagues, the car wash attendant, the grocery cashier, while they mindlessly washed the dishes or vacuumed or washed their faces in the bathroom. They were performing their Americanness, perfecting it to a gleaming hard veneer to shield over their Chinese inner selves. Please and sank you.

Sometimes, thinking I was one of the church ladies from the Chinese Christian Community Church, she would ask me to pray with her. Even though I had given up praying since high school, when my father passed, I clasped my hands and bowed my head. I took her requests and prayed whatever she wanted me to pray.

Dear God, I began in English. Please bring back Zhigang, beloved father and husband, back from the hospital. Please help him recover quickly and come home soon. Amen.

Keep going, my mother urged.

Okay, I relented, and put my hands together again. Don't allow a senseless accident to take away his life. He had the right of way when he crossed the street. Because as it says in 1 Corinthians 10:13, *But God is faithful; He will not suffer you to be tempted by more than you can bear*, I recited imperfectly from memory. We believe that whatever you ordain, it will not be more than we can bear. That is why we ask you to bring back Zhigang, because we would not be able to bear it. I exhaled, a shaky breath. In Jesus's name we pray, Amen.

Amen, she repeated, then smiled at me. Let's do it again.

No, that's enough, I said.

My father had worked hard his whole life, taking late hours at the office, coming home to cold leftovers in the fridge. He received

Ling Ma

promotion after promotion, in part because he went into the office on weekends too. His work ethic was like that of many other immigrants, eager to prove their usefulness to the country that had deigned to adopt them. He didn't get to enjoy his life nearly enough. One exception that I remember: The afternoon my father and I passed our U.S. citizenship test together, he took us to the KFC across the street and ordered a deluxe combo of fried chicken with all the sides. I wasn't particularly hungry, but because he never treated himself, I ate a few pieces alongside him, feigning a festive, abundant appetite. We sat in a booth next to the window, and it was there, with the view of trucks ambling down the freeway, that he seemed to lose himself in memory. He told me that when he was a kid, growing up in the Fujianese countryside, meat and eggs were so scarce that they were only consumed during Chinese New Year. He grew up with his grandparents, tenant farmers. During the New Year festivities, his grandmother would prepare two eggs per person, fried on both sides with soy sauce on top, with crispy edges. That was his favorite dish when he was a kid. It was hard to conceive of anything better.

But when we moved here to Salt Lake, he added, your mom and I went to that buffet restaurant, Chuck-A-Rama. I had never had fried chicken before. And I thought, this is better. Fried chicken is better.

My father rarely spoke of the past, and perhaps it was only after having officialized his severance from China that he felt free to speak openly of his life there. I kept quiet so as not to break the spell, hoping he would say more. And he did. He spoke of the mornings in the Fujianese countryside, waking up early and walking through the mountains to collect firewood with his lucky pet goat. In the afternoons after school, he taught himself English using a translation of the French novel *The Red and the Black*. He looked up every single word in a Chinese–English dictionary.

What's the book about? I asked.

188

It's about a man from a poor background who wants to better his life.

Does he make it?

My father smiled. He does, but it comes at a cost. There's no happy ending.

By this point, the sun was low in the darkening sky. Across the freeway, the USCIS office had closed and its employees, the same ones who had officiated our U.S. citizenship, were pulling out of the parking lot. There was a pile of discarded bones on the table. We had ruined our appetites and my mother would be annoyed if she'd already prepared dinner. But KFC was his victory lap and I couldn't interrupt it.

Strangely, the memory of eating eggs on Chinese New Year was one that my mother later told me as well, except in this version, it was she who had grown up in the countryside—even though she had actually grown up in Fuzhou city proper. It was as if she had absorbed her husband's memories as her own. Or maybe she was trying to speak for him, to keep his memories in circulation.

Trying to discern my mother's slippery logic was like trying to grasp a stream of water. Yet even in those last days I still detected glimmers of understanding, moments of lucidity. We used to be so close, she would say, periodically, apropos of nothing. There was a tinge of wistfulness, but that was all.

Yes, I confirmed, though she could have been speaking to anyone. We used to be so close.

When we lived in China, she pressed. And you were small.

Yes, I remember, I said, clasping her hand. Her skin was softer than a baby's.

She had stopped eating, and according to the nurse, all that was left to do was wait. Though death always seemed near in those final days, when the end drew very close, her fog seemed to lift entirely. She knew it was me, and addressed me with solemnity in Chinese.

Your father is an ambitious man. He wanted a better life for you, and it is only possible in America. You are the only child. You must do better or just as well as him.

But what do you want me to do? I asked, afraid to admit how much I didn't know.

She closed her eyes. For a moment, I thought she had gone to sleep. But then I heard her breathe, a long, shaky exhalation that rattled her frame.

I just want for you what your father wanted: to make use of yourself, she finally said. No matter what, we just want you to be of use.

17

I got up. I went to work in the morning. On the J crossing the Williamsburg Bridge, I noticed that the sky looked different. It was yellowed, some kind of yellow I'd never seen before, an ir- regular jaundiced chartreuse like a bruise trying to heal. Later, trying to pinpoint the beginning of the End, I'd think about the way the sky looked that day.

I hadn't slept well the night before. I had lain in the cheap bed of my Bushwick studio, listening to the sound of my breath. I thought about the next day at the office, and the day after. When- ever I couldn't sleep, I would torture myself by creating a com- pletely hypothetical Bible production scenario to troubleshoot. I would calculate the cost of using Swiss Bible paper in place of the Chinese paper that the client insisted we buy, should the latter prove too flimsy to prevent ink from bleeding to the other side, the Psalms obscuring the Proverbs, Matthew contradicting Mark, Peter preempting John. I would estimate the time this theoretical setback would delay the production schedule, then the shipment schedule. I would know that I was alone.

Before the train tunneled underground, my phone buzzed in my tote bag, alight with another text from Jonathan: *Leaving Sunday. Talk to me plz.*

What if I texted back: *I'm pregnant! It's yrs lolz.*

I needed to find a way to break the news. We hadn't seen each other in a month, the last time being when he had informed me he was moving out of New York. He had texted, called, and emailed a bunch since then. I hadn't meant to ghost, but it was just easier not to deal with it. Especially since I didn't know whether I was going to have it.

I put my phone on silent.

I took the J to Canal, where I transferred to the Q up to the Times Square stop. Crowds were thin on the morning commute. When I walked out onto the street, the yellow of the sky had deepened. Its tincture infected everything. Even in Times Square, there was only a slight scattering of tourists. The lobby of the building was empty, except for Manny.

What are you doing here? he said.

I'm going to work.

Wait. Did you check your—

Sorry! I called out, as the elevator doors closed. I wasn't in the mood to hear cracks about my unusual punctuality. It was 8:44 a.m. on a Thursday, which, admittedly, was pretty early for me.

The elevator screeched to a standstill. It paused in suspension, emitting a mechanical moan. It always did this between the twenty-sixth and twenty-seventh floors, some kind of glitch. Then something clicked and it glided up smoothly to the thirty-second floor. I held my breath, willing the doors to open.

They opened to reveal a darkened office floor. Spectra was entombed, blinds drawn across the floor-to-ceiling windows, our cubicles small, silent sarcophagi. A lone beam of light emanated from a bank of offices at my left.

I swiped my key card and opened the door. Hello, I called out.

The light was coming from Blythe's office. Navigating through the tangled maze of gray cubicles, I found her inside, typing on her computer. The glare of the screen bounced off her straight, equine features, her long, blond hair pulled back in a low pony-tail.

Hey, she said, not looking up. Can you believe this shit?

What shit.

The email that they sent out this morning, at like six. The of-fice is closed. There's a major storm advisory. You didn't check your work email?

No, I said, feeling guilty. Why are you here?

This is what I get for breaking my phone, she said, almost to herself. She looked up. There's going to be a storm. Here. She swiveled around her computer screen toward me, and Googled *ny weather*. There was a superstorm warning for the entire tristate area. A category 3 hurricane, named Mathilde, was closing in. Certain train lines would be closed in the afternoon. Flash floods were expected in Brooklyn and lower Manhattan.

The mayor had held a press conference earlier that morning. Blythe played the video: *New Yorkers,* he said, in front of a bank of microphones. *Our job here in the mayor's office is not to alarm you, but it is to prepare for the worst. The fact is, while we have our emergency services on standby, we may be stretched beyond capac-ity tonight. Please—*

Anyway, Blythe said, swiveling the screen back toward her, I'm going to get some files and take them home. She looked me up and down. You might think about doing the same.

She opened up her file cabinets, rummaging around for proofs. Locating the project folder, she spread out the proofs across her desk. The proofs were for *New York Mirror*, a compilation volume of New York photographers.

Splayed out on her desk was a Nan Goldin photograph, *Greer and Robert on the Bed, NYC*. I could recognize it on sight.

I love Nan Goldin, I said, lingering in the doorway. She was my favorite artist when I was a teenager.

Blythe glanced up. Maybe you can take a look at this proof, give me a second opinion.

Sure, I said, uncertain whether she was asking me out of courtesy or because she genuinely wanted a second opinion. Blythe was hard to read in that way, like a WASP version of Kourtney Kardashian.

Do the colors look off to you? Blythe asked. She turned on the color-correcting lamp. A woman lying down next to a man, clutching her wrist as if measuring its thinness. He was looking away, beyond the frame. They were bathed in the warm, yellow light of the room. She was in love with him; he didn't seem to care.

I don't know, I finally said. It's supposed to be a warm image, isn't it?

Look. Blythe indicated the woman's arms, her neck. Doesn't this look weird?

It took a moment for me to see what she was saying. The flesh tones are off, I confirmed. There's maybe too much Y in the CMYK.

Good. She produced her proofing pencil and marked it up with satisfied, incisive lines. She turned the proofs, page by page. More than the other Art Girls, Blythe had a sharp, exacting eye.

Take a seat, she said, not looking up.

I rolled someone's desk chair into her office, and she produced another proofing pencil for me as I sat down beside her. We slowly paged through the images, images by Peter Hujar, David Armstrong, Larry Clark, marking up repro imperfections.

There were other Nan Goldin photographs, her earlier work taken in the seventies and eighties. They were all of her friends; they existed on highly emotive planes, socializing in cars and on beaches, posturing at good-bad parties, picnicking chaotically, cleansing themselves in milky baths, sexing and masturbating and visiting each other in hospitals, lit up by the bald glare of the camera flash. When they laughed, they threw their heads back to reveal crooked, yellowed teeth. The city back then was almost bankrupt.

Day and night seemed indistinguishable, the dividing line between them membranic. The party spectacles gave way to hospital scenes gave way to funeral tableaux. The AIDS epidemic seemed to strike overnight.

I first encountered Nan Goldin's photographs when I was a teenager, and hoarded a copy of *The Ballad of Sexual Dependency* under my mattress. So many of the people depicted seemed freakish or other in some way; they didn't fit in. But that didn't matter, the photographs seemed to say. What mattered was, they styled and remade themselves in the way they wanted to be seen. They inhabited themselves fully. They made me want to move to New York. Then I'd really be somewhere, I had thought, inhabiting myself.

We went through all the proofs, marking up color corrections.

Thanks for helping, Blythe said.

No problem. I thought Lane was working on this title, though.

Lane's taking a leave of absence.

Oh. I looked at her, waiting for her to say more.

Blythe paused, choosing her words carefully. Lane is sick. She's, uh, fevered.

Wait, really? I searched Blythe's face for a reaction.

Yeah, it's pretty shocking, Blythe said with feigned nonchalance. But her voice caught and she looked away.

I'm sorry. You never think this kind of thing happens to anyone you know.

It's happened to a lot of people, Candace, Blythe corrected me. But with Lane, it's really surprising. Lane wore her mask everywhere. After her neighbor was found fevered, she had her apartment sprayed with that antifungal treatment all the time. She took every precaution, and still it didn't . . . Blythe swallowed, trailed off. She undid her smooth, sleek ponytail and then redid it. She checked her phone. Think I need to get going. Better get home before the storm starts.

Yeah, me too, I echoed. Do you want to split a cab?

She hesitated. I was just going to take the subway. They're not shutting down for another few hours.

Somewhere in the office, a phone was ringing.

Would you get that, please? she asked, gathering up the proofs in her bag.

I left Blythe's office and went toward the ring, grappling through the maze of cubicles. It led me all the way to the other end of the floor and back to my office. It was my phone. Someone was calling me.

Spectra New York. This is Candace.

Finally, you pick up, Jonathan said.

I paused. I guess you really wanted to get ahold of me.

I called Spectra and punched your last name in the directory. I was worried.

The light went off in Blythe's office. She had put on a trench coat and was walking out the glass doors to the elevator bank. I could hear the rain on the windowpanes. Suddenly, the rain intensified so drastically that the pane shook. On the streets below, tourists in white sneakers and Crocs scattered.

There's going to be a storm, he added.

I heard. I was about to leave.

Can I stay over at your place? The landlord says my basement needs to be evacuated in case of flooding.

In the distance, I heard the elevator doors ding as Blythe left. I envied her her free time, her evening of carefree plans. I needed to tell Jonathan my news. I couldn't put it off forever.

Okay, come over, I finally said.

It was early evening by the time Jonathan came over. All day, it had been raining intermittently. After I buzzed him up, I listened to his footfalls echoing up the staircase and through the hallway, heavy and careful, as if treading a bridge that might give way.

I waited for a few beats before opening the door.

Hey, he said. He was wearing his one nice shirt, a button-down plaid needled with rain. And, I couldn't help it. My heart barked confusedly with love.

With mannered formality, he placed a pair of tidy, whiskery pecks on each side of my face, leaving behind an unfamiliar citrusy aftershave scent.

Hey, I echoed. You smell like a men's magazine.

Where do I put this? he asked, indicating the white mug in his hand. It was his overnight retainer, soaking in green mouthwash. He held the mug level, by the handle, his palm over the top. He'd walked from his apartment to the station and boarded the train this way.

I shrugged. Wherever you want.

I watched as he opened up the medicine cabinet in the bathroom and placed the mug carefully inside. It was where he'd always placed it. Asking was just a pretense.

Are you all packed for your move?

Almost, he said, and went into detail about his day: How he had sold his mattress and record player on Craigslist. The remaining belongings he had packed and left with the upstairs neighbor, a middle-aged bachelor whose only act of storm preparation was to muzzle his dog.

I also found some of your things in my apartment, he added. Your toothbrush, some books. I'm sorry, I forgot to bring them with me. They're at my neighbor's. You want me to bring your stuff back here tomorrow?

I'll pick them up, I said, even though I probably wouldn't, then changed the subject. Are you hungry? I'm kind of starving. You want to go to El Paradiso?

He hesitated. Um. I really don't want to be caught out there when the storm worsens.

Come on, I have an umbrella. Plus, it's not even that bad outside right now.

We went downstairs and bounded outside, forgetting the umbrella. We walked along the street underneath the subway tracks. The rain was supposed to worsen later, but now it was clear enough that everyone was outside. The world was exploding into a party. Revelers spilled out of bars that advertised #mathilde drink specials: five-dollar Dark and Stormys. On rooftops, hipsters congregated in little gatherings, surrounded by masses of beer bottles. In bodegas and convenience marts, strangers chatted with one another as they waited in line, stocking up on bottled water and batteries. Old men sat on plastic milk crates, enjoying the show. Music blared from competing boom boxes and sound systems. A black sports car, its open trunk stuffed with soup cans and boxed wine, barreled down toward the intersection, pumping Ginuwine. Passing the open doorway of a hipster honky-tonk bar, I caught a bit of an old song. Waylon Jennings, "Crying," the man's voice one big pitcher of water being relieved.

Finally, we reached El Paradiso, this Puerto Rican chicken place. A druggy blast of air-conditioning greeted us as we walked in, bells tinkling. It was a pretty casual place: fluorescent lighting, red tile floors, the smell of industrial cleaners. The dishes were served cafeteria style; you went up to the counter and told them what you wanted while they ladled the food on a plate.

We went through the counter with our trays. As usual, Jonathan ordered chicken and rice, and I got oxtail stew.

For here or to go? Rosa asked. She was the owner.

For here, please, I said.

We sat down at the hard Formica tables. El Paradiso was almost completely empty. I wasn't used to seeing it this way. We used to come here a lot, Sunday afternoons when it was packed with churchgoers just out of service, resplendent in their Sunday finery.

I don't understand this festive mood, Jonathan said, indicating outside the window.

Well, they won't have to work tomorrow, I explained.

So? he asked, cutting a plantain with a plastic knife.

I was like everyone else. We all hoped the storm would knock things over, fuck things up enough but not too much. We hoped the damage was bad enough to cancel work the next morning but not so bad that we couldn't go to brunch instead.

Brunch? he echoed skeptically.

Okay, maybe not brunch, I conceded. If not brunch, then something else.

A day off meant we could do things we'd always meant to do. Like go to the Botanical Garden, the Frick Collection, or something. Read some fiction. Leisure, the problem with the modern condition was the dearth of leisure. And finally, it took a force of nature to interrupt our routines. We just wanted to hit the reset button. We just wanted to feel flush with time to do things of no quantifiable value, our hopeful side pursuits like writing or drawing or something, something other than what we did for money. Like learn to be a better photographer. And even if we didn't get around to it on that day, our free day, maybe it was enough just to feel the possibility that we could if we wanted to, which is another way of saying that we wanted to feel young, though many of us were that if nothing else.

I don't know if you get that though, I said.

Of course I get that. I worked in an office. He took a bite of a plantain.

We ate in silence for a while.

When do you move again? I asked.

On Sunday. So that's in . . . three days. He looked at me. I kept trying to meet up with you. You didn't answer any of my texts.

Well, we had a fight.

We didn't have a fight. I told you of my plans to leave New York, and then you stopped communicating.

Yes, I said, because you made a decision that affected us and only told me after you decided. It seems very easy for you to walk away.

You have to know that I'm leaving because of New York, not you. You know why I don't want to live here. I don't want to hustle 24/7 just to make rent. He let his gaze drift outside the window. Then you have global warming and these seasonal hurricanes. This whole city is falling apart. Whatever happens, this place gets what it deserves.

That's a little harsh, even coming from you.

He narrowed his eyes at me. You know this Shen Fever thing is only going to get worse, right? Some are saying more than a third of the population in China are fevered. It's way worse than avian flu.

I shook my head. If that were true, then we would've heard a lot more about this.

The state media in China controls the optics of this, so we don't know the real statistics. Maybe they don't want to incite mass panic, but I'll bet it's also because they don't want foreign investors to pull out of their economy. They need to save face.

That sounds like a conspiracy, I dismissed. One of Jonathan's constant critiques of me was that I didn't keep up with the news enough, but I wondered if he wasn't overinformed, deep-diving into obscure articles and message boards, seeing connections that weren't there.

He looked at me expectantly. And Shen Fever is spreading here too. It tends to move the fastest in coastal areas that see a lot of trade, a lot of shipping, imports. The whole tristate area should be on red alert or something.

Well, I guess you're leaving at the right time. I drank my water.

He softened, struck a more conciliatory tone. You could be leaving too. You could just come with me, he said, reaching for my hand across the table. We'll settle down somewhere new, somewhere cheaper. We'll figure it out.

I moved my hand away and said: No matter where we move, it would be the same thing for me. I'd need to hold down a job. I'd need to make rent. I'd need health insurance.

Jonathan gave me a hard look. Why do you want to work a job you don't really even believe in? What's the endgame of that? Your time is worth more than that.

I returned his look. The way you choose to live is a luxury. It's only possible for a while, when no one depends on you. But it's not sustainable.

He leaned away from me, defiant. But no one depends on you either. Neither of us have a family to support. And yet you choose to be tied down to a job you don't believe in or even respect.

But what if you had kids, like, tomorrow? I asked, trying to sound neutral. It could happen. How would you take care of them?

That's not going to happen to me, at least not anytime soon, he said, so obliviously confident that I wanted to laugh.

Instead, I ate my rice, focused on chewing each and every grain. I wasn't going to tell him, I decided right then and there. It flared up without warning, this protective feeling toward an indeterminate bundle of cells inside of me. In that moment I knew.

Rosa came over to our table. I'm sorry, but we decided to close early today, she said. The storm. She gestured to our plates. I can wrap up your leftovers.

I looked down at my plate. I had barely touched my food, but I was no longer hungry. That's okay, I said. Thank you though.

Of course we'll wrap it up, Jonathan corrected.

Fine. You eat it then, I shot at him.

Rosa hesitated. You guys used to come here, right? I remember, on the weekends.

We used to, I said.

You're a nice couple. Whatever you're fighting about, it's not worth it. She looked worriedly outside. A storm, you know, these forces of nature, they put things into perspective.

How are you getting home? Jonathan asked her.

My niece and her husband are picking me up. They should be here soon.

Sorry for arguing in your establishment. Jonathan boxed up the leftovers in a Styrofoam container and put it in a plastic bag. He put down a tip. We stood up to leave.

Have a nice night, I added. At the door, I turned around and saw that she was wrapping up all the unserved, uneaten food behind the counter. I thought about her taking the food home to her niece and her husband, and eating the day's leftovers.

Come on, he said, grabbing my hand.

It had darkened outside. The parties had dispersed due to the rain, the rain that started dropping in bigger pelts, faster and steadier, as we ran home. The houses outside, each window flickering with the light of the TV screen, sat in tidy, orderly rows, obediently being cleaned with a good whiplashing. Pretty soon, it was hard to see anything. We clasped hands as we ran, so as not to lose each other along the way. When we reached my building, we were thoroughly soaked. I fished around for my keys and we heaved ourselves up the stairs.

I took a shower first, then Jonathan. While he showered, I pulled out my laptop and checked Facebook, Instagram, Twitter. Everyone was posting about the storm. Craigslist Casual Encounters exploded with urgent booty calls. People posted selfies in front of the window, with storm views outside, and filed the pics under #mathilde, the top trending thread on Twitter. Another was #netflixstorm because Netflix was hosting a viewing contest. Participants tweeted their viewing selections during the storm, and a hundred would be selected for complimentary annual Netflix subscriptions. Extra points to those who included a screenshot of their viewing choices.

Watching twister during #netflixstorm cuz I'm basic

#Mathilde is mother nature's wrath for airing Jersey Shore
   #netflixstorm

Showgirls #netflixstorm #lifechoices

Watching #Mathilde outside window > Watching movies for
   #netflixstorm

Jonathan sat down beside me, on the floor cushions. He wore a clean T-shirt and boxers that he'd left at my place last time.

What are you looking at? he asked, speaking with a slight lisp. He had just put his retainer in.

Look at this, I said, swerving the screen around to show him a photo someone had posted on Twitter. It showed a picture of the East Village partly underwater, with only the awnings of storefronts visible. Boxes of Tide and hot dogs floated erroneously all around. Broken electrical wires flailed.

He shook his head. It's fake.

How do you know?

The light in this photo is plain daylight, afternoon light. But the storm didn't really begin until it started getting dark.

I studied the photo. There was no yellow sky. I scrolled through the comments. Others had picked up on the same thing, labeling the picture #stormhoax. One commenter wrote that it was a picture taken on the set of an apocalyptic movie and reappropriated as reality.

People have too much time on their hands, I said.

Okay, I think we've reached weather-news saturation, Jonathan said, reaching to close the laptop. Let's do something else.

Hold on, I said, still clicking. Let's read the real news. On the *New York Times* homepage: *Blackout Affects Millions in Manhattan*. Mathilde was escalating. Electricity had been lost in parts of lower Manhattan: Battery Park and Wall Street. There were satellite images showing the tip of the island almost completely dark. On other sites, we read, *Storm Barrels Through Mid-Atlantic Region, Alert Extended*. The storm alert had been extended from 6:00 a.m. to 2:00 p.m. the next day. Hurricane-force winds were up to 180 miles per hour. The hurricane level had been upgraded from category 3 to category 5, the difference between "devastating damage" and "catastrophic damage."

At that moment, the lights in my studio flickered, then shut off.

Shit, I said.

I looked out the window. The darkness was total out there too. The only light came from my laptop, which only had a seventeen percent battery charge. It was only 10:13 p.m. The neighbor's Wi-Fi, KushNKash, which I siphoned, had also succumbed, and Spotify stopped streaming.

Jonathan closed my laptop before I could protest.

Let's just go to bed, he said. Come on.

We lay down on my bed, on top of the covers. I could barely see his face. He put his arm around me. There were too many terrible things happening in the world. His embrace felt familiar and comforting, as I listened to the sound of our breaths. And the intensity of the rain coming out of tempo in fast, hateful waves, viciously attacking the glass. A car alarm went off in the distance, then another. Pretty soon he was kissing me. His lips were chapped. He never thought to buy himself simple things, like ChapStick. It made me feel tender again toward him, the same throbbing ache as when we first met. I could feel his retainer, the clack of it in the dark. He moved slowly, so that I could stop him at any point, as he removed my T-shirt and bra, a scalloped black lace thing with an elastic that seared into my ribs. It was my best bra.

Candace, he said.

I couldn't see his eyes. He pulled his shirt off. He had a thin body, hairy and slimy and squishy. I can honestly say that it was my favorite body, his dick an ugly sea cucumber, veiny and brown and wretched. He handled me as if separating egg whites from yolk. He kissed my breasts and stroked the innards of my thighs, reaching into me. I sucked his dick and put it inside me. First I was on top, then I was on bottom, then in front on my hands and knees as he pulled my hair back hard. The hair pulling was new. Maybe he'd changed up his porn viewing, or maybe he had been with someone else in the month I'd been avoiding him, some rail-thin, high-pitched blonde—I bit his neck, he bit my breast—who liked it hard but not as hard as I did, someone who moaned and gasped a lot.

I was moaning. I was gasping.

Oh god, he lisped, pulling my hair back.

He didn't give any warning when he came, something he used to do. Oh, fuck, he moaned. He jizzed all over the place. He jizzed inside me, and on instinct I cried, Wait. Stop.

We lay under the covers on our backs, side by side but not touching, looking up at the ceiling. His breathing was slow and steady, like a bass line against the relentless rain that continued coming down hard on the windowpanes.

What's wrong? he asked. I have this feeling like you want to tell me something.

I don't know how many times I can tell you I'm not going with you.

I guess I have a hard time believing that. We don't have to go to Puget Sound. We can go anywhere, as long as we don't stay here. I just want you to come with me.

I'm not like you, I said.

What I didn't say was: I know you too well. You live your life idealistically. You think it's possible to opt out of the system. No regular income, no health insurance. You quit jobs on a dime. You think this is freedom but I still see the bare, painstakingly cheap way you live, the scrimping and saving, and that is not freedom either. You move in circumscribed circles. You move peripherally, on the margins of everything, pirating movies and eating dollar slices. I used to admire this about you, how fervently you clung to your beliefs—I called it integrity—but five years of watching you live this way has changed me. In this world, money is freedom. Opting out is not a real choice.

I didn't say these things because we had fought about this before, or some variation of the same issue. I didn't want to fight on our last night. I didn't want to hurt him. Maybe he sensed what I was thinking, because he was silent for a minute.

He said, There has always been this stubbornness to you that I can't break through.

I still love you, I said.

Whenever you say you love me, it sounds like a criminal confession.

I laughed sadly, my tired, hoarse voice cracking. After a moment, he began to laugh too, despite himself. We were both laughing, the last few weeks of our fight breaking like heavy clouds finally discharging rain, and for a moment, it felt like the way we were at the beginning, when we didn't take things too seriously.

I have a request, he said, out of the blue.

Okay. You want to store some of your belongings here?

No, it's for after I leave. You know that photo blog you used to have?

I paused. NY Ghost?

Yeah. You had a good thing going with it for a while. Well, my request is that I want you to start updating that blog again. I'm going to be checking it after I leave. I want to see new work.

I can't even remember the last time I posted, I said, amazed. It's just—the photos aren't that great. Not fishing for compliments. I just know they're not good.

They weren't that great in the beginning, he admitted. But they got better though. And I remember, you started it the summer when we met. I had a crush on you after that shark fin party, and I used to kind of online-stalk you. The photos on your blog were what drew me in. It's just something I think you should keep doing.

Thank you.

We lay there in silence for a while. How many nights have we stayed up, talking in the dark side by side? I wanted to say more. My mind kept searching for words—words to unite us despite, words to bond us in spite—and coming up empty.

Soon, his breathing slowed and deepened. He was falling asleep.

Me, I couldn't sleep. I kept my eyes open, looking at all of the belongings in my apartment, all of the things that would still be there after he had left. I would get rid of some of the furniture to make room for a few new things. I was going to have this baby.

18

Due to Storm Mathilde, the office was closed on Friday. When we came in the following Monday morning, we found out Seth, Senior Product Coordinator of Gifts and Specialty, had come down with Shen Fever. He had managed to return the morning after the storm, as security cameras showed, and been sequestered in his office for the full weekend, sitting at his computer, surrounded by coffee mugs. His email history showed a series of errant messages, sent to the Hong Kong and Singapore offices, about previous projects that had been printed years ago. One of the cleaning ladies had found him.

So they shut down the office for the remainder of Monday. Some men from an antifungal service came in and treated the office with a kind of spray. They sprayed the walls, and the crevices in the corners. They dusted some kind of powder on the carpets and gave them another vacuuming. Afterward, we fastidiously avoided the corner where his office was located, even avoiding those in his department who worked nearby.

An email notice came around that it was now company policy for all employees to wear N95 masks in the office (before, this had only been suggested). Spectra would provide each employee with two N95 masks. If we wanted more, we could buy extra from HR for a cheaper, subsidized fee.

We talked about Seth the rest of the week, our voices muffled by the masks, in elevators in the mornings, in our select cliques during lunch, and later in the afternoons. We sent him—his family, really—a Zabar's gift basket of fruits and nuts and salamis and cheeses, as if for a summer picnic. A grief basket, Blythe called it. A sympathy card was passed around the office, and we all signed it in our best handwriting. GET WELL SOON, it read, even though that message did not seem to apply to the fevered. There had been no reports of recovery, at least not amongst the patients whom we knew, friends of friends.

In the afternoon, we talked about him as we gathered around the espresso machine, as Frances from Cookbooks made everyone impeccable afternoon Americanos. Our voices, amplified by the masks, sounded deeper and more grievous.

So I went to visit Seth in the hospital, Frances said. At New York-Presbyterian.

How is he doing? someone asked.

Frances shook her head. They only let me see him for a few minutes. He was strapped down to the bed with these wrist things. He looked like he wanted to get up.

Everyone muttered vague, blurry sentiments of sympathy that muffled our fear of getting it ourselves.

At least we've only had one fevered in our office, someone else said. At Random House, the whole publicity department became fevered. Can you imagine?

I looked at Blythe. She shook her head, warning me not to mention Lane, who was, as far as anyone knew, taking some personal days.

We sipped our Americanos warily.

I went back to my desk, pulled up the news. For the first time, the *New York Times* homepage listed a count of U.S. victims of Shen Fever, from Boise to Topeka. An official at the Centers for Disease Control and Prevention stated that since the storm, the number of cases had multiplied. What had seemed like a fringe phenomenon was now regarded as something more serious.

I Googled *Shen Fever*.

The fungus *Shenidioides* had originated in Shenzhen, then spread to nearby regions of China. The reigning theory, first disseminated by a prominent doctor in the *Huffington Post*, was that the new strain of fungal spores had inadvertently developed within factory conditions of manufacturing areas, the SEZs in China, where spores fed off the highly specific mixture of chemicals. To predict the transmission of the fever, the blogger claimed, wind patterns may be analyzed. Not only that, but the holiday traffic surrounding the mass commute of migrant factory workers back to their home villages, such as during Chinese New Year, should also be limited. Traffic carries spores.

If the United States is to avoid the same situation, the blogging doctor claimed, then the country should quarantine whole regions, especially during Thanksgiving, Christmas, and other holidays that usually prompt mass travel.

Further in my Googlings, the *New York Times* reported that a travel ban was passing through Congress to prevent citizens of Asian countries from visiting the United States. A list of the banned countries was provided, China at the top of the list.

In the month after Jonathan left, New York became an impossible place to live. It seemed to happen gradually, then suddenly. I got up. I went to work in the morning. Outside the office windows, the city thinned out.

Tourists roamed through Times Square in scattered flocks, wearing useless face masks printed with I ♥ NY. It was amazing to me that they still came to visit. With cameras hanging around their necks and socked sneakers, they dressed like 1980s Japanese tourists, except they weren't from Japan. They were mostly European visitors, from lesser-known countries such as Malta and Estonia, who were taking advantage of the drastically reduced hotel rates, reduced everything rates. They bought hot dogs and chicken rice plates and pretzels from the half-dozen remaining food trucks. They cheesed with the handful of character impersonators still working, all Marvel superheroes. They looked up and took pictures, the flashes from their cameras bouncing off windows of semiemptied office buildings, off the billboards advertising Broadway shows that were on hiatus, soft drink and fitness water brands that were no longer trucked into the city. Supposedly the influx of these tourists kept the reduced operations of the city functioning. It was more their city than ours, at least for now.

I got up. I went to work in the morning. New York Fashion Week was still being held, but on a smaller scale. Designers sent models down the runway in face masks, gloves, and even scrubs, many branded with designer logos. The accessories industry exploded. The last show of Fashion Week was Marc Jacobs, whose spring collection eschewed obvious references to Shen Fever and aimed for something more subtle. Held at the Lexington Avenue Armory, the show featured the drop-waist, boxy dress silhouettes of 1920s flappers, rendered in muted shades of stone, black, baby blue, the gentlest seafoam. If these were party outfits, they were for the most somber party.

Most noticeably, the clothes incorporated translucent materials, from the cellophane organza of the tiered skirts to the see-through plastic of the boots and pumps, which left parts of the models' bodies incongruously, uncomfortably exposed. Reviewers commented on how the transparent features highlighted the way that we had all begun assessing each other's bodies, in fruitless attempts to detect Shen Fever. Fashion was beside the point.

We didn't look at a woman to appreciate her outfit, we looked at her to evaluate her potential sickness.

At my desk on an especially uneventful afternoon (production jobs placed at Spectra were slowly drying up), I watched a video of a backstage interview. He spoke in his low, characteristic drawl: I didn't want it to feel real.

One Sunday, I woke up to the sound of church bells ringing in unison. At first I thought they were alarm bells, but after scanning the news online, I realized that they were commemoration bells. It was the morning of September 11. They began ringing at 8:46 a.m., the moment when the first plane struck the north tower.

There was an elaborate ceremony being held at Ground Zero, with a recitation of the names of the dead. President Obama addressed the crowd by quoting the 46th Psalm. *Come behold the works of the Lord, who's made desolations in the earth. He makes wars to cease to the end of the earth; he breaks the bow, and cuts the spear in two; he burns the chariot in fire.*

I went out for a walk. I remembered how, after it had happened, President Bush told us all to go shopping. All through the morning, church bells rang at times corresponding to the moments when the planes hit and when each building fell. The north tower, the south tower, the Pentagon, the crash in Pennsylvania. The streets were quiet.

Later that night, I thought to get in touch with my relatives in China. I hadn't communicated with them much since my mother's passing. I would send them gift boxes during every Christmas season, which they celebrated only in the most secular sense. The packages, addressed to my aunt, who would dispense them as she saw fit, were filled with Clinique and Godiva chocolates, replicating what my mother would give them on her trips back. Every Chinese New Year, in response, an aunt would send me a card, signed by everyone, with a few U.S. dollars in a red envelope.

I waited until ten at night to call my aunt's number, the only phone number I could easily find. My first aunt was the one who had some working knowledge of English. It rang and rang. I calculated the time difference again. It was ten in the morning there. I let it ring for another half-dozen times. It went to voicemail, but the voice mailbox was full, or so the automated Chinese message seemed to convey. I hung up.

The remainder of my family, distant genealogical lines, dimming.

The other contact info I had was for Bing Bing. It was a WeChat username. I had joined WeChat, this texting service he used, just to talk with him. Though I spoke Mandarin fluently, I had lost my reading comprehension of Chinese characters—yet by the wonders of technology we managed to text back and forth. I would use Google Translate to transform my English into Chinese, which I would then copy and paste into WeChat. Using that convoluted method, Bing Bing and I would occasionally hold stiff, rudimentary conversations, which would eventually peter out into a rash of emojis, both of us too tired to translate.

Using this same method, I texted Bing Bing awkwardly, *Is the family okay? I am worried. Has anyone contracted Shen Fever?*

I closed the app and waited.

Later that week, protests had erupted in and around Wall Street. Hundreds of demonstrators set up camp in Zuccotti Park. They called themselves Occupy Wall Street, and they were protesting the bank bailout that President Obama had signed after the subprime mortgage crisis. Day and night, they chanted, Banks got bailed out! We got sold out! For a few elated days, there was a strange hopeful, charged atmosphere around New York. I found myself thinking of Jonathan, wishing that he were here. If he'd have stayed, he would have joined.

But Occupy Wall Street lost its glow pretty quickly. At first a media darling, it became a hot-button debate issue in editorials and cable news shows. In light of the rapid dissemination of Shen Fever, the movement was deemed decadent and out of touch. The images of young, healthy protesters chanting, not wearing their masks so their voices could be heard more loudly, only seemed to enrage the public.

Within a week, the protests in Zuccotti Park waned. Several of the protesters had succumbed to Shen Fever. The city bartered with protesters to provide free medical aid to the remaining demonstrators, most of whom did not have health insurance, in exchange for their leaving.

Zuccotti Park resembled a deserted refugee camp. It was left this way for several days before the diminished maintenance crews came to clean it up. In news photos taken before the cleanup, abandoned tents, tarps, and pieces of clothing littered the grounds. You could read their discarded protest signs: PEOPLE BEFORE PROFITS. DEPRIVATIZE DEMOCRACY. WE ARE THE 99%. EAT THE RICH.

The Death Knell, as we called the *Times* homepage victim count, was eventually pulled at the request of government officials, who cited its potential in inciting mass panic. By the end of August, it was difficult to get an accurate victim count—and by difficult, I mean that you couldn't just Google it anymore. The last public count had been at 237,561. It had become so obscure and shrouded in controversy that journalists filed FOIA requests. The seriousness of the epidemic varied depending on which news source you trusted. Some claimed that the disease was experiencing exponential growth, others that it was spreading at a slower, more contained rate. Either Shen Fever was no bigger an issue than the West Nile virus, or it was on the level of the Black Plague.

On the *Times* homepage: The travel ban of visitors from Asian countries had passed. It would go into effect immediately.

After the abolishment of the Death Knell, in early October, employees at Spectra filed for leaves of absence en masse. Though there had been no Shen Fever victims other than Lane and Seth, it was a preemptive move. Everyone wanted to stay home, supposedly safe, or move back to their hometowns and work remotely. In response, Spectra took its cue from other companies facing the same demand and introduced a work-offsite program. To be eligible, the employee had to fill out a questionnaire, comprised of twenty-seven questions that ominously hinted at his or her dispensability.

> In a hundred words or less, describe the role you fulfill at
>   Spectra.
> On a scale of 1 to 10, how would you rate your work quality?
> How effective would you describe your job efficiency? Very
>   effective, Effective, Neutral, Ineffective, Very ineffective.

After filling out the questionnaire, the employee would have an interview with Michael Reitman and the HR head, Carole. They would make a decision on his or her eligibility for the work-offsite program by the next day.

One day at work, someone tapped the back of my chair. It was Carole. Michael would like to see you now, she said.

What's this regarding? I asked. I haven't filed a work-offsite request.

There are some details we'd like to discuss regarding your future at Spectra. She smiled.

I followed her down the halls to Michael's office. I wondered whether this was about my transfer to Art. I had filled out that form more than a month ago and hadn't thought about it since. I regretted not wearing a nicer outfit.

I hadn't been inside Michael's office in a while, though I'd often passed by and glance at the black leather chaise longue through the glass walls, fantasizing about napping on it while everyone else carried on around me. If they offered me the transfer to Art, could I request a chaise longue in my new office?

Michael stood up upon my arrival. He looked weary, dark circles under his eyes.

Have a seat, Candace, Michael said. It's nice to see you.

I sat in front of his desk.

We wanted to discuss the details of your future at Spectra, he said, echoing Carole's words. You have done a tremendous, tremendous job during your time here—coming up on five years now, right? We've all been very impressed. Like the way you managed to find that last-minute supplier for the Gemstone Bible.

Thank you, I said.

Now, he said as if reciting a script, extenuating circumstances force us to evacuate this office.

We're closing down? I asked.

No, not closing down, Carole chimed in, next to him. Just putting things on hold. We're letting the whole office go on the work-offsite program. All of management is also moving. This is how we're going to move forward in light of Shen Fever.

But we're still planning on keeping the office open. We're putting together a select group to oversee day-to-day operations while other employees are on leave, Michael said. He straightened his tie. We'd like you to be part of this interim team.

I sat up straighter. What would that entail?

Just to keep doing what you're doing, Michael said. Oversee the production jobs, you know, keep them running. We'd like you to take over some of the jobs others in your department may need help with, along with your own. He looked to Carole, as if for affirmation.

Carole jumped in: You would work here in the Spectra New York office. We'd prefer to keep our main office open. This is partly an optics issue. It gives our clients confidence that we're still open when our competitors have closed their offices. All the documents and prototypes will be sent here. You and others here will serve as the point contact team for those working remotely. They may ask you to send certain samples out, for instance.

I nodded. Well, I appreciate that you considered me for this, I said. But to be honest, when you first brought me in here, I thought this was about the transfer to Art.

At this point, all transfers are on hold. We're not looking to fill any positions right now. However, I will revisit this issue once things get back to normal, after all this is over, he said.

We'll discuss the Art transfer later, Carole cut in. For now, let's just focus on this temporary arrangement for the foreseeable future. The bottom line is, we're willing to offer you this. She slid a packet of papers over. This summarizes the offer.

It was a contract.

Spectra will deposit the agreed-upon amount after the termination of the agreement, November 30, 2011. It will be direct deposited to your bank account in arrears on this date. Spectra holds the rights to extend the contract, if necessary.

It was a delirious offer. I turned the number around in my head. I wrung it dry. It rained with Crème de la Mer moisturizing creams, Fendi handbags, and Bottega Veneta sandals—luxury items that my mother wanted but never allowed herself to buy.

The HR lady slid the pen toward me, an emerald-green Montblanc with a tiny white star at its cap. The amount meant a drawerful of Montblanc pens. More realistically, it meant I could take cabs all the time, without cramming into dirty train cars. It meant an air conditioner, a window unit in every room. It meant a larger apartment. It meant that I could afford more for the baby. It meant that I could eventually take some time off to do other things. Take an extended maternity leave. Read more fiction. Take up photography again.

I picked up the pen. I flipped to the last page, to the dotted line.

Wait. Michael leaned over. He put his hand over the contract. I looked up at him, and for a disorienting moment I could see his brother's face. He looked sorry for me, which I couldn't take, the condescending expression so similar to Steven's. I wondered if Michael knew his brother and I had been involved. Probably.

You're going to want to think about this, he said. Read it before you sign it.

It's okay, I said. Everyone who's taking this work leave, they're going back to their hometowns, they want to be with their families. But I don't have any living family—in the U.S., I mean. So I would have stayed in New York anyway. I've lived here for five years—it's home to me by this point. This arrangement—my eyes flicked to the contract in front of me—just makes my time more worthwhile.

I surprised myself as I spoke; I was frighteningly lucid.

Michael's expression changed from condescension to a particular paternalistic concern that reminded me of Steven. A family man.

Still, he said gently. Take your time.

Sorry. I'll look it over at my desk, I conceded, then changed the subject. How's your brother doing?

Michael looked surprised. Steven is sick, he finally said. He's fevered.

Now I was taken aback. Oh, I'm sorry.

Thank you, he replied. We're all praying for recovery, but you know.

The odds are slim, I said, before I could stop myself.

He nodded, impassively. Right. The odds are slim to pretty much nonexistent.

I'm sorry, I repeated, and then, trying to think of something nice to say, I added: I think of Steven fondly.

Well, this is the world we live in now, Michael said shakily. Anyway, just think this offer over. I'd obviously like for you to do this, but you should make the right choice for you.

I stood up, and with the sheaf of papers gripped in my hands, I saw myself out and walked the length of hallway toward my desk, where, not even bothering to sit down at my rolling chair or read the whole thing through, I laid it out and scanned it—the hours I would be at the office, the direct deposit payment, the liability disclaimer in the event that I contracted Shen Fever—and signed it, my signature riddled with seismic tremors caused by my shaking hand.

The office was almost empty by the end of October.

19

The days begin like this: They wake up in the morning. They wash and dress and descend to the first floor, in the atrium in the middle of the mall. They cluster around the table and wait for Bob for the breakfast meeting. When he arrives, they say grace before their meals of cereal and canned fruits, their voices rising and falling. From my perch behind the metal gate of L'Occitane, I can hear their voices echoing up to the second floor.

As they eat, Bob proceeds to give them instructions for the day. There are various projects under way to make the Facility more habitable. They are cultivating a vegetable garden near the windows of the food court. They are converting Old Navy into a communal entertainment room. They are planning to stalk the Ikea in nearby Schaumburg for new pieces of furniture. They debate whether it is worth the risk to clean the mall's skylight now, frosted with cold, or wait until warmer weather. They draw up a list of hardware stores in the greater Chicagoland area for more electric generators, once the supply runs out.

Usually, it is Adam and Todd who are sent outside the Facility after breakfast. Sometimes Genevieve or Rachel accompanies them, depending on the complexity of the task. But Evan always stays behind, doing any number of domestic chores. I'm not sure what giving up my secret to curry Bob's favor has earned him. He works like everyone else. Even worse than everyone else, and he has no leaving privileges. He does the laundry, running the Sears washers and dryers. He cooks and he cleans.

In the mornings, Evan walks by my cell on his way back upstairs from the meetings. When he passes, he never once looks in my direction. He keeps his eyes averted. Once, I banged on the metal gate, and he quickened his step. Another time, I said hey and he said hey back and continued walking, avoiding my face. I like that my presence makes him newly ashamed every time. It gives me a perverse sense of power.

I want him to feel like he owes me something.

Sometimes, when I am feeling at my lowest, I think about asking Evan for Xanax. I'm pretty sure he still has it, since he seems so calm and placid as he goes about his day, doing domestic chores with Rachel or Genevieve. I'd like at least six pills, seven to be sure. It is not a serious thought, but the option is there.

In the end, we have come to the Facility to work. We work on the weekdays, rest on the weekends. Adhering to the typical work-week schedule, however ridiculous, feels strangely comforting. Even though I am exempt from working.

I sit in L'Occitane, day in, day out. The light, streaming in through a dirtied skylight, moves throughout the mall during the course of the day. It is one of the few indications of time passing.

Not working is maddening. Bob understands this. The hours pass and pass and pass. Your mind goes into free fall, untethered from a routine. Time bends. You start remembering things. Past and present become indistinguishable.

Day passes into night.

One night, when I still lived in my Bushwick studio, I opened up the medicine cabinet, searching for Clinique skin exfoliant, and saw Jonathan's mug. Inside, there was his retainer, soaking in old green mouthwash. My heart leaped, and for a wild, inexplicable second I thought he must've not left New York after all.

I stood over the sink and eased the thing into my mouth. It was too big. His teeth were not my teeth. I looked at myself, my freakish, grotesque self, a mouthful of metal and plastic jutting out, and knew that I was alone.

I spit the retainer out. I washed it, filled the mug with fresh mouthwash, and placed it back in the medicine cabinet. I thought, absurdly, that I'd keep his retainer fresh, for when he returned. That's where it still is, in my old apartment.

I wonder where Jonathan is now. Maybe he is on the yacht somewhere. Maybe he made it to Puget Sound and has joined a band of other survivors. Maybe he is fevered, or, more likely by this point, deceased.

Long after everyone is asleep, my remembering is interrupted by the sound of someone crying. It begins as a soft, suppressed sobbing, and then, as if moved by unconscionable suffering, erupts into a moaning—or something more primitive, a keening. It cycles through again, various iterations of despair, frustration. Then silence again.

I don't feel sympathy toward Evan, not even in his wrenching, humiliating despair. What I feel instead is a small, dense bud of anger, wedged tightly inside my chest. The idea that he and I could have just gone off and escaped together, to find other survivors and perhaps join a new group, now seems ridiculous.

Like Evan, I also have late-night lunacies. Mine is a recurring dream: It's of a retainer in green mouthwash, in the same white mug. I'm looking inside the mug, looking at it moving and clattering around of its own volition. But after a moment, I realize that it is speaking. I put my ear to the lip of the mug, as if listening to the ocean through a seashell. Maybe Jonathan is sending me secret messages. Maybe he wants to come and save me.

Except instead of the sound of ocean waves, my mother's voice comes out.

She says, You're not doing too well. You barely eat. You don't sleep enough. You don't do things to keep your mind active. You don't read.

She says, Only in America do you have the luxury of being depressed.

She says, Change your clothes. Brush your teeth. Wash your face. Moisturize. Exercise. Get yourself together.

She says, Now is not the time to give up. It's only going to get harder. You need to figure this out.

And sometimes I say things back. Figure what out? I ask, but she doesn't answer. Figure what out? I repeat, and the sound of my own voice jars me awake. I have been talking in my sleep.

Night passes into day.

The only way to metabolize time, I decide, is to partition it into digestible packets. I wake up in the morning. I lie in bed, meditate for a few minutes. I do my morning stretches, replaying a memory of a YouTube yoga video in my mind. I brush my teeth and wash my face, using the water jug. I moisturize, applying the only thing available, stretch-mark belly cream. There is a sink in my cell, once used for demonstrations of skin-care products. The faucet no longer works. I spit out mouthwash down the drain. The water circles clockwise before disappearing.

I watch things that happen outside my cell. Today, I see Evan and Bob standing across the mall in front of Hot Topic. Evan looks like he's cracking jokes, and they're both laughing, lightly. Then Evan holds his hand out mischievously, as if he was waiting to be given something. Bob shakes his head, smiling.

Evan always tries to suck up to Bob. It's a daily occurrence. Sometimes he walks into Hot Topic with a mug of what looks like hot chocolate. Or he fetches Bob some requested items, such as an extra pair of socks, or a pen. It's all so obvious and desperate.

But today, the pace of the conversation quickens. The discussion seems to escalate, though both make an effort to keep their voices quiet. I can see Bob shaking his head. When he begins to walk away, Evan grabs him. The fighting looks playful, but then I realize they're actually struggling. Their voices rise.

But it's been three weeks! Evan says. He is trying to wrestle the key chain connected to Bob's belt loop. He's trying to take it, with amateur desperation. There is the sound of some scuffling, some struggle.

Finally, Bob wrests free. Evan plays it off with a laugh, but Bob doesn't join in.

Don't do that again, Bob says.

Three weeks. Has it been that long since we'd arrived at the Facility? That must mean we're well into December. There is a discernible change in the weather. Though it has not begun snowing, the cold is unmistakable in its intensity.

Dressed in a North Face coat zipped up to her chin, Rachel brings me my lunch: a can of fruit cocktail, two trail-mix bars, a few strips of beef jerky, bottled water, a prenatal supplement for the baby. It is the same lunch every afternoon. We communicate in looks and nods.

Looking around to check that the coast is clear, she slips two packets of HotHands warmers out of her jeans pocket and stows them underneath the bedcovers. We rely on space heaters for warmth, but it is nearly impossible to heat up such a vacuous space as a mall on only a handful alone. Bob is wary of overusing our supply of electric generators. I am only allowed to run the space heater at night.

I nod at her in thanks; she gives me a tight-lipped smile before leaving, locking the slide-down metal gate.

When Rachel first served as my escort, she would keep up a steady patter of chitchat, despite the rules. She said that this solitary confinement thing was a charade, that it would blow over in a few days and we'd play along until it did. But after a while, she seemed to be increasingly observant of Bob's requests, including his rule that others limit their interactions with me. She began to disengage from our conversations, even as she accompanied me on daily walks to the restrooms, or brought me my meals. Secret favors, however, never diminished: a fresh change of clothes, a Pop-Tart warm from the toaster. She had given in somewhat to Bob's rule. I resented the change in Rachel's behavior but couldn't totally blame her.

Things I know about Rachel: In her past life, she worked in the publicity department for a cable news channel. Her job was to disseminate YouTube clips of reactionary political debates by random talking heads on various shows, generate controversy, and make the clips go viral. The more "sticky" these clips could be, the more it generated publicity for the shows. It was incredibly stressful and incredibly meaningless, she once said.

Day passes into night.

It gets dark early in the winter. The skylight above us grows dim. And then in another few hours, the flashlights and LED lanterns are turned off in each cell one by one, and the entire mall is once again submerged in darkness so complete and absolute. It is a primitive darkness. It has always been here, after all the city lights have gone out, carrying its own time with the sun. And as I lie here in a vacuum, it feels like a miracle I exist at all. And I realize that, given the odds, with New York wiped out, it is indeed a miracle I am still here. I am alive, I think to myself, and my baby is alive.

Under the covers, I break the disc of a HotHands packet and keep it on my stomach, trying to keep the baby warm. I've begun to think of it as a girl. She sleeps during the day and awakens at night, like the moon. I call her Luna for her nocturnal habits.

At night, Bob comes out and takes a walk. It's dark enough that I can't see him, but I hear him. The ring of car keys, which he keeps hooked onto his jeans at all times, jingle and jangle. He is the designated keeper of all car keys, which he grudgingly doles out to others undertaking his assignments.

He walks through the mall alone. I track his location by the sound of those keys clanging. When he gets to the end of our floor, he descends the still, deadened escalators and takes a lap through the first floor. It is the first of several laps he makes around the mall.

The only way to metabolize anger is to direct your focus to things at hand. Like my breath, which comes out in fogs. Like the whirring of the space heater, its thin heat disappearing out the cell as soon as it is made. Like Luna's nocturnal activity inside of me. Sometimes her movements are like a flurry of butterflies unleashed all at once, their wings giddily fluttering. Other times, she's a teakettle at full boil, whistling shrilly at fever pitch, as if enraged. Tonight, she is enraged.

I feel a strange intimacy with Bob as I hear him snaking around. To despise someone is intimate by default. I understand that he feels under a tremendous amount of pressure, relieved only by the act of doing one simple, mind-clearing thing, over and over. As Bob walks, he mutters to himself, sayings repeated like a Buddhist mantra over and over. Sometimes I can make it out: *We need more inventory*.

Other times, his thoughts are strung together. He worries about the weather, the days growing colder and colder, the deep freeze that pervades the nights. He takes mental stock of our supplies, from the water gallons to the batteries. He goes over the next day, the tasks he'll assign, with the goal of making this mall a sustainable home.

The Facility means more to Bob than just a place to live. It is the manifestation of his shoddy ideology. He dictates and enforces the rules, rules that only he fully knows and understands. He sees us as subjects, to reward or to punish. He compliments you when he wants to control you. He doesn't see you. It doesn't mean he's not a person. It doesn't mean he's not vulnerable. In certain moments, he's just vulnerable enough that you feel sympathy for him. You make excuses for him, often to yourself. You think that if you just work with him a little, then eventually things will get better. Even if he makes you pray, or breaks your iPhone, or makes you shoot at fevered. You think things will be different, more comfortable once you arrive at the Facility. But he doesn't work that way. Or you wouldn't have ended up locked up in a cell.

Whatever happens to me, I don't want Luna to be in this environment. I don't want her to grow up here, in a group controlled by someone like him. I don't want her to be within his reach. Even if the threat isn't immediate, when it becomes immediate it will be too late.

As Bob cycles through his route, coming closer to this side of the mall, he's become silent. Only the sound of the car keys in his belt loop is clear.

I can hear it no matter how far away Bob is. It beckons me. All I need is one key to unlock one car. Then I hit the gas. Then I am gone. If I make it into another city, I can disappear inside of it.

Night passes into day.

It begins to snow in the morning, lightly at first and then intensifying over the course of the day into a raging blizzard. Rachel comes in and wakes me up.

Bob wants you to come downstairs, she says, touching my arm.

I look back at her, confused. Am I . . . Am I allowed out?

Only for this morning. It's a special occasion.

Is it Christmas or something?

That's already passed, she says gently, with unbearable pity.

I look back at her blankly. The surprise I feel is not just that they celebrated without me, but that it actually stings.

I'll come back in fifteen minutes, Rachel finally says. Get dressed and clean up.

I do as I'm told. I psych myself up: Don't screw this up. Maybe

Bob is letting me come out on a trial basis. I comb through the dresser, clothes pilfered from past stalks. There are no pregnancy clothes, only large sizes to accommodate my belly. I put on a Lacoste sweater over a new pair of black trousers, rolling them up as they are too long for me. Over this, I throw on a Marmot parka.

Rachel comes back and opens the metal gate. She leads me down the escalator, like a crazy aunt coming down from the attic for Thanksgiving. They are also dressed a little nicer, business casual attire. When I smile at each face, they either look away or give me a slight nod. Everyone is here, except Evan. He has been increasingly late to these breakfast meetings.

The table is decorated a bit more elaborately, with a boho-chic floral tablecloth and crochet place mats pilfered from Anthropologie, which means Genevieve decorated. There is even a centerpiece of fake flowers in a pitcher. But the food spread is the most impressive: There are pancakes upon pancakes, with a gravy boat filled with maple syrup. And slices of fried Spam and Vienna sausages, charred on the sides in a frying pan. In lieu of fresh fruit, there is a bowl of canned fruit cocktail, mixed with multicolored marshmallows.

Genevieve is asked to say grace.

Lord, we thank you for this meal, she says. And on our one-month anniversary at the Facility, we would like to thank you for providing for us so generously.

Amen, everyone echoes.

Happy one month! Rachel says. We clink our mugs of coffee, made with Evian and freeze-dried coffee granules.

From the head of the table, Bob looks around. Evan's not here. Can someone get him?

I'll go, Todd volunteers. With that, he bounds back up the escalator and disappears inside Journeys.

We all eye the food, waiting.

229

Before we begin eating, Bob says, I'd just like to say a few words about our guest of honor today.

Everyone turns their heads to me.

Candace, Bob says, addressing me, you've been through a trial during this confinement period, perhaps longer than you had expected. But I believe that this time has provided you time for reflection, for seeing the error of your ways, and, we hope, for correcting your duplicitous nature.

He looks around the table. As we accept you back into this group, you'll be receiving the privileges previously revoked. Leading up to the birth of your child, we will return these privileges one by one. Today, we've allowed you to join us.

Everyone in the group claps, as if on cue.

Since you're the guest of honor, why don't you begin to eat, Bob says.

But I can wait for Evan. I glance up at the second floor, expecting to see him.

Well, we insist. You're with—you're with child, he says, his voice stumbling at the word *child*, as if it were a foreign word.

I look around at the table, the few people left assessing my state of compliance. Well, of course, I say, and fork two Spam slices onto my plate. But this choice is a mistake, I realize too late. Because meat is typically reserved for special occasions, and it is what everyone wants, and I'm eating it right in front of them. Well, good.

Bob! We look up to see Todd's face, looking down at us over the railing from the second floor. His expression is somber. Bob!

Bob looks up. What is it? he says, annoyed at being interrupted.

I can't wake him, Todd yells down. He's not . . . He's not breathing.

Bob looks at Adam. Wordlessly, they get up and go up the

escalator. We hear them going into Evan's cell, together. Minutes pass.

Genevieve, Rachel, and I remain frozen at the table, looking uneasily at one another, pushing the food around on our plates. Then I put my fork down, unable to eat, already sensing what they will find.

At the table, Genevieve begins to cry.

In the end, there was the empty office. It was dark inside, smaller and more sparse. They had closed the lower floor. We, the remaining employees, circled around in our smaller confines, bumping against locked rooms we weren't allowed to enter. Like the glass offices of upper management. As we walked past these offices on our way to and from our desks, we glimpsed their belongings sealed off and entombed behind glass like emperors' afterlife provisions, the photographs of their wives and children smiling out at us. Their framed motivational prints hanging on the walls, dispensing career advice. YOUR GREATNESS IS NOT WHAT YOU HAVE, IT'S WHAT YOU GIVE. Or AS LONG AS YOU'RE GOING TO THINK ANYWAY, THINK BIG.

In the end, there were a half-dozen of us left to man the course. We were a ragtag crew of younger employees, including Blythe and Delilah, many of whom remained out of ambition, in the hopes of career advancement after this catastrophe passed. We shared an unspoken understanding that Spectra would once again resume at full capacity. Every Wednesday, the antifungal cleaning company still came to spray down and vacuum our offices for microscopic fungal spores.

Management had left without establishing a clear hierarchy of our positions, so inevitably there was competition and jostling. Our camaraderie was uneasy; everyone was keeping score. Like who would get to compile and send the weekly productivity reports to management, who arrived on time and who arrived late, who heeded corporate policy by wearing those hideous N95 masks, who was taking the initiative for the greater good by re-stocking the coffee filters. When we passed each other in the hall-ways, in our ridiculous professional outfits of wool trousers or pencil skirts and button-up shirts, we instinctively smiled tight-lipped smiles—which of course weren't visible behind our masks. Only the stiffened cheeks.

Me, I kept to myself. I stayed in my office. I hated the whole scene, partly because I could so easily see myself joining their petty games of one-upmanship if I got too involved. I preemptively eliminated that possibility by alienating myself. I was there to work, I reasoned, so I would just work.

And yet there was no work. It had dried up by the second week. Clients asked for estimates but refrained from placing any new jobs, and the remaining production jobs had been palleted and shipped out to sea. The only thing to watch out for was to make sure customs didn't turn them away at the port, since they increasingly rejected shipments of export goods from China, or even Asia in general. Correspondence with Spectra Hong Kong was sluggish and infrequent, as all Spectra offices had reduced their in-house staff. It was all getting pretty boring.

Instead of going through the Hong Kong office, as was proto-col, I sent an estimate request for a reprint directly to Phoenix Sun and Moon Ltd., the printer that had done the initial printing of the Daily Grace Bible.

I received an email from Balthasar right away, unusual consid-ering it was nearly midnight in Shenzhen. I had forgotten about his ever-courteous, slightly British way of correspondence.

Dear Candace,
    I am pleased to hear from you. Unfortunately, Phoenix is

no longer accepting new print jobs at this moment. My apologies. I do hope you are doing well, given these trying times. I wish you the best.

Sincerely, Balthasar

It wasn't all that surprising, but I had a job to do. I clicked Reply. My response was carefully calibrated in my usual office-speak.

Dear Balthasar,

It's great to hear from you as well. Let me just clarify: This estimate request is not a new job, but a reprint of a job that Phoenix has already done, the Daily Grace Bible. You should have all the files and plates on hand from the original printing. We only have to update the copyright page. As the initial printing was a great success, it makes sense that we work with you again.

I want to emphasize the scale of this project, and the opportunity that you may be turning down on behalf of your company. You are right that these are trying times, to say the least, but we are still in business and looking forward to working together.

Best,

Candace

I clicked Send, knowing it was fruitless. Two of the Chinese printers we worked with had also closed, another one in Singapore. Like them, Phoenix was suffering from a diminishing supply of migrant laborers. Due to federal efforts to curb mass panic, most media outlets collectively agreed to limit their coverage of Shen Fever, but the consensus was that the level of Shen Fever in China was worse than in other places. How bad the situation was depended on whom you asked. Maybe the whole city of Shenzhen was fevered. Maybe the whole province of Guangdong.

But I sent the email anyway. I owed it to the client, Three Crosses Publishing. I owed it to Spectra. I owed it to my contract. I was just doing my job. Balthasar would probably send a polite but sidestepping note in response to my blundering insensitivity.

I walked around the office, looking out the windows. I hadn't expected that there would be such little work to do. Maybe I should just go home in the middle of the day, even if Big Brother was watching. Our key cards kept track of our comings and goings. Carole or someone in HR received automated emails whenever we keyed in or out, monitoring us from afar.

Hee hee hee.

I looked around, trying to figure out the source of the laughter. It was girlish laughter, disembodied and tremulous, as if someone were being bounced around from knee to knee.

There was no one else in the hallway. I walked around, following the sound. It led me to the glass staircase, which connected the thirty-second floor to the now-vacant thirty-first floor. The entrance of the staircase was blocked off with a dusty burgundy velvet rope. As an energy- and cost-reducing measure during this interim, Spectra had closed that floor, switching off its lights and closing its blinds.

Hahahahahaha. Someone else was now giggling. It was definitely coming from the floor below.

I peered down the length of the staircase, its lower half submerged in shadow. The skunky scent of leftover beer, the aroma of cheap weed. Tinny music coming from a laptop or an iPhone. There was the same laugh, and another voice. They were having a mini party.

I unhooked the velvet rope and descended the staircase,

following the voices in the dark through the empty Accounts, IT, and HR departments, until I arrived at the employee lounge, a haven of vending machines and sectional sofas. It had been converted, years ago, from a conference room, at the advice of consultants hired by the company to boost morale, and to encourage a communal office spirit. Almost no one ever used it.

I opened the door.

Sprawled out across the sectional sofa were Blythe and Delilah, drinking out of red Solo cups. It looked like they had ransacked the party-supply closet: a champagne bucket on the floor, some crumpled Amstel Light cans. The flat-screen played *The Mary Tyler Moore Show*. Regular programming had ended that week, so all the channels played sitcoms on an infinite loop, deep cuts across all seasons and eras. *Malcolm in the Middle. Seinfeld. Friends. Family Matters. Who's the Boss? Will & Grace. Caroline in the City. Boy Meets World. Saved by the Bell. Full House. Perfect Strangers. Murphy Brown. The Cosby Show.*

Hey, I said, still holding the door.

Heeeeeeey. Delilah glanced up, surprised. Where's your mask?

Oh. I guess I must've have forgotten it at my desk, I said, though the truth was that I didn't wear it that much. I didn't like the way it made my mouth feel hot and suffocated, a bacterial cesspool.

You should be more careful, Blythe chided. It's company policy for a reason.

If the masks actually work, don't you think maybe there wouldn't be an epidemic? I asked, facetiously polite.

Come in. Close the door, Delilah said, playing peacemaker. Want something to drink? Not waiting for my response, she grabbed the champagne bottle from the ice bucket on the floor and poured it into a red Solo cup.

I sat on the sofa and took a lukewarm sip. How have you guys been? I feel like I haven't seen anyone in a while.

A lot of people quit. We thought you'd already left, Blythe said, proceeding cautiously.

Blythe. If I'd have left, I would have at least said bye, I said, looking at her. We've worked together for too long.

She softened. I know.

What do you mean, quit? I pressed. Everyone else is gone except us?

She shrugged. Some said they had finished their projects. Others just left and didn't come back. I guess they're forfeiting their fulfillment checks.

I took another sip. Where did they say they were going?

Most were headed back to spend time with their families, Delilah said. Apparently, Amtrak's down, but Greyhound's still running.

I've made it this far, so I'll probably keep going. I took another sip of champagne. I'd like to get paid.

Blythe and Delilah exchanged glances.

Does it even matter at this point? Blythe snapped, with a quick annoyance that made me feel oddly fond of her. It takes us two hours to get to work in the morning. The buses do absolutely nothing.

After Storm Mathilde, the city had suffered a series of smaller rainstorms, and though none of them were as severe as Mathilde, arguably they did more damage. With only a skeletal operating crew, the hydraulic pumps of the subway system were quickly overwhelmed, and after the storms ceased, the train lines were never restored. The city offered shuttle buses in lieu of subways, but they were never really that consistent.

Candace, so many stores have shut down, Delilah added. The only place to get any groceries are the bodegas or those vending machines that the city has put in everywhere. My neighbors had their electricity cut off. There's barely any Wi-Fi.

But how is that different from anywhere else? How is New York worse than any other place?

Delilah persisted: Did you hear about the tower crane that fell on a group of pedestrians the other day? This city is crumbling because there's no labor infrastructure to maintain it.

Blythe cut in again. We've been planning on leaving the city, to Connecticut. You should think about coming with us.

I'll think about it, I said. But right now, I'm still thinking I'd like to fulfill the terms of the contract. I don't have anywhere else to be.

You'd be alone! she snapped, increasingly angry. Who would take care of you? Candace, don't be stupid.

How are you guys getting out of the city? I asked, addressing Delilah.

We're going to rent a car, Delilah said. We already reserved something at Enterprise for tomorrow. It's their last one, this Lincoln Town Car, so we're leaving in style. All the vans and utility vehicles were already taken.

How did you guys decide that now is the right time to leave? What if things start to improve? Maybe not now, but in another few weeks?

Blythe studied me coldly. Candace. We wait an hour for the shuttle bus already. The hospitals are short-staffed. What is Michael going to do, fault us for leaving when the management have already left? There is nothing keeping us here. And they probably won't even notice when we leave. When's the last time you received an email or a phone call from upper management? I haven't heard from anyone for two weeks. They've forgotten about us. Even Manny's gone. When Manny leaves, you know it's serious, because that guy never takes a sick day!

I have a friend who works in the mayor's office, Delilah added. He says they're having a problem with city employees leaving, across the board. They know it's not going to get better. My friend's leaving too.

I didn't respond. I took another sip of the champagne.

So anyway. We're leaving tomorrow, Blythe said. Think about it. Seriously.

Okay, I said. All the air had left the room, had left my body. I went over to Blythe and Delilah and extended my hand.

Really? Delilah said, taking my hand. Well, good luck.

What the fuck, Blythe said, and threw her arms around me in an uncharacteristic hug and squeezed me hard. Just think about it some more, Candace.

Thank you for teaching me how to do this job, I told her. With that, I stood up and walked away, a lump forming in my throat. I walked out of the employee lounge and up to the staircase, back to the thirty-second floor, back into my office, where it was bright and orderly. On my desk, all of the items were arranged in a row: the Swingline stapler, the ruler I used to measure spine widths, a magnifying glass, a mug holding all of my Muji pens, a green tube of Weleda Skin Food that I used on my hands in the winter. The sun was low through the single window. I thought about what I would eat for dinner. In my fridge, there was leftover penne. I had been eating a lot of penne lately, since bags of dried pasta were light and easy to transport. Mixed in with that shelf-stable Kraft Parmesan and some dried herbs, it had become my main subsistence dish.

Sitting down again at my desk, I saw a new email from Balthasar.

Dear Candace,

Thank you for your response. You are candid with me, so I will be candid with you. Seventy-one percent of our workforce has become fevered. As you know, there is no cure. We have had to close the residence buildings. Phoenix

Sun and Moon Ltd. will cease all operations at the end of this week.

As for myself, I will be taking leave from Phoenix starting tomorrow. I am sorry to say that my daughter is also fevered, and our family is spending her last days together. There is no need for condolences. Almost all of my colleagues here at Phoenix Sun and Moon Ltd. have experienced something similar.

I am pleased that we have worked together. You are good at what you do. In these sad, uncertain times, however, it is important to be with people you love. I do not know the details of the epidemic in New York, but my suggestion to you: Leave. Spend time with your family.

Yours, Balthasar

The morning they discover Evan's body, snow piles onto the mall skylight throughout the day, snuffing out any trace of sun. I hope it keeps snowing. I hope it snows so much that the skylight breaks in a shower of glass shards and the snow heaves in and obliterates everything.

From my cell, I watch as Todd and Adam take Evan's body, swathed in blankets, out of his cell. Todd carries his head and shoulders, Adam the socked feet, which peep out from the blankets. They carry it down the stilled escalators, toward one of the exits.

Rachel comes to take away my half-eaten bowl of Frosted Mini-Wheats and condensed milk.

What happened to Evan? I ask her, breaking our no-speaking rule.

She hesitates, then finally says, They don't know. He wasn't breathing. They found some pills nearby.

Were the pills Xanax?

I don't know, she repeats, as if to herself. I really don't know.

So where are they taking his body?

She hesitates. They're taking him outside.

So they're burying him.

She nervously tucks her hair behind her ear. They're going to put him in the trunk of one of the vehicles in the parking lot. But it's just for now, she adds hastily. They're thinking that the body will keep better in the cold.

I nod thoughtfully, as if my approval matters. I guess that's reasonable.

He's going to get a proper burial. It's just that we're waiting until the blizzard lets up. Maybe tomorrow, or the next day. She touches my arm. I'm sorry.

Why are you apologizing to me? Evan is the one people should be apologizing to. He's the one who's dead, I say, laughing a little at the end.

I know you and Evan were good friends. And Janelle and Ashley.

I think he was better friends with Bob.

They're not good friends, Rachel says. Evan wasn't allowed to leave the mall. He wasn't allowed to take any of the cars out, on stalks or anywhere. He was trapped in here, like you.

All of the day's planned tasks are canceled. Bob stays inside Hot Topic for the rest of the day. Left to their own devices, the group huddles together in the communal Old Navy on the first floor. At first, I think they're holding a memorial service, but then I hear the TV playing. They're watching DVDs of *Friends* on a giant, monolithic plasma screen. A citywide blackout forces Monica, Ross, Rachel, Phoebe, and Joey to hang out together. They light candles and talk about the weirdest places they've had sex. Phoebe sings a song. I hate *Friends* but I've seen most of the episodes.

The laugh track reverberates throughout this mostly empty space, echoed by their laughter.

I drift off to sleep in the middle of the afternoon. At some point, in a visitation too lucid to be a dream, my mother comes in and sits next to me. The bed compresses under her weight. She is wearing the navy skirt suit, the outfit in which she was buried. I feel her cool hand on my forehead, checking for fever. Like the Sunday mornings when I'd pretend to be sick to get out of going to church.

What are you doing, she asks, lying here in the middle of the afternoon? Are you sick?

I'm not sick. I'm just tired, I say softly, shyly, lest she disappear into thin air.

Now is not the time for napping. Sit up. You need to figure this out.

Figure what out?

She shakes her head at my incompetence. What happened to your friend Evan. How did he die?

I don't know. He was found dead in his cell. He wasn't breathing.

Ai-yah. You don't know, she says incredulously. You don't know. Well, you need to know.

Evan had a lot of Xanax, I finally say. It's possible that he self-medicated and accidentally overdosed.

Or maybe he meant to kill himself. She looks pointedly at me. This should trouble you. What do you think that means for you?

I don't know.

Your group of friends, Janelle, Ashley, Evan, are all gone. What do you think that means for you? she repeats.

But as long as I'm pregnant, Bob is invested in my well-being, I argue hollowly.

My mother tsks. Listen to what you're saying. As long as you're pregnant. Let's say you have the baby. Do you think you'll even have the chance to escape after that?

I look at her, keep listening.

As long as you carry this baby, he's interested in making sure nothing happens to you. But what comes after that? She looks at me empathetically. Do you hear what I'm saying?

You're saying that I should try to escape while I'm pregnant.
You should escape now, she says.

When Rachel comes in to bring me my dinner, a peanut butter
and jelly sandwich with a side of canned peas, she gives me another
one of her tight-lipped smiles and gets up to leave.

Wait. I grab Rachel's arm so hard that she loses her balance.
She pulls away. Candace, stop.
Sorry. But can you let Bob know that I'd like to see him?
She pauses. I'll pass the message on. But you know, he might
not come. He shows up when he wants to show up.
I'm not feeling well. Tell him it's about my health, I say, then
correct myself: Tell him it's about the baby.

That night, after everyone is asleep, Bob comes into my cell. I
hear the keys as he makes his way from his cell across the mall to
mine.

I lick my dry, chapped lips.

Slowly, he raises the metal grating and lets himself inside. He
turns on his flashlight, a dim beam that shows me just enough,
his face.

Candace, he says quietly. Are you awake?
Yes, you can turn the lamp on, I say, sitting up.
Sorry to barge in on you this late. How are you? he asks, pulling up a chair to sit next to the bed. Up close, I take in the ten
o'clock shadow and the dark circles under his restless eyes; he
looks thin-skinned and almost vulnerable. There's a jitteriness to
his demeanor. He hasn't been sleeping regularly. I have to tread
carefully.

I've been better, I reply, sitting up. I mean, given the circumstances.

What happened to Evan was a tragedy. He looks down, almost abashed. Anyway, Rachel said you wanted to see me. Is this what you wanted to discuss? Because I don't have any answers as to what happened to Evan.

I didn't call you in here to talk about—

Because Evan was the one who gave you up, he says, with impassive vehemence. He was the one who told me your secrets. I would be surprised if you were so concerned—

Bob, I interrupt. I didn't ask you here to talk about Evan. I need more from you than this.

His breath catches at my reprimanding tone. He's caught off guard. I can't read his complicated expression, but this tiny hesitation gives me confidence.

It's about the health of myself and my baby, I continue, moving swiftly. That's what I wanted to talk to you about.

He watches me carefully. And how is your health?

Well, I am feeling flu-y right now.

Bob places his fleshy hand on my forehead, which I warmed all night by pressing HotHands packets to it. You are a bit warm, he observes. Have you told Rachel?

I mentioned it to her earlier. But it's not just that. It's the dizziness. It's the back pain. And the mental toll of—well, seeing what happened to Janelle, Ashley, and now Evan. The stress is getting to me.

So what do you need? he asks, his voice neutral.

I'd like to discuss what it would take for you to release me.

This is hardly a prison cell, he says, unmoved. Rachel takes you out for walks every day. We provide you with all the food, all the prenatal vitamins you need. I don't see how your situation can get any better.

You've locked me into a tiny space, I press. Maybe you don't call it captivity, but I feel like a prisoner. It's hard to stay healthy under this kind of duress, especially when I'm pregnant.

Bob doesn't say anything. His silence encourages me.

I'd like to have the same privileges as anyone, I say. I'd like to be able to freely move through the Facility.

He looks away for a long, awful moment. Candace, he finally says, slowly, as if thinking aloud. What do you really know about the Facility, aside from the fact that I've forced you to live here? Why do you think I chose this place, of all places we could've settled?

Because you co-own this place.

True. But that's not the whole story. This place—and here, he looks around in the dim nothingness—holds a great deal of sentimental value for me. I used to go to this mall when I was younger.

It takes me a moment to understand what he is saying. So you grew up around here? In Needling?

He nods. My parents would drop me off here, and I'd spend hours just walking around. I've probably spent more time here as a kid than anywhere else.

What about the house you grew up in?

My parents sold it after they divorced, and it was razed to build a retirement home. So there's nothing left. But I never used to hang out much at home anyway. My parents fought a lot, and so I'd come here a lot. I'd just walk around. When I was hungry, I'd eat free samples in the food court. When I was bored of walking, I'd play games in the arcade. The employees knew me. They'd give me extra tokens.

In this light, at this closeness, Bob's facial expression seems more legible. There is a fragility about him, apparent in his delicate, paper-thin gray eyes.

So what I'm trying to say, he continues, is that this place is special and important to me, even if it's just a nothing mall to you.

I didn't say—

I know what you think about this place. You don't respect it.

You don't respect me. You don't respect our rules. You or your friends. You put yourselves in danger, meaning you put the whole group in danger. And I can't just overlook that.

We made a mistake when we went off to Ashley's house, I concede. But I'm the only one left. I'm just surviving.

He watches me observantly. And how do I know that you wouldn't escape?

I pause now, choosing my words carefully. Bob. Look at me. Do I look like I'm going anywhere? People take care of me, they feed me, they do my laundry. There's no reason for me to leave.

He looks away again, in silence. I don't know, he finally says.

Please, I say.

I got up. I went to work in the morning. I got on the shuttle bus and looked out on the emptying streets, the unused subway tracks on the Williamsburg Bridge. The first bus took me to Canal, where I transferred to another shuttle that headed north to Times Square. There would be a half-dozen commuters on each shuttle, wearing a variety of fashion masks, in all black or leopard print or emblazoned with the Supreme logo. The masks seemed to preclude any conversation. Sitting by the window, I listened to music on my iPhone, to a nineties mix of sweet-sad songs that Jonathan had sent me before leaving. Pavement, the Innocence Mission, Smashing Pumpkins. I walked through the quiet streets and bought a cup of coffee from the street vendor on Broadway.

The empty lobby greeted me.

I pressed the button and waited for the single elevator that now serviced the entire building. I sipped my coffee and reflexively glanced at the security desk for Manny. He was long gone. In his place were extra security cameras, mounted in every corner of the lobby ceiling. Someone was still watching.

The elevator had seemed to take longer than usual to arrive that morning, but then everything seemed to take longer. The city was operating on a different kind of time. The shuttle bus service was spotty at best. I had taken to buying all my household supplies off Amazon, but the boxes, carrying anything from batteries to deodorant, took at least two weeks to deliver, whether the service was FedEx or UPS or USPS or DHL. Making a quick grocery trip to the nearest open bodega meant walking two miles. Everything kept closing.

When the elevator arrived, I stepped inside and pressed the button for 32. The doors closed behind me, and we began to move. I stepped out of my sneakers and slipped into a pair of office flats.

The elevator suddenly shuddered, a plane hitting turbulence. The lights cut out. My feet lifted off the floor. Coffee splashed out of my cup, burning my hand. I dropped it.

Then silence. The emergency light bathed everything in orange.

The monitor indicated that we were around the twenty-sixth floor. I took a breath. The elevator always caught between the twenty-sixth and twenty-seventh floors. It was an old glitch. I took another breath. But it had never lurched so violently, nor had it stood still for so long. I could feel the elevator wavering, as if undecided what to do.

I hit the 32 button again. I hit buttons for other floors. I hit the Door Open button. I hit the Emergency Call button. The terrible sound of a phone ringing filled the darkness. It rang several times before the call went to voicemail.

This is City Services of New York. We are currently operating at full capacity. Please leave a message detailing your address and the situation. We will address it at our next available time.

Hi, hi! I yelled, afraid that my voice wouldn't carry. I'm trapped in an elevator. I gave the address. I gave my name. I explained what had happened. I said, inexplicably, that I had money. Then, without warning, the voicemail cut me off midsentence.

I glanced up at the newly installed security camera in the corner. Maybe someone, some security guard in Jersey or wherever, was watching. I grabbed a notebook from my tote bag and in my largest, most demonstrative print wrote, *Trapped! Elevator broken.* I shoved the sign up toward the lens and waved it around.

The elevator lurched.

I dropped the notebook, the pen, the tote bag. They splashed into the puddle of coffee, splattering my legs. I crouched and grasped at the handrail, crushingly sick to my stomach, awaiting a plummet. *Please don't drop, please don't drop, please don't drop.* Several minutes passed. My ears popped. *Please don't drop, please don't—*

Abruptly, the lights flickered on and the elevator resumed operation, smoothly ascending to the thirty-second floor.

The doors opened. I walked out, dragging my tote bag.

Relief washed over me in cold, prickly sweat. I swiped my key card. My shoes sank in the familiar plush carpets as I wound through the processional of glass offices and dimmed cubicles.

Sitting down in my office, I picked up the phone and called 911. It rang nine times before someone picked up.

Nine-one-one, what's your emergency? It was a woman with a tired voice.

Hi, I just want to report an elevator malfunction. I was, uh, just trapped inside.

Is anyone hurt or in danger at the moment? Are you hurt or in danger?

No, I said, adding, I managed to get out. I'm okay, just a bit, uh, worried.

Okay. Where is this?

Times Square. I gave her the address.

I heard the clacking of keys as she input the data. Wait, she said. Is this an office building?

Yes, I work here.

We'll send someone to check it out, she finally said. But, if you don't mind me asking, what are you still doing in there?

I'm working, I said, as if it were obvious.

It's just that most of midtown is deserted now, except for the stray fevered that we pick up.

I have a contract that stipulates I have to work in the office until a certain date, I explained stiffly, defensively.

Sure, I've heard about some companies that do that. But let me ask you a question. Where is your building management?

What do you mean?

Is there a building superintendent who still works in the building? Because if not, then you really shouldn't be in there. It's not safe.

I'll double-check on that, I said, though I knew there was no superintendent in the building. So does this mean the elevator won't be fixed?

She sighed. We'll send someone to take a look at the elevator. But I don't have an ETA. We're short-staffed. The fact is, more people are leaving this city than there are staying. The city is curtailing all its services. You may want to consider that if you intend on carrying out this contract.

The city should do its job, I said, suddenly angry, frustrated.

Ma'am, she said, her tone sharper and more irritated, if I told you the number of issues we're facing in the city, you'd realize a malfunctioning elevator is the least of our problems. Now, I'm adding this elevator malfunction to our queue, and that's all I can really do for you. What's your name?

Candace. Candace Chen.

Thank you, Ms. Chen. Someone will be on the way. But think about what I said.

I hung up, then picked up the phone again and dialed the number that Michael Reitman had left us for his cell phone. I thought about conveying what the 911 operator had told me, that it was no longer safe to work in the building. While I was at it, I might as well update him on the fact that the entire office had cleared of employees.

It rang a half-dozen times and then went to voicemail. I wanted to leave a recording, but an automated message informed me that the mailbox was full. I hung up.

My reflection in the computer screen stared blankly at me. I opened Outlook, which showed no new emails. I typed up an email to Michael Reitman and Carole, with the subject line *elevator malfunction*, that detailed my morning's travails and the steps I took to implement a solution. I wrote that I would let them know of any updates. It was satisfying to finally execute a task, but the satisfaction was fleeting. I needed more to do.

I looked out the windows. For the first time, I noticed that Times Square was completely deserted. There were no tourists, no street vendors, no patrol cars. There was no one. It was eerily quiet, as if it were Christmas morning. Had it become this way without my noticing? I walked around the perimeter of the office, trying to spot a fire truck or a police car pulling up outside, trying to discern a siren in the distance, something.

It wasn't just the emptiness. In the absence of maintenance crews, vegetation was already taking over; the most prodigious were the fernlike ghetto palms, so-called because they exploded in prolific waves across urban areas, seemingly growing from concrete, on rooftops, parking lots, any and all sidewalk cracks. I'd Googled *ghetto palms* after seeing them everywhere. Known by their scientific name, *Ailanthus altissima*, which translates to "tree of heaven," but informally called "tree of hell." They are deciduous suckering plants that originated in China, were cultivated in European gardens during the chinoiserie trend before gardeners became wise to their foul-smelling odors, and were introduced to America in the late 1700s. They have lived on this land almost since the formation of this country.

Looking out the windows, I imagined the future as a time-lapse video, spanning the years it takes for Times Square to be overrun by ghetto palms, wetland vegetation, and wildlife. Or maybe I was actually conjuring up the past, the pine- and hickory-forested island that the Dutch first glimpsed upon arriving, populated with black bears and wolves, foxes and weasels, bobcats and mountain lions, ducks and geese in every stream. Initial European explorers had viewed Manhattan as paradise. Here, I would lead a horse to drink. There, I would build a fire. And there still, I would seek refuge from the sun and rest in the shade.

In the midst of this imagining, I heard, out from nowhere, the distant sound of sleigh bells. I was going crazy.

But there, right in front of me, across the street, was a horse—chestnut, with white spots—trotting down the street. It trotted along purposefully, cheerfully, unhurried, down Broadway. Holding my breath, I managed to find my phone and snap a photo before it disappeared from sight, obstructed by other buildings.

Did I really see that?

I looked at the photo on my phone. It was a former carriage horse, with its blinders still on, and a harness decorated with bells, jingling with every trot. Once enlisted to give tourists carriage rides around Central Park, it was now free. I wanted to show someone, for someone to marvel at this with me, but there was no one left in the office. There was no one left in sight.

Sitting down in front of my computer again, I looked up my old NY Ghost photo blog, Googling myself because I had forgotten the URL. It still existed, still showed the same old tired images I'd posted. I tried to log in to the WordPress platform, but it'd been so long that I couldn't remember my password and had to fill out a request to create a new one. I waited for the password-request form to go to my email. The connection had been slow and staticky since the office emptied, but finally, the form arrived and, after creating a new password, I accessed my blog and created a new post.

I uploaded the photo I just took. I added a caption: *If a horse rides through Times Square and no one is there to see it, did it*

*actually happen? If New York is breaking down and no one docu-
ments it, is it actually happening?*

I clicked Publish.

I got up. I went to work in the morning. It took forever to get
there. On the shuttle ride over, I thought about moving somewhere
closer to the office, maybe within walking distance. The rents had
decreased so significantly that I could definitely afford something
in Manhattan.

In the lobby, I waited for the elevator but it never came. It had
still not been fixed. I took the stairs instead, all thirty-one flights.
It was my morning cardio, I rationalized, as I huffed and panted,
sidestepping the cigarette butts and gum that littered the concrete stairwell, stopping once or twice to take a break. They used
to call the stairwell the Smoke Dungeon, because it was where
covert smokers, usually the Art Girls, would light up instead of
taking it outside during harsh winters. I could still see the soot
marks of the Parliaments they smoked before dashing the lit butts
against the concrete walls.

The empty office greeted me. I swiped my key card. The green
light came on, and I opened the glass doors.

The Spectra office was effectively the headquarters of NY
Ghost Ltd., I decided. It was a thing now. I focused my efforts
entirely on the blog. It was my new job. If there was no work for
me to do, then I would make my own work. I wasn't afraid of being found out since there was no one else around. I couldn't remember the last time that the antifungal cleaning service had
come to spray down the office. Maybe management had stopped
paying them, or maybe they had fallen victim to the fever themselves.

I posted on NY Ghost twice a day, once when I arrived in the office in the morning, and once in the evening. During lunch hour, I would leave to take more pictures documenting the deserted city.

The lunchtime walks reminded me of my first summer in New York, when I'd roam for hours. It was colder now, and I wore a jacket with many deep pockets to keep my iPhone, a battery charger, my ChapStick. I also carried my wallet, though there were few places to buy anything. As I walked, ideas for the blog snowballed. I took pictures of the meadows where carriage horses congregated, eating grass. I took pictures of all the obvious landmarks, now indefinitely closed: MoMA, Rockefeller Center, Carnegie Hall, Lincoln Center.

There was a haunted look about all of these places. Ambling through midtown, I thought of the Robert Polidori photographs of Chernobyl and Pripyat, a ghost town that formerly housed the nuclear-plant workers. Or the Yves Marchand and Romain Meffre images of Detroit, the images of abandoned auto plants and once-grand theaters. And the Seph Lawless images of the vacant, decrepit shopping malls that closed after the 2008 crash.

The main difference from those images of decrepit places was that New York hadn't given up yet. It was deserted but not abandoned. The institutions here were still being maintained, as if someone expected everyone to come back eventually. They were guarded by security guards, uniformed in black muscle tees and pants, emblazoned with the Sentinel logo of a guard dog silhouette. Except for their discreetly holstered guns, they looked like waiters. Often the Sentinel guards were the only nonfevered people I would see for days on end; their presence was both eerie and comforting.

I devoted a blog post to Sentinel, a security firm that had primarily served as a military contractor in Afghanistan and Iraq. The city had contracted Sentinel to protect public institutions from looters. Private owners also hired the company to guard evacuated homes. One time, walking down Fifty-fourth Street, past my favorite row of town houses, I looked up and glimpsed a Sentinel guard at the top window. He was a glorified house-sitter. He probably watered the white orchids in the windows, slept in the feathery sheets with million-thread counts, and upon waking up made himself petite espressos that he drank out of dainty, gold-rimmed espresso sets.

I waved, he waved. I snapped a picture.

The only indication by which he could tell, from his distant vantage point, that I was not fevered was that I wore a mask. And though Sentinel guards did not wear masks (given the scope of the epidemic, we had begun to understand that the masks were not fever-preventative), wearing a mask meant something. It was a visual shorthand that I was fully cognizant, that I understood the distinction. Thus I always wore a mask outside, to mark myself as unfevered.

Another time, I ran a photo series of various subway stations. One afternoon, I went as far down the Times Square station steps as I could, pushing aside the caution tape, until I reached the water's edge. I raised my iPhone and took pictures. The flash bounced off the floating, waterlogged candy bars and magazines, drowned rats, and all the trash that cluttered up the surface. You couldn't even see the water beneath all the garbage, but standing on the steps, you could hear it, like an enormous animal lapping thirstily. The deeper you tunneled down, the bigger the sound, echoed and magnified by the enclosed space, until this primordial slurp was all that existed.

The resulting post was called *No One Rides the MTA Anymore*.

By late October, all major media outlets, including the *Times*, had stopped publishing. Visitors trickled in to NY Ghost. Overwhelmingly, they were from Kihnu, Iceland, Bornholm, and other cold-climate islands I had never heard of, where the fever had not reached. They requested photos and updates of their favorite places. It was as if they still couldn't believe New York was breaking down, and needed confirmation. Everywhere else could fall apart, but not New York. Its glossy, reflective surfaces and moneyed environments seemed invincible. Even after 9/11, even after the attempted bombings, even after the blackouts and the hurricanes and the rising waters due to global warming.

I have always lived in the myth of New York more than in its reality. It is what enabled me to live there for so long, loving the idea of something more than the thing itself. But toward the end, in those weeks of walking and taking pictures, I came to know and love the thing itself. This was partly because I loved the work of documenting it. Even if capturing the city in deterioration was an insurmountable task—New York was too vast and I was too small; there were places too far or too dangerous for me to reach—I didn't want to stop.

I treated readers' requests as assignments. Each assignment, I turned into a blog post. I organized requests by neighborhood and charted a schedule for fulfilling them. There was a pleasure in doing this, a pleasure in knowing that every morning, upon waking, I knew my agenda for the day.

Once, I went to the Strand bookstore and wandered with a flashlight through overturned aisles of books, reporting on the titles that I took to read. Once, I ate my lunch by candlelight at a booth inside Bemelmans Bar. I took pictures of the mural, to try to preserve as much of the idyllic park drawings as possible. Afterward, I crossed Central Park, with its fleets of horses and rats, and "shopped" for dried goods and prenatal vitamins at the giant Fairway on Broadway.

Once, I managed to get into Walter De Maria's Earth Room installation, a huge interior filled with dirt on the second floor of a SoHo loft building, but left quickly after discovering the deceased attendant still sitting behind the reception desk. He must have been fevered, doing his job until the end.

The fevered stumbled around New York in ever-diminishing numbers. There was the fruit vendor near Ground Zero who moaned indecipherable language, hawking browned bananas. There was the old lady in her nightgown, pushing her food cart back and forth in front of Gristedes. Or the homeless teen couple in Tompkins Square Park, jiggling coffee cups of change to attract nonexistent passersby. I rarely photographed the fevered for NY Ghost because it had seemed disrespectful to depict them without their consent, and they weren't in a position to give it.

There had been one exception though. I had been walking down Fifth Avenue, hurrying back toward the office before it got dark. When I passed the Juicy Couture flagship shop, it looked so pristine that, for a second, I actually thought it was open for business. Many retail spaces had been looted, which was why it was odd that it looked untouched. Not just untouched but immaculate. It was sealed up like an enormous glass time capsule, its racks of trademark velour and terry-cloth sweat suits arranged by color into a candy rainbow.

I noticed movement inside. It was a saleslady, folding and refolding pastel polo shirts. She was clearly good at her job, even in her fevered condition. The wall of bedazzled sunglasses gleamed. The wall of handbags was artfully arranged, by model and by color.

The subsequent post was a thirty-second video of the saleslady folding T-shirts. I tried to show it from a distance; I didn't want the video to be too graphic. Half her jaw was missing. But the way she folded each garment, with an economy of movement, never breaking pace, generated a sense of calm and ease.

It became the most popular NY Ghost post, but also the most controversial. I felt conflicted about it. Some readers expressed their sorrow and concern for my safety. They wrote about their situations—how their countries had closed off most imports and banned most foreign travel, to alleviate the spread of fever. They expressed regret that they could not extend invites for me to stay with them.

Others accused me of posting disaster porn. They questioned why I hadn't left New York, why I was compelled to keep going with this.

How do we know, one skeptical reader wrote, that you're not fevered yourself?

One morning, I waited so long for the shuttle bus to arrive that I ended up calling the dispatcher at Yellow Cab. The call went to an automated recorder, which gave me the direct numbers of a dozen or so drivers still working. I listened to all the names, hoping to hear a woman's name, but they were all male cabdrivers. Finally, I called the last number. After half an hour, a taxi finally pulled up in front of the apartment.

I slid into the backseat, avoiding eye contact with the driver. Given the minimal law enforcement, I tried not to be alone with a man if I could help it. We drove in silence, past boarded-up storefronts, the overgrown community garden where I foraged for vegetables, assorted vending machines that Brooklyn had set up to deposit dry foodstuffs, the library where I'd forgotten to return my last batch of books. We went underneath the train tracks, whited over with splattered pigeon feces and feathers.

Nice day out, he remarked, finally breaking the silence.

I glanced up at the rearview mirror and caught his gaze. He was a middle-aged Hispanic man, wearing a loosened mask decorated with goofy *Simpsons* decals. This relaxed me.

I lowered my mask too. Yeah, it's nice out, I echoed cautiously. For the sun was shining on my arms, some of the trees had turned russet and crimson and saffron, and even though it was fall, the temperature was warm and balmy.

Do you mind if we take the Brooklyn Bridge? The Williamsburg is closer, but I heard the city closed it. They don't maintain that bridge anymore.

I nodded. Go ahead. Whatever you think is safer.

I guess if you're going to preserve any bridge, the Brooklyn is the one to preserve, he said, more to himself.

Do you still get a lot of passengers out of Brooklyn? I asked politely, thinking maybe I could make a NY Ghost post about taxi services.

Honestly, not that many. You're my first pickup today. But sometimes, especially on a day like today, I get in the cab anyway. It's too beautiful not to enjoy. I just like to drive around with the windows down, take a look at the city. Gas is expensive, but taxi drivers get a subsidy and, you know, it's not that bad. You gotta do something, right?

I like to walk around the city and take pictures, I offered. I post them on my blog.

Oh yeah, what's your blog? Maybe I'll look it up sometime.

It's called NY Ghost. It's mostly just—

He swiveled around. No kidding. I've been on your site before. He turned back. It's very nice what you're doing, keeping people informed. The places you post about—I would've never thought about. Like that one inside the subway. I don't even want to ask how you got down there.

We crossed the Brooklyn Bridge, which was majestic and resplendent in the sun. It occurred to me that in all my years of living in New York, I had never walked or biked or even driven across the bridge. How was that possible?

Your blog makes me appreciate New York even more, he continued. And I'll tell you a story. I just got back from Massachusetts last week. My cousin's out there. He's part of this group—

they call themselves a colony, which, I don't know about the terminology—and they all squat in one of those rich abandoned old houses together. They grow vegetables and make art and sing songs around the bonfire. I was supposed to move in with them out there.

Huh. So why did you come back?

They didn't like me! He burst out laughing. No, I mean—I've lived in New York my whole life. I've lived in Spanish Harlem, in Morningside, in the Bronx. This place is home. What am I going to do at this point, go sailing in Martha's Vineyard? He laughed again, a little uneasily this time. Besides, now that all the white people have finally left New York, you think I'm leaving?

I smiled.

You should put on your blog something about how New York belongs to the immigrants, how it was once the first point of entry for foreigners. The history of it, you know?

I was thinking about doing a post about Ellis Island, but none of the ferries run out there anymore.

Well, I guess we shouldn't be surprised. It's not like there's a tourism industry anymore. The type of people who are still here, they're either very old, fevered, or random solitary types like us. Well, I'm assuming. I apologize—he glanced at me in the rearview mirror—if I'm being presumptuous here.

It's not too bad here if you can stand being alone, I corroborated.

We drove around in silence for a while. As we arrived in midtown, he said, There's something I like about being in midtown Manhattan. Sometimes I drive here just to remind myself.

Remind yourself of . . . ?

That there's still civilization. In midtown more than anywhere else, there's infrastructure. You've got the Sentinel guards, guarding our prized institutions. There's less crime in midtown. The electricity still works. You can still get Wi-Fi here. You can still get a cell phone signal. Being here gives me a sense of stability when I think everything is coming apart.

Yeah, there's something reassuring about being here.

So, you're going to Times Square, huh? Going to a musical tonight? He chuckled at his own joke.

Yeah, I'm going to see *Wicked*. Dinner and a show.

That's the way to do it, he said, and he didn't push further in asking about my plans. Okay. I'm going to pull up right in front.

When he pulled up to the Spectra building, he hesitated. It's gonna be seventy-two fifty. If you'd like, I can knock twenty dollars off of it or something. They really hiked up our fares.

It's okay. I pulled out my wallet and gave him a hundred-dollar bill. Keep the change.

Hey. My name's Eddie.

I shook his hand, his fingertips, through the divider. I'm Candace. Nice to meet you, Eddie. Maybe I'll call you up again when I need a ride.

Sure thing. See you later, Candace. With that, he drove away.

By November, I had moved into the Spectra offices. I could have easily moved in earlier after Blythe and Delilah had left and the office was my own, but I was a creature of habit, as it turned out. It was only the shutdown of the shuttle buses—without notice or warning—that catalyzed me. One Monday morning, I packed clothes, toiletries, my mother's keepsakes, and whatever else I could fit into a suitcase. I called Eddie to drive me in his cab, but no one picked up. So I called the Yellow Cab dispatcher again and found another driver. When he arrived, I locked up my apartment for good.

I slid into the backseat with my suitcase and asked, Hey, do you happen to know this cabbie named Eddie? Is he doing okay?

Doesn't sound familiar to me. The driver turned around, his

voice muffled behind his dirty mask. Just because we drive cabs doesn't mean we all know each other, you know.

Sorry, I said, and we drove the whole way in silence.

The empty office greeted me. I spent the rest of the move-in day doing inventory.

In the storeroom, there was a generous bounty of coffee, refill water bottles for the water cooler, packets of coffee creamer, which, combined with water, could make a milk substitute. There were also cleaning supplies, two Dyson vacuum cleaners, rolls of paper towels, and refill vats of pink hand soap I could use to wash my body at night.

In the employee snack room, there was a vending machine full of healthful snacks: roasted honey peanuts, dried fruit assortments, nutrition bars, yogurt-dill kettle chips, lentil crackers. I took a three-hole punch from the copy room and heaved it repeatedly at the glass, which slowly splintered, cracking open as it fissured. When it finally came down, I took all the food items, a fox stealing hen eggs. I rifled through abandoned desks and found chocolate bars, microwavable Kraft mac and cheese, Maruchan Instant Lunch noodles in shrimp flavor, saltine crackers, packets of Heinz ketchup, and, randomly, a box of Manischewitz matzo ball mix. I took all the food items I found and placed them in the cabinets of the employee snack room, organizing them according to their expiration dates. In Blythe's desk, I found half-filled bottles of Kiehl's Ultra Facial Cleanser and Ultra Facial Moisturizer, along with a Mario Badescu Facial Spray, all of which I lined up on the counter of the bathroom for my daily skin-care routine.

The move-in day was long and draining. I was exhausted by evening.

To secure myself a proper bedroom, I took the three-hole punch and threw it at the glass walls of Michael Reitman's locked office, which shattered on the third or fourth try. Inside, I vacuumed the glass shards glittering on the carpet, crunching underneath my shoes. I dusted the glass from his enormous desk, which was now my enormous desk, and from his beautiful chaise longue, which was now my beautiful chaise longue. I Googled it. It is called the Barcelona sofa, designed by Mies van der Rohe. Rifling through his desk, I found his portable Braun clock, which I would use as my alarm.

It had grown dark without my noticing. I turned off the lights.

I took off my office outfit, slipped on a nightgown. I didn't intend to go to sleep, I just wanted to see how lying down in this new room felt.

Above me, cut into the ceiling, was a skylight. In all the years I'd worked there, I'd never noticed it, and now that the city no longer lit up as brilliantly with electricity, I could see the stars. They were so bright and clear that the sight of them felt astringent against my tired eyes. So I closed them. Before falling asleep, I felt the baby move for the first time.

In my new Sephora space, I tell Bob about the last days I spent in
New York. We sit across from each other at a little table, sipping
tea from cup-and-saucer sets, like old friends who have been
through things together. A battery-powered LED lamp emits a
cool, dim glow in the darkness. We speak softly because our voices
echo in this new space, only half-filled with new furnishings.

So, in the end, you lived in your office, Bob summarizes.

And I worked there too.

Right. NY Ghost. That makes sense. But, he continues, putting his teacup down, I don't understand why you stayed for that
long when it was no longer habitable.

It was still habitable to me.

But those stairs you took, though. How many, thirty flights
every day? That's like running a marathon every morning. He
smiled opaquely.

Yeah, it was my cardio, I quip, playing along. I would've had
to leave eventually, if for those stairs alone. That and the readership
fell off when, you know, everyone got fevered.

Is that why you left, because your blog no longer had a readership? he asked, the mocking now unmistakable in his voice—and
something else: a hard contempt, resentment.

I left because I was pregnant, I reply, which is not exactly the truth, but bringing it back to the baby seems to quell Bob's moodiness.

Do you regret leaving? he asks, then catches himself. You don't have to answer that. I assume that you do.

It wasn't sustainable to stay in New York, I say, not alluding to all that has transpired since I joined the group. Should I finish the rest of the story? There's not much left.

No, let's save it for tomorrow. You can keep me in suspense. He takes another sip of tea.

Bob. I hesitate. What's it like being back?

Back, he repeats. You mean where I grew up? Or do you mean this mall specifically?

I'm not sure. Both, I guess. But this mall in particular, where you spent so much of your time as a kid. Does it still seem the same? Does it seem worth it?

He looks at me. Believe it or not, yes. It even smells familiar, the way it smelled when I was a kid.

Can I ask why you walk around the mall at night? I always hear you.

I don't know what you mean, he says, emptying the last gulp of cold tea.

Before I can question him, Todd ducks into the room. Hey, Bob?

Bob glowers at him. What did I say? Knock first.

Sorry, Todd mutters. He returns to the entrance, where Adam also stands, and raps his knuckles against the side wall. Bob looks at me.

Come in, I call out.

This time, Adam enters and addresses Bob directly. We need the keys to one of the cars. We're going to get those batteries.

Right. Bob nods. You don't need a big vehicle, so I'll give you the Nissan. He removes a key from his chain, hooked onto his jeans. Next time, you should make sure to get all the supplies in one go.

Ideally, Adam says. We might be back late. How do you want us to give you the key when we return?

I'll be sleeping. Just leave the key outside of my door when you get in.

Will do. Adam nods at Bob, then me. Good night.

Perhaps due to their presence, Bob is gruff with me again, authoritative. Have you taken your folic acid pills today? he asks. He frowns. Rachel was supposed to make sure you take them. I specifically asked her to do that.

She reminded me earlier.

Well, she was supposed to make sure you take them, not just remind you. They prevent birth defects, they help your body generate new cells.

Right. How impressive. You too have read *Pregnancy 101*, I want to say. But don't. Instead of arguing with Bob, an unnecessarily risky move, I get up and go to the dresser, where the bottle of folic acid pills is kept, along with packages of diapers, wet wipes, cans of formula, and baby outfits.

The whole Sephora space is filled with new Ikea furniture, hastily constructed by Todd and Adam. They had brought me a catalog and I picked out everything I wanted. There's a queen bed with a Tempur-Pedic mattress, and, though I'm not due in the immediate future, all the baby furniture has been set up: a yellow crib with a musical mobile, a matching changing table, a little swing. The best part, however, is the massive bookcase, holding all the books I want to read. And if none of the books suit me, I am now allowed to freely roam to other parts of the mall, to the entertainment room (the Old Navy), to the library (the Barnes & Noble, with its leftover cache of titles).

Lately, I have been reading *The Arabian Nights*, in which the narrator of the tale, Scheherazade, keeps herself alive by telling

King Shahryar tales night after night, withholding the ending of each story until the next night.

I sit down again at the table. In full view of Bob, I put a pill in my mouth and wash it down with the rest of my cold tea. Thanks for reminding me, I tell him.

He nods. Should we pray before I leave? I'll pray for you.

I nod. In our chairs, we bow our heads and clasp our hands in prayer, like I used to do in Sunday school.

Dear Lord, Bob begins, there is a humility in our prayers to you. In asking for what we want, we acknowledge the limits of our power. To that end, please help us keep this child safe and healthy. We would very much like this opportunity to bring this child to term, despite the missteps of the mother. Please help Candace continue to see the error of her ways, to understand that her newly granted freedoms are privileges. Please help us lead her back from her deviated course and set her right in our group. Amen.

Amen, I echo emptily.

After Bob leaves, I wait for a few beats before I turn off the lamp and get into bed. For a long time, I just lie there. My heart beats so hard I feel it in my fingertips.

It's not long until my mother comes over. I feel the weight of the bed shift as she sits down. She doesn't say anything.

I know what you're going to say, I tell her, but let me just think this through.

You have to get the key, she presses. You get the key, you get the car, then you get out.

You think it's that easy?

I think it's an opportunity and you don't have many opportunities.

Tonight? Is it the right time?

My mother scoffs. Ai-yah, yesterday was the right time. Last week, last month. Things will change for you after you give birth.

She hashes out the details: Stay awake. Wait for Todd and Adam to return. Todd will place the car key on the floor in front of the Hot Topic entrance. I will retrieve it. The timing has to be right. If I do it as soon as possible, Bob might catch me on his walk, or notice that it's missing. But be careful: Even if I manage to grab the key and get into the car, it will likely still be dark when I make my getaway, dark enough I'll have to turn the headlights on. If they notice I'm gone, I'll be easy enough to spot on the roads.

Better to wait, then, until early morning, when there's enough light to drive without turning on the headlights. The sun will be barely peeping over the horizon. And everyone will still be asleep as the engine turns over and I quietly pull out of the parking lot. There will be other survivors out there.

But what if I get caught? I ask.

My mother's voice turns cool. You're just taking a stroll around the mall, just like Bob does at night sometimes. You're uncomfortable because the baby was shifting around and you needed to stretch your legs. That's plausible deniability. What?

I've just never heard you use the term plausible deniability in real life before.

May you live long enough to see how little your children think of you.

I didn't mean it like that. It's just strange now, how you speak perfect English.

Well, I can't communicate with you in your terrible Chinese, she deadpans. Anyway. She gets up. Be careful.

As she is about to leave, she turns back. If you do manage to escape, then it will be a long time before I see you.

Just like that? I ask.

Just like that, she says, and goes.

I wake up. It is so silent. I could fall through the cracks of such silence. There is nothing to do but wait. And wait. And wait.

I don't know what else to do, so I close my eyes. I begin to pray.

One morning, I left the office at the same time as usual, to take more pictures. Just as the door closed, I realized I had forgotten my key card. I reached to grab the handle, but it was too late. It had shut with a click.

Shit, I muttered. I double-checked the pockets of my coat, making sure I hadn't misplaced it. I tried not to get angry at myself. The fact that it hadn't happened before, given the numerous times I'd forgotten my wallet or iPhone, was a miracle. But it was still a shock.

I stood at the entrance of the office, assessing the situation. I should have placed a doorstop at that door, something that had been on my to-do list for too long.

The enclosure and the door were made of glass. I could go outside and find a big heaving rock, a concrete block, or something I could throw at the doors. It wasn't the tidiest solution, but it would do the trick. It would be a pain, though. I thought about going to other floors to scrounge for something heavy, but I knew they were either vacant or locked like the Spectra offices.

I went downstairs. At some point, around the seventeenth floor, I had to sit down from dizziness. The dizzy spells came and went, and I ascribed them to the symptoms of pregnancy. As I sat there in the stairwell, lights buzzing, I thought about how I could not do this forever. As my pregnancy advanced, I couldn't go on taking such enormous flights up and down every day.

I stood up. I went downstairs.

Outside, the sun shone at a low, friendly angle of light. It was colder than I expected, so I quickened my pace. I had a lot of work to do.

I headed north toward Central Park, with the idea of finding a throwing rock. I passed all the places I used to frequent, now closed. I passed the Starbucks where, for a whole disgusting summer, I used to buy a Frappuccino a day. I passed my regular lunch buffet, which featured daily holiday banquets of rotisserie chicken, haricots verts, glazed sweet buns, all garnished with intricately cut carrot flowers and zucchini flowers. My stomach rumbled in memory.

At that moment, I spotted a rare food cart, the basic kind that sold coffee and pastries, usually frequented by Sentinel guards on their breaks. It was located two blocks away. I didn't have any cash, but there was a Chase Bank on the corner. I checked all five ATMs in the lobby until I found one that worked.

I withdrew a hundred dollars in twenty-dollar bills. The screen asked me whether I wanted a receipt, and on instinct I punched Yes. It took a long time to print. I folded the receipt up and put it inside my wallet, behind the bills.

As I was about to leave, something stopped me. I opened up my wallet again, unfolded the receipt, and squinted to read the barely visible printing. The amount listed under my checking account was insane, bloated, more than I'd ever had. There must have been some mistake, some system glitch. My eyes scanned toward the date, something about the date. November 30, 2011. November 30, 2011. I kept running it over in my mind. My heart quickened, my body understanding before my mind.

November 30, 2011. The day my contract was up.

Shit, I muttered.

Wait, was it true? I took out my iPhone. Carole from HR had sent the contract as a PDF attachment, which I opened again.

Spectra will deposit X after the termination of the agreement, November 30, 2011. It will be direct deposited to your preferred bank account in arrears on this date.

It was true. Today was my last day.

I walked out of the Chase and onto the empty street, cautiously, as if a meteor might strike me. The expansive valley of midtown engulfed me. Broken windows of high-rises whistled with wind. For the first time, I felt scared. I hadn't thought of what I would do when the contract ended. I hadn't thought that far ahead. Why had I been getting cash again? Right, the food cart. It was right in front of me. Instinctively, I walked toward it. Coffee and pastry. My intention had been to get coffee and pastry.

Maybe I had meant to lock myself out, with the subconscious knowledge that today was my last day. Maybe I was telling myself it was time to stop. But even if I was no longer contracted by Spectra, did it matter? My father used to say: Work is its own reward. It was also its own consolation.

Reaching the food cart, I asked, Can I get a coffee and pastry, please? Any pastry is fine, just give me your freshest.

I took a twenty-dollar bill out and placed it on the counter before I realized. In the display cases, the bananas were completely brown, desiccated. Flies had collected. The pastries—muffins, croissants, Danishes—had grown mold, were putrefying, liquefying in their plastic bags. I peered inside the food cart. There was no one there.

Shit, I muttered.

I walked away. I wandered in a daze, forgetting my plan to go toward Central Park. I'd heard somewhere that to prevent shock, you're supposed to bite down on lemons or limes. And of course, I needed rocks too. That's what I had come all the way out here for. Rocks, lemons, and limes. I needed rocks, lemons, and limes.

I was muttering aloud until I stopped myself. I kept wandering.

At some point, I looked up and saw that I was standing in front of Henri Bendel. I looked inside the windows; it had been ransacked and looted, with upturned cosmetics tables, the Annick Goutal perfume display, handbags.

The last and only time I'd ever been inside the Henri Bendel store was when I tried to resign from Spectra. Having only been there for a little longer than a year, I'd considered carefully the decision to leave. I couldn't see myself as a product coordinator forever, coordinating Bibles, shaving razors, Nike sneakers, or whatever, from my desk in New York to various plants across Southeast Asia. Just because you're adequately good at something doesn't mean that's what you should do.

Before leaving the office that day, I had handed my two-week notice to Michael Reitman. He had been perplexed; we had never discussed it before and I'd given no indication that I was planning to leave.

Have you given thought to what you'll be doing next? he'd asked.

No, I had replied. I just don't see myself doing this long-term.

When did you decide this? he asked, studying my resignation letter like a piece of evidence.

Just last night, I said. Then added, I'm sorry.

You don't have to apologize to me, he said, so calmly that I wondered whether he was actually seething inside. But I'm sorry to see you go. You've been a great product coordinator.

I made the decision last night, but it's been on my mind for a while.

You've learned fast, he continued, and you've managed to take on new projects of increasing difficulty. The team in Hong Kong speak highly of you. We've noticed your troubleshooting work on many Bible projects, and your ability to run impactful, large-scale production jobs is an asset to our company.

Thank you.

The next words he spoke carefully. But you're young. You haven't worked here for much longer than a year.

About a year and three months, I said.

You're young, he repeated. You're maybe under the impression that everyone gets to do what they want for a living.

I just . . . I floundered, trying to find the right words. I just don't want my life to narrow so quickly. This job is fine. I just don't see myself here forever.

He folded the resignation letter and put it back into its envelope. It's your choice, but I want you to be sure. If you're lucky enough to find something you're good at, where people appreciate you, don't thumb your nose at it. If it's an issue of salary or benefits, I'm open to discussing. He handed the envelope back to me. Why don't you take until Monday to decide. Take Friday off. Spend the weekend thinking. You should be sure.

I am sure, I said hastily.

Be very sure, he said.

I left the office quickly and walked around midtown to clear my head. It was a cold Thursday evening. Faced with Michael's arguments, I felt insecure in my decision. Trying to talk myself out of my job felt like trying to justify an extravagant purchase I couldn't actually afford. Unnervingly, he had undercut my certainty so briskly, in just a few minutes.

At some point, I wandered into Henri Bendel and somehow, after looping up the spiral staircase, skirted into the lingerie department, its racks of teddies, nighties, bras, panties. I felt wary, now that I was basically jobless, of being caught by a sales clerk and asked whether I could be helped. Yet I slowed my pace, marveling at these alien delicacies and confections; the flimsy swaths of expensive fabrics, the abnormal growths of lace, seams of fringe, stitched hard leathers. I wondered about the manufacturing process. Such beautiful frivolities could only be produced by specialty artisans in Italian foothills, fed a diet of soft, runny cheeses and flowered honey. Maybe nuns.

I touched a Victorian-style lavender teddy and glanced at the label sewn in the back: Made in China. Of course it was. I looked at a powder-blue camisole printed with bluebells. Made in Bangladesh. And a set of panties. Made in Pakistan.

No matter where you go, you can't escape the realities of this world.

By Monday, I was back at Spectra.

By this point, the sun was low in the sky. I was just wandering around aimlessly, in circles, never venturing farther than midtown, where I never saw anyone, not even the Sentinel guards standing outside the landmarks and cultural institutions. In fact, I couldn't remember the last time I saw a Sentinel guard standing on duty. Had they all left?

I burrowed deeper into the collar of my coat. My teeth were chattering. I kept my hands stuffed in my pockets.

Across the street was Juicy Couture. It was no longer the pristine, untouched jewel box I had seen and documented for NY Ghost. The glass had been punctured, and approaching it from across the street, I saw that, like Henri Bendel, it had been looted. Inside, the wares were in disarray, a velour and French terry-cloth rainbow explosion, strewn with sunglasses, handbags, smartphone covers. I peered inside the puncture of glass. I saw the saleslady almost right away, lying on the floor. Dried blood stained the wares. She had been bludgeoned, hit upside the head.

Jesus, I said.

At which point I fell down. Or rather, I backed away from the scene and tripped over the curb, hitting my tailbone in a clumsy landing. I could feel the pain—immediate, jarring—all the way to the bridge of my nose. For a long time, I didn't move, just stayed there on the ground, half on the sidewalk, half in the street. The metallic scent of blood filled the air. I checked my nose for blood and confirmed the nosebleed.

The baby moved inside of me, fluttering frantically.

It came to me in a rush, my understanding: I needed to leave. Not just this scene, not just midtown, but New York. I needed to leave New York. I needed to go now. Today. This minute.

As if by teleportation, I found myself standing at the mouth of the Lincoln Tunnel.

I walked timidly inside the tunnel, taking the walkway along the right-hand side, fenced in by a metal railing. I ventured inward for only a few yards, maybe half a mile, but reversed my tracks. The darkness was too overwhelming. Most of the lights had burnt out, a few still flickered, casting a light on some of the abandoned cars. I didn't want to think about what was inside.

Frustrated, I tried to summon up the courage to walk into it again.

At the mouth was a billboard for New York Life, some insurance company, that greeted all traffic entering the city. It showed a picture of a grandfather hugging two grandsons, next to the slogan LIFE IS KNOWING WHAT YOU LIVE FOR.

At that moment, in the distance, I saw a single cab driving down the street. It moved slowly, at a school-zone creep, swerving sluggishly across lanes. The whole day was so dreamlike, so riddled with signs, that I thought I must've been hallucinating.

Nevertheless, I raised my arm to hail it.

Miraculously, the taxi stopped, sort of. I looked inside.

Eddie? I said.

He didn't look at me. He kept looking straight ahead. The car kept moving, at a snail's crawl. I opened the driver's door, unleashing a strong scent of body odor, and reached over and pulled the parking brake, bringing the car to a stop.

Eddie, I said again. It was him, I was sure of it, though his face was more gaunt than I remembered. He wasn't wearing a mask. I touched his shoulder, but there was no reaction, just the blank stare straight ahead. His foot was still pressing on the gas pedal. By this point, I had seen enough people who were fevered. I knew what it looked like.

So maybe that justified the fact that I pulled Eddie out of his own cab, out of his livelihood. There was no struggle.

I climbed into the old, shaky Ford and drove away.

That is the true story of how I left New York.

And yet. It's possible that there is another true story. In this version, maybe he wasn't fevered. Maybe he had been trying to get out of the city like I was. Maybe, despite his frail, weakened state, he had stopped to help me, a familiar person he knew by the side of the road, and maybe I had misidentified him as fevered. It's possible. I can't be sure. Because I wasn't really all that careful. All I thought about was myself. It got me where I needed to go.

25

It is time.

I get out of bed. I begin to change out of my flannel pajamas but think better of it. The change of clothes would give me away, should anyone catch me. Instead, I just throw on my big Marmot coat. I'm just going for a stroll. I'm just talking a walk because I'm restless and I can't sleep. Because everyone knows how pregnancy messes up your sleep cycles.

The one concession I make is to put on sneakers. The floors are cold.

My heart is pounding so hard I can feel it in my fingertips, throbbing, throbbing. Luna moves inside me, unusually alert this morning, her motions like frantic popcorn popping. She's nervous too. Don't worry, I tell her.

Sell the story to yourself. Believe in this story up until the moment you can't anymore. You're just going for a walk at five in the morning. You're in your pajamas, and the only reason you're wearing shoes is that you need to use the porta potties in the parking lot. Who would go out into a parking lot without shoes? You're having trouble sleeping, and you have to use the bathroom.

In order to get from Sephora to Hot Topic, I have to cross about half of the second floor, go past two escalator stations, pass about a dozen shops. The recent snows have melted off the skylight, letting in a bit of daybreak. I scan the second floor; it looks safe, empty. I almost feel silly.

I want to break into a run, but I don't. I walk purposefully, not too fast, not too slow, the gait of someone who doesn't have anything to hide, who has no ulterior motives. Peering over the balcony, the first floor also scans as empty. Maybe I've even hidden my intentions from myself. I'm surprised by how relaxed I feel.

There is Hot Topic, a massive black storefront to my right.

From afar, I don't see anything on the floor. My heart sinks. I try not to panic. Maybe it's there but I can't see it from this distance. It is a small key, and perhaps it blends into the beige tiles. I'll find it. I'll find it, and I'll bend down and close my fingers around it, finally betraying my intentions.

I hold my breath and approach. It isn't until I am right in front of Hot Topic that I see that the key is not there. There's no key. There's nothing.

The sound of jangling keys.

Oh god. I look up.

Bob emerges from Hot Topic.

I swallow. Bob, I say, as he walks toward me, his face betraying no emotion.

I'm looking back at him, ready to make up lies, ready to deny all accountability. I have seen his face in its many variations. I have seen it when he's angry, when he's satisfied, when he tries to project control. I have been on his good side and his bad side. It is a face I have spent a lot of time trying to read, trying to appeal to, trying to capitulate to, trying to pretend for. I have always positioned myself in relation to him, thinking I could toe the line, thinking it would be fine if I just cooperated, thinking if only I compressed myself a bit more.

But this expression on his face now—I have never seen it like this before. It is blank, not angry or disappointed or frustrated. There is nothing.

He comes closer and closer. Instinctively, I step back. And he walks past me.

Could he be sleepwalking? Could I be that lucky?

I turn around and watch him in disbelief. His body language does not seem to acknowledge my presence. I watch as he walks away, his motions smooth and unselfconscious, as he turns around to descend the escalator.

The car keys, dangling from his belt loop by an aluminum carabiner buckle, catch the early-morning light coming in through the skylight. They glint, beckoning me.

I exhale, a deep, shaky breath. I begin to follow. I trail behind Bob, descending the escalator swiftly to bridge the distance between us. A part of me is afraid he'll snap out of it somehow, that he'll awaken, so I walk as soundlessly as possible.

When I reach the first floor, he is already several paces ahead of me, passing the Old Navy. There is a coffee stain on his white T-shirt. I have never seen Bob in a T-shirt, actually. He takes care not to dress casually around us. The material of the shirt is thin, so I can see his pink skin through it.

The keys jingle and jangle.

I get closer and closer. I can see the back of his neck, the hairy tufts sticking out of the collar. His fleshy shoulders. I get so close that I catch his morning breath, sour and acrid. I think of teenage Bob, aimlessly wandering through the mall to escape his parents' fights at home. And I think of his walks at night, the walks he says he doesn't take.

The keys jingle and jangle. It dawns on me.

I run out in front of Bob, facing him. Uncomprehending, he approaches me, not even a flicker of recognition in his hooded eyes. His gaze is unaffixed to any specific object but to a vague middle distance, as if he is watching a secret movie projecting in front of him. As he comes closer, I am certain. It is the gaze of the fevered. I have seen it before, on Ashley's face the night we tried to stalk her house, which was the last time I saw her, which was the last time I saw Janelle.

All of my blood pumps to this pulse. All of my blood rises to my head. There is an uneven jagged sound, and it takes a moment to realize that it is the rattle of my trembly, angry breathing. My sudden rage surprises me.

You have done a tremendous, tremendous job, Michael Reitman says.

I shove Bob and the force pushes him back. Again and again, until he topples backward, skidding across the floor. He is on his back, a crumpled beetle, his hands clutching the air. The idea is to quickly snatch the keys, but instead I kick him in the ribs, in the stomach, in the groin, in his face, in all of his soft parts. It's a fury of kicks and blows, quickly, furiously accelerating before he even has a chance to react, if he can even react. Because he doesn't so much as raise his arms in defense. Which only makes me redouble my efforts. I spit on his face, on his eyes that don't even blink. The sounds this kicking makes, squelches and crunches, are unreal video-game sounds.

Candace!

I look up. It's Adam, standing a few feet away. He has appeared out of nowhere. His incredulous expression quickly reassembles, neutralizes into one that's controlled, authoritative.

Candace. Stop before you do something you regret, Adam says loudly, enunciating every word as if speaking to a child. We can fix this if you stop now.

He must find his words very funny because I hear the sound of trembly, jagged laughing. Except his face hasn't changed, his mouth isn't even open. Someone is laughing. This familiar laughter, like gargling gravel, like rocks in a washing machine, the laughter that doesn't go over easy at office parties. It's me. It's actually me laughing. I'm laughing because I have never had a personal conversation with Adam in all this time and he is telling me what to do. That's pretty funny.

In full view of Adam, I lean over Bob's body and unhook the carabiner key chain from his jeans. There is blood on the floor.

When I stand up, we look at each other. Don't follow me, I say.

With that, I walk deliberately toward the parking lot doors, bluffing the role of victor. Then there is some confused shouting, and at the first invocation, I burst into a run. Rachel comes out of her cell, her expression inexplicable except for the despair. Come with me! I scream at her. She recoils as I get closer, ducks back inside, as I furiously pound my feet toward the exit, where I slam against the doors—maybe I hear them after me or maybe it's the bark of the push bar—and bound out into the parking lot.

The Nissan Maxima is only a few paces away in the parking lot, parked, with all the other vehicles, in a handicapped spot. I stab desperately toward it, propelled by my own momentum, stopping only to throw up gashes of vomit across two parking lanes on the dirty asphalt. The door isn't locked. I get inside and shove in the key. The engine roars to life.

I look behind on the chance that maybe Rachel has followed me, that she too is looking for an escape route. But no one comes. The doors remain closed.

I pull out of the parking lot and I get the fuck out.

26

For a long time, I just keep driving and driving, not knowing where I am going, just wanting to put as much distance as possible between myself and the Facility.

It isn't until I merge onto Illinois Route 21 that I begin to think about where I am going. It is an eight-lane road, which gives me more than enough space to drive. The roads are surprisingly clear, mostly uncluttered with vehicles. I go in the direction of Chicago, following the signs. The light glimmers out of a bank of trees, which obscures a river embankment. Jonathan once told me about the rivers of Illinois, how the land adjacent to a Great Lake is rippled with rivers. On my right side, the land is riddled with corporate parks, auto-parts stores, new housing developments with colonial-style homes, public storage compounds, a Benihana, pancake houses, crab shacks.

Periodically, I check the rearview mirror, paranoid that there might be headlights behind me. Soon, there's no need for headlights. The sun comes gradually and then suddenly, all at once, shining into my eyes. Rifling through the glove compartment, I find a pair of sunglasses. They were Ashley's fake Chinatown Chanels. I crack open the window, and the rush of crisp air douses me in cold. My hair billows around, blowing everywhere.

For a while, I don't see a single building. I think I must be driving in the wrong direction; away from the city, not toward it. But then Illinois 21 narrows, turns into the four-lane Milwaukee Avenue and I think, I feel, that this must be the right way. From the stories Jonathan told me, I know it is a big street that runs the span of the city and its outer suburbs diagonally, cutting a cross section through several neighborhoods.

Glenview. Niles. I decipher the names of each suburb from the names of various car dealerships, furniture showrooms, banks, bakeries, and bridal boutiques that pass outside my window. For what seems like a whole mile, I drive alongside what I think is an overgrown golf course but turns out to be a cemetery, inexplicably littered with abandoned camping tents pitched in the middle of its grounds.

The trembling of my hands on the steering wheel has calmed. My breathing slows. My heart has slowed.

Passing underneath a highway overpass, I'm startled to see makeshift Catholic shrines, decorated with Virgin Mary and saint iconography, strewn with burned-down candles. They are accompanied by abandoned sleeping bags and plastic lawn furniture. From then on, I seem to spot these same accoutrements, shrines and sleeping bags, under every overpass. As people made their exoduses out of the city on foot, these spaces must have served as makeshift sanctuaries. They prayed and slept beneath them.

The sun disappears. The sky becomes heavy with clouds. It is going to rain. The tank is under half full. It'll take me only so far. I'll get to Chicago and then take a long rest, load up on supplies, and figure things out from there. A city has so many crevices in which to burrow.

As I near Chicago, the lanes become increasingly cluttered, jammed with stilled, empty vehicles, squeezing me into the right lanes. Whenever an opening comes up, I consider exiting and merging onto another route, but instinctively, I right myself before making the turn, jerking back into my lane. I can't leave Milwaukee Avenue. It is the one thing that feels familiar.

Even if it is a secondhand familiarity, it is a familiarity all the same. As if all of the stories Jonathan told of his years in Chicago, while we lay drowsing in bed, had seeped into my own memories. Right before sleep when the brain is at its most porous and absorbs everything and weeps chemicals indiscriminately, I must have been deep in his reminiscing, his intricate, lacelike memories inlaid in me. I have been here in another lifetime.

The sounds of Milwaukee Avenue from his apartment at night: the owl-service buses that stopped below his window, the fire trucks with their blaring horns, gunshots from warring gangs. Inevitably, the panicky shriek of ambulances. The street seemed to exist in a perpetual state of anxiety, its jittery lanes of traffic diffusing and reorienting at every siren call of emergency vehicles trundling down its outstretched, grandiose expanse. He lived in that apartment for three years, during which time he had distanced himself from his family in southern Illinois, avoiding their drunken calls, declining to return for Christmas. He considered Chicago his real home, and like any place, it was changing. As the neighborhood gentrified, the gunshots at night grew increasingly faint, gang warfare pushed to streets farther west until, over the years, he couldn't hear them at all. By that point, the taquerías he used to frequent, selling mangoes and carnitas and cream-pumped pastries that looked like horns of plenty, had also disappeared. Other night sounds took over: the soothing hum of whirring washers and dryers from the twenty-four-hour laundromat below the apartment, its reverberations coming up through the floorboards until finally, he would fall asleep.

The first place you live alone, away from your family, he said, is the first place you become a person, the first place you become yourself.

I have been an orphan for so long I am tired of it, walking and driving and searching for something that will never settle me. I want something different for Luna, the child of two rootless people. She will be born untethered from all family except me, without a hometown or a place of origin. I want us to stay in one place. Maybe Chicago, the city her father loved, in which he once lived, could be the place.

The sky buckles and it begins to rain. The windshield puckers with droplets. I turn on the wipers, but they're broken and I squint my way through the blurring scenery.

I don't notice when I enter the city limits of Chicago—no immediate skyline announces itself—but at some point, I sense it. It feels different. And it looks different, a dense amalgamation of strip malls and brick buildings with faded business awnings. Bus stops every few blocks. I pass old immigrant grocery stores, wholesale produce centers, MoneyGram depots, mattress warehouse outlets, a car wash with splashy old signage, and old-world delicatessens and bakeries, their window displays still intact with dangling sausages and tiered wedding cakes, respectively.

Ding ding ding ding ding. The fuel light blinks, warning me that the gas is running low.

But I stay on Milwaukee Avenue all the same. It is so straight and smooth, easy to drive. Rarely does it make turns that you can't predict, though often it gets entangled in confusing three-way intersections. The farther south I drive, the more gentrified the neighborhoods become. The Western Unions give way to banks, the dive bars give way to glossy cocktail lounges, the diners to sushi restaurants, the chiropractor centers to yoga studios, the Payless shoes and Gap outlets to clothing boutiques, the bakeries to cupcakeries. There are newer developments, the scaffolding still up. To my right, I glimpse a subway train on an elevated rail, suspended between stations, raised high above the houses and buildings.

In the distance up ahead, the skyline comes into view, just barely. It is shrouded in mist, hazy through the rain-speckled windshield. I can pick out the Sears Tower, the Hancock, and it isn't until I see the skyline that I realize I have actually been in Chicago before.

It had been a long time ago, when I was a kid, during the year when my mother and I would follow my father on his business trips, making it a vacation for ourselves. We had gone to New York this way, but Chicago must have been before that. I was about eight. The trip had been two days, if even that. There's not a lot I remember, except how it had drizzled intermittently the whole time we were there, and between that and the overcast skies, my impression of Chicago was of being inside a perspiring gray cloud. The downtown area, where my mother and I roamed as my father attended his conference, was a tangle of black buildings. We periodically ducked inside restaurants and hotels and stores whenever the storm started up again.

And it must have been spring. My mother and I had sought shelter in the lobby of a corporate office building, which consisted of all reflective black surfaces, except for the seasonal decorative centerpiece: an enclosed white clapboard hutch, strewn with pastel ribbons. We approached the hutch and looked inside. It held a mass of live white bunnies, squirming in sawdust. A banner above the hutch read HAPPY EASTER!

The receptionist came over. The rabbits are for Easter, she explained, enunciating loudly. Then, looking at my mother, she asked, Does she know what Easter is?

My mother stiffened. Yes.

You can hold one if you want. She picked up a bunny, white, with gray spots, out of the hutch and attempted to place it in my arms.

No, thank you, my mother politely declined for me, then

gripped me by the shoulder and guided me out the revolving doors. Outside, we stood underneath the awning of the building, watching the pedestrians crossing the bridge, shielding themselves from the rain with umbrellas or newspapers over their heads.

What do you think it would be like if we lived here? she wondered, reverting back to Chinese. I would work, and then what would you do?

You would work, and I would play, I said.

I would work and you would cook, she decided. You would cook and clean. Do you know how to cook rice in the rice cooker?

Yeah. You just put the rice and water in, then hit the button!

No, you have to wash the rice first. So it doesn't taste dirty. You wash the rice in cold water for at least a minute. If you could learn how to do that, and also how to steam a fish with ginger and scallions, then I could work.

What would you work at?

She was quiet for a moment. Finally, she said, personal wealth management. She said this stiffly in English, as if rehearsed for a job interview. I would manage people's money, help them afford homes, plan for retirement. I'd work in a building like this one.

She looked at me, suddenly stern, as if I were holding her back: But if I do that, you'd have to stay home. You'd stay home and I'd go to work. Okay?

Okay, I had agreed.

All along the street as I drive, there are stops for the 56 Milwaukee bus. In another life, in my mother's alternate life, I would take the 56 bus directly downtown, to one of the office buildings, and all of its nearby pleasures: the coffee from Lavazza, the off-street diners with wood-paneled interiors, the shops on State Street. I would sit in the back, wear sunglasses, watch the other passengers.

I would go to work in the morning. I would return home in the evening.

To live in a city is to live the life that it was built for, to adapt to its schedule and rhythms, to move within the transit layout made for you during the morning and evening rush, winding through the crowds of fellow commuters. To live in a city is to consume its offerings. To eat at its restaurants. To drink at its bars. To shop at its stores. To pay its sales taxes. To give a dollar to its homeless.

To live in a city is to take part in and to propagate its impossible systems. To wake up. To go to work in the morning. It is also to take pleasure in those systems because, otherwise, who could repeat the same routines, year in, year out?

The first toasty cigarette of the day, leaning against the outside of the building, near the entrance of revolving doors, before heading upstairs to the office. The cold of a winter morning, and the smell of exhaust from all the cars and trucks down Lake Shore Drive, and the wind from the lake.

As I drive farther downtown, Milwaukee Avenue becomes more congested, denser with rusting vehicles, taxis and buses that never reached their destination, until it becomes difficult to go farther. It's as if they all abandoned their cars during a giant rush hour. I am forced to drive off-road on the sidewalks, bypassing clumps of cars. The pileup stretches for what seems like a mile. The Nissan emits a groan. The fuel light blinks furiously.

Still, I keep pressing on, at a painful crawl. Up ahead, a tower crane has toppled onto the trisection, smashing all the streetlights and cars, blocking several routes. It is the cause of the frozen traffic. I attempt to maneuver around the fallen crane and turn onto the only street that isn't blocked off. I'm not on Milwaukee anymore. The car manages another few blocks, until it stops with a lurch. I hit the gas hard, but it only makes a terrible sound in protest, then nothing. The engine stops.

Silence. It's dead.

Up ahead, there's a massive littered river, planked by an elaborate, wrought-iron red bridge. Beyond the bridge is more skyline, more city.

I get out and start walking.

ACKNOWLEDGMENTS

Thank you to Jin Auh, whose conviction changed everything, and to Jessica Friedman at the Wylie Agency.

Thank you to Jenna Johnson and Sara Birmingham, whose insights surfaced the deeper story. You made this a better novel! Much respect to the hardworking team at Farrar, Straus and Giroux, including Rebecca Caine, Jane Elias, Debra Helfand, Peter Richardson, Rob Sternitzky, Stephen Weil, and Chandra Wohleber.

The MFA program at Cornell University provided the funding and resources that allowed me to finish this novel. Thank you in particular to J. Robert Lennon, Stephanie Vaughn, and Helena Viramontes. And much praise to the English administration office for their organizational prowess.

Thank you for your kindness and generosity: Melody Flahart, Lee Froehlich, Isabelle Gilbert, Baird Harper, Jacob Knabb, Elizabeth Merrick, Katie Moore, Hajara Quinn, Kirsten Saracini. Ed Park, thank you for letting me steal NY Ghost (RIP the New-York Ghost)!

My family relieved me from the immigrant pressures of traditional success. I am grateful for their love and unreasonable acceptance.

Finally, thank you to Valer Popa, who has been swimming alongside me all this time.